A TASTE OF
Midnight

Books by Shannon Page

Eel River
Our Lady of the Islands (with Jay Lake)
I Was a Trophy Wife (essay collection)

The Nightcraft Quartet:
The Queen and The Tower
A Sword in The Sun
The Lovers Three
The Empress and The Moon

Island of Second Chances:
A Taste of Midnight
Love and Lemongrass (forthcoming)

Collaborations, as Laura Gayle

The Chameleon Chronicles:
Orcas Intrigue
Orcas Intruder
Orcas Investigation
Orcas Illusion
Orcas Intermission

Tales from the Berry Farm:
Orcas Afterlife
Orcas Aliens (forthcoming)

A TASTE OF
Midnight

BOOK ONE
ISLAND OF SECOND CHANCES

SHANNON PAGE

ALOT
PRESS
A Little of This, Inc.

ALOT
PRESS
A Little of This, Inc.

"Never settle for Beaujolais Nouveau when there is a well-aged vin d'Avignon on the menu, my dear."

—Countess Lucinda Devonryshireton,
The Countess's Exceedingly Perfect Guide to Love and Romance, Volume II

Chapter 1

JULIE

The mid-October meeting of the Orcas Island Semi-Monthly Sunday Soup Symposium was about to get underway. Julie Pessel lifted the lid on the big red Dutch oven on her stove and gave the fragrant mixture a stir, then grabbed her tasting spoon. More cumin? More red pepper flakes?

More salt?

She blew on the spoon, then tasted. Mmm. Perfect: tender Midnight Black beans, just the right amount of heat, and a rich, hearty broth.

As she replaced the pot's lid, she heard a knock at her front door.

"It's open!" she called out, stifling a sigh. Who was early *this* time? Probably Ron and Alicia. Didn't anybody respect a schedule around here? Luckily she was nearly ready.

To her surprise, Matt Richards shuffled into her kitchen, ducking under the low, wide doorframe even though he was in no danger of hitting his head.

"Hey," Julie said. "Have a seat." Then she glanced behind him. "Is Heather meeting you here?"

"No, she…" Matt started, and then his voice choked as he sank into a chair at her table. Julie was even more surprised to see tears gathering at the corners of his eyes. "She…left."

Julie practically fell into a chair as well. "She what? What do you mean, left? Is she off-island?" But it was clear from his face that that wasn't what he'd meant.

Matt took a deep, steadying breath before looking up at Julie. "She left, like, for good. She said she still loves me, but she can't keep on doing this—" he waved a hand vaguely "—anymore."

"'This'? Meaning your dad?"

Matt grimaced. "She says not—that she loves him too, and wants to help—but, well, that's got to be a factor. It can't be easy."

"No, I'm sure it's not. For either of you."

"But what she *says*—which is probably also true—is that she can't live in such a remote place anymore. The ferries, the winter power outages, the lack of a night life…"

"The lack of sushi," Julie added, wryly.

"Yeah. She says she gave it her all, but she's just not happy. She's staying with some friends in Seattle till she figures out something more permanent."

"Wow." Julie shook her head, taking this all in. This was completely out of the blue—for Matt as well as her, obviously. "I'm so sorry, Matt." She glanced over at her small counter where she had a bottle already opened, breathing. "Can I get you a glass of wine?"

"A wine glass, sure—but empty." He reached down to his messenger bag and pulled out a bottle of something amber, with a complicated label. The words "single malt" stood out, though she couldn't read much else. "I brought this."

Julie raised an eyebrow even as she was getting two glasses out of the cupboard over the sink. "I have snifters."

"Snifters are for brandy." He cut the paper seal with his pocketknife and cracked open the bottle.

"And wine glasses are for wine," she said, but set them on the table anyway. It wasn't as though she had whiskey glasses. "Whoah—just a half-inch for me."

He gave her an inch, and himself several. Then he raised his glass. "To being single," he said, with a brave, if wavery, smile.

"To being single," she echoed, and they clinked. "It really isn't that bad, I promise." Then she cringed. "I mean, eventually."

He took a generous gulp of his whiskey while she sipped. Then another. "I'm sure it isn't, but I'm not looking forward to finding out. Especially right now."

Julie patted his hand, both to try to comfort him and to prevent him from taking yet another slug from his glass. "Hey, slow down there, tiger. The others aren't even here yet—and you'll be in no shape to drive home if you get smashed."

He set his glass down. "Sorry I was early. I wasn't sure how long it would take to walk down here."

"You *walked?*"

He shrugged. "Yeah. I needed to clear my head; I was going crazy, in the house, and I didn't trust myself to drive. So when Ramona got there to stay with Dad for the evening, I just headed out."

"Wow." Julie sipped her whiskey again. It was smoky, peaty; very smooth. He must have spent a fortune on it. Well, he could afford it—just as he could afford to pay the certified nursing assistant to come and stay with his dad when he needed to leave the house. "How long *did* it take you to walk to town?"

"Maybe forty minutes? Something like that." He shook his head. "I didn't really look at a clock or anything."

A commotion in the front of the house resolved itself into Ron and Alicia bustling into the kitchen. "I know I said I was going to do the cheese bread but I ran out of time to bake so I got a hearth loaf, but it needs slicing and maybe we could heat it up in the oven for a few minutes, oh good the wine's open, are you guys drinking *whiskey?*" Alicia announced in a breathless rush as she dumped a fragrant paper bag onto the counter and pulled two wine glasses out of Julie's cupboard. Ron, businesslike as usual, lifted the wine bottle, examined its label critically, then filled the glasses, handing his wife one. Alicia pulled out a chair across from Matt, only then focusing on him. "What's wrong?"

Matt gave Julie a helpless look.

"Heather left him," Julie told the newcomers, "and he's a little fragile right now, and maybe we should wait for the others to get here so he doesn't have to tell the story five times?"

"It's all right," Matt said, though he took another fortifying swig of his drink before filling Alicia and Ron in. "Maybe saying it over and over again will help it become more real," he added, when he'd finished.

"Oh, honey," Alicia said, getting up and leaning over Matt, pulling him into an awkward hug. She held on to him tightly, then ruffled his hair before letting him go and standing back up. "Oh, that's just awful. I never liked her."

"Yes, you did," Ron put in quietly, sipping his wine. "We all did."

"Well, I don't like her now. How could she do this to our Matty?"

"I hope you didn't start without us!" came a cheerful voice from the front of the small house, and into the kitchen came Lynne and Steph. They lived next door to each other, so they generally drove in together from Deer Harbor for Sunday Soup meetings.

"We did," said Julie, getting up and taking the big salad bowl from Lynne, "but just with drinks. Special circumstances. Oh," she added to Steph, "you can put that on the coffee table—let's go into the living room, it's too crowded in here."

Out in the house's main room, Steph took the lid off a giant tray of homemade appetizers: caviar toasts, tiny quiches, bacon-wrapped scallops, stuffed dates, and what looked like miniature pepperoni pizzas, perfect in every detail down to the pencil-eraser-sized dots of spiced meat.

"Wow," Alicia said, "did you stay up all night, Steph?" She put a date into her mouth and hummed with delight. "These are amazing—I'm glad I skipped lunch."

"And played an extra hour of pickleball," Ron added in an undertone. "In case anyone was wondering why she 'ran out of time' to bake."

After handing full wine glasses to Lynne and Steph, Julie glanced over at Ron. He was known for his sharp tongue, but tonight he seemed a little spikier than usual. She gave him an inquisitive look, which he didn't see, as he had turned to watch his wife take a scallop.

Lynne settled on the sofa and raised her glass. "Before I call the official meeting to order, who is going to fill us in on these *special circumstances?*"

Julie chuckled. 'Official meeting' indeed—if you called a themed potluck dinner 'official'.

Matt gave another brave smile and launched into his news again.

Julie watched her friends as they listened with sympathy and support—and another avowal of *She's not good enough for you* from Alicia. They were a good group, some of the best friends Julie had ever had. Well, most of them; she'd never quite been able to crack through Ron's prickly reserve, but everyone else was as dear to her as her own family.

Julie had met Lynne when she'd first moved to Orcas Island eight years ago. Lynne, widowed with a grown son, had struck up a conversation with Julie as they shared a volunteer table at the island's film festival, selling tickets and checking in the movie-goers. Julie, long divorced with two grown daughters, had welcomed the friendship of another single "older" woman—in her late fifties, yes, but not at all ready to stay home and putter around her garden. Lynne had soon introduced her to her younger neighbor Steph, who might as well be single (Julie could never figure out her relationship with her husband David; they seemed content to lead entirely separate lives); and then to Ron and Alicia.

It had been Alicia's idea to organize regular get-togethers, and

Julie's suggestion that these meetings could be a book group. She'd loved her book group back in San Francisco. Surely these interesting, smart new friends would enjoy the same here.

However, it had gone poorly almost from the start. Nobody could agree on what to read; then, once that had been settled (after much acrimony), nobody could agree on whether what they'd read was any good. Except that instead of this disagreement leading to stimulating intellectual discussions, as had been Julie's experience in the past, it seemed to just make everyone feel peevish and dissed. Within the first year, half the membership had stopped even reading the books. And when Alicia had invited her new web designer, Matt, and his lovely girlfriend Heather to join the group, hoping to inject a little more positive, youthful energy into the endeavor, he had announced that he never read fiction, but would be interested in meeting to discuss biographies of inventors or even successful businessmen. Heather, for her part, claimed to not read at all. "I do listen to podcasts."

Meanwhile, sparked by Steph and her kitchen-based enthusiasms, the culinary accomplishments of the group had begun to level up, leading to a little friendly one-upsmanship. The second winter, after a string of amazing soups, Alicia had said, "We should just forget the books and rebrand this as the Sunday Soup group."

"Hear, hear!" cried Steph, and the measure was adopted by general acclaim.

Now, Julie sipped her wine and nibbled at a tiny quiche, glancing at all the lovely volumes of poetry on her shelves, the many novels—a whole shelf devoted to Libby Perrine, and full runs of several other favorite authors. She loved the soup group, and couldn't wait for them to try her Spicy Midnight Black Bean Chowder, but...it would still be nice to have someone to talk about books with.

Oh well.

"So, shall we eat?" Lynne asked after everyone's glasses were empty, as well as the appetizer platter.

"Sure thing," Julie said. "I'll get the bread sliced, and then you can all come in and start dishing out your soup."

At the end of the evening, Julie was relieved to see that Matt wasn't as blitzed as she'd feared he'd be. Lynne and Steph had offered to drive him back up Enchanted Forest to his home at the top of the hill. Yes, he could walk, but then Ramona, the CNA who came regularly to sit with his father, would have to stay out later than she was comfortable doing. Matt's dad had been struggling with the slow but steady progression of dementia over the past few years, and could no longer be left alone for even a few hours, particularly after dark. Matt's mother had succumbed to breast cancer in her early fifties; Julie had never met her, and still gave a shiver when she thought of dying so young.

She stacked the plates and soup bowls in the dishwasher, scraped the rest of the black bean soup into a container, and wrapped up the heel of bread—it would make fine toast in the morning. Then she got out the bag of fancy kibble from under the sink and gave it a shake. "It's safe now, Fergie," she called. "All those scary monsters are gone, you can come out now." She filled a clean cat bowl, set it on the floor, and waited.

Within thirty seconds, her calico emerged from somewhere in her closet-sized bedroom—probably under the bed, as there was barely anyplace else large enough to contain even a smallish cat. Fergie gave her a disdainful glance before approaching her food bowl.

"You really should give them a chance, though I know you won't," Julie said, wiping down the counters. "Let someone else in. You might like it."

And what about you? the cat didn't need to say. *A life full of friends who all go home at the end of an evening? Who should be giving advice to whom here, cat lady?*

"At least I am not a *childless* cat lady," Julie said, mock-primly.

"Megan and Lori are the living proof that, at least at one point in my life, I managed to have a marriage and a family. And I could have a partner again if I wanted to, easily. I like my life the way it is."

You just keep on telling yourself that, cat lady, Fergie did not answer.

Julie stepped into the living room and gazed at the framed photos of her daughters on the mantelpiece while Fergie crunched her food in the kitchen. Megan and Lori were not just proof that Julie wasn't an old spinster; they were fine, beautiful, creative young women, intelligent and accomplished. And a source of unending joy to their mother, of course. Neither of them were married, though as with Julie, they could have had life partners if they'd wanted; this was the career-building, figuring-themselves-out part of their trajectories. They had plenty of time. Julie was nothing but proud of them for not rushing into marriage and motherhood as she had.

I'll just keep telling myself that too, Julie thought with an inner rueful smile. She tried hard not to be one of "those" mothers, but there were times when she ached for grandchildren so badly, it stunned her. Apparently, the biological clock didn't stop ticking at menopause; it just shifted from *Become a mama* to *Become a grandma*.

"Someday," Julie whispered, giving the photos one last fond look before heading back to the kitchen. Fergie had stopped crunching; Julie needed to take the bowl up, or Fergie would push it around the floor all night. Someday Julie again would rock a baby, snuggle a toddler, chase a leggy kindergartner giggling around a room…

THE NEXT MORNING, Julie rose early. She wanted to get the stitching finished on her latest batch of books—the books she made, not those she read. Her day job, which she sometimes still could not believe was real, was running a gift shop in the tiny building at the front of her lot on North Beach Road, just across from the Orcas Island Museum. At the back of her lot, of course, was her little cottage, entirely hidden from view by the store and a well-placed big-leafed maple tree.

Paper Magic was no ordinary gift shop; she sold only items made by herself or a few other crafts people on the island. Julie's handmade sketchbooks and journals—constructed from paper she also made herself—fairly flew off the shelves, faster than she could replenish them, especially during the summer months. They had started selling so well after she got the idea to put images of Orcas Island, the San Juans, and orcas on their covers. Visitors always wanted a souvenir of their time in this magical place. And if it could be lovely as well as useful, all the better.

Her shop opened at eleven, Tuesdays through Sundays, though starting in November she would switch over to her winter hours: Fridays through Sundays, and closed the entire month of January. Summers on Orcas Island were glorious, and everyone who ran the shops, hotels, and restaurants relied on a flood of visitors for their livelihood, but the winters were in many ways her favorite time of the year. The whole island seemed to let out a long-held breath, and the town of Eastsound belonged to the locals again. If it weren't for the twice-monthly soup group, Julie didn't think she'd see any of her friends between April and November.

She finished a pile of small blue-and-green notebooks, attached discreet price tags to their backs, and carried them up to the shop, arranging them on a front table. Then she made a final sweep around the store, making sure everything was tidy and the wood floor was swept, before turning her sign to "open" and unlocking the door.

"Can we bring these in?" Her first potential customers stood in the doorway holding dripping ice cream cones, despite the chill in the air.

Julie gave them an apologetic smile. "I'm sorry, I've too much that could be ruined. Feel free to sit on the bench on the porch while you finish them, though."

The couple shrugged and glanced at each other. "We'll come back," the woman said.

Julie nodded. They would indeed likely be back; Eastsound only had so many places for tourists to shop. If they'd parked down on Main Street, along the water, they wouldn't venture much past the hardware store before turning back around. Either way, it was fine. Other customers were already stepping in to browse. A teenage girl picked up the entire pile of notebooks Julie had just stitched and sighed with delight. "Mom! Look!"

It was easy to lose oneself in the flow of commerce; only Julie's growling stomach let her know that half the day had gone by. She did not like to close during regular business hours, even with a "back in ten minutes" sign on the door like so many other shops did, so she made sure to have plenty of snacks handy, plus a big thermos of tea.

She was rummaging under the counter looking for a granola bar when the bell over the shop's door rang yet again. "I'll be with you in a sec," she called out, shifting aside a box of blank receipts and several rolls of cash register tape. Ah, there it was: one last bar. She made a mental note to replenish her supply and rose to her feet, nearly bumping her head on a strong male chin.

Her eyes widened; above the chin was a very kissable mouth, and above that was a strong nose framed by gorgeous gray eyes, and atop all that was a tousled mop of salt-and-pepper curls. She registered all this in an instant before realizing with a sinking heart that all these elements belonged to Gavin Jones.

"Oh." She took a step backwards, nearly bumping into the wall behind her. But why was he leaning over the counter?

"Sorry." He drew back and frowned at her. "Wasn't sure where you were."

She tucked the granola bar into her skirt pocket and forced a smile. "I was right here. What can I help you with?" Surely he wasn't here to buy a sketchbook.

Gavin worked at the library, and though he wasn't completely incompetent at his job, Julie had run out of patience with him years ago. The Orcas Island Library was a marvelous resource, with a rich and varied collection and a robust interlibrary loan program. Julie had spent many, many hours combing many, many books to choose pithy, amusing, or profound quotes for another part of her shop's offerings: her line of coffee table and back-of-the-toilet books. Gavin, as the fellow behind the desk during most of this time, should have been her greatest ally.

Sadly, he either never understood what she was trying to do, or (as she suspected) disapproved of the project. Was it because she was making the books to sell, and therefore an ugly odor of commerce clung to the endeavor, in contrast with the lofty aims of the public library? Was it simply because he was a snob, or disapproved of fun? Julie never knew. What she did know was that when she changed her method of coming up with the quotes and stopped visiting the library, her blood pressure had returned to a more healthful level. As an added bonus, the books had started selling even better than before—and she had a lot more fun making them.

Thus, she hadn't been to the library in forever.

Why was Gavin here now?

"I just wanted to bring you this," he said, setting a sheet of paper on her glass counter. "Thursday evening, at the library. Come if you can."

"Well, I'll have to see," Julie hedged, squinting at the flier. Without her reading glasses, she couldn't quite make out the small printing, so it wasn't clear what the event even was.

Gavin gave a soft snort. "I mean, if you care, that is." Without waiting for an answer, he turned and walked out, leaving the bell jangling behind him.

"Wow," she muttered to the empty shop, shaking her head. "Who peed in your Cheerios?" She dug her glasses out of her pocket and scanned the flier. "Oh, not *this* again."

Last year, a consortium of business owners—*newer* business owners, as it happened, led by a wealthy vacation-rental developer—had made a formal proposal to the county council. The proposal had been laughed off; the council hadn't even taken it up. Now, rather than taking the hint, the consortium was back, collecting signatures to put the measure on the ballot.

"Parking meters!" Julie muttered. "We're not Seattle."

The flier announced, as Gavin had said, a meeting at the library to discuss this dangerous and divisive plan. "Preserve Eastsound's historic character!" read the banner across the top. "Come and help us brainstorm how to keep our community safe and pleasant, and welcoming for all."

The bell over the door rang again, and Julie tucked the flier below the counter as she greeted her newest customers.

STEPH

STEPH HANCOCK SAT on the burgundy sofa in her den, going through a stack of cooking magazines. She'd agreed to host this month's neighborhood association meeting, and though it was a potluck, the host was responsible for the anchor dish.

She flipped through an older issue of *Gourmet*, then tossed it onto the coffee table with a sigh. She was sure that had been the one with the flank steak recipe she'd flagged, but she couldn't find it now.

Of course, Steph didn't really need recipes; she cooked by smell and taste and instinct and long, long practice. But it was nice to have a guideline, a starting point; recipes in general were great for inspiration. Spices she wouldn't think of putting together; methods that were different from what she was familiar with.

What was it? It had sounded so good, and easy. Grilled, and with something like a chimichurri sauce, but not quite… Was it too summery, for this time of year? But that actually sounded like a good thing: a streak of bright flavor as the weather turned darker, colder.

She heard a quiet *clunk* at the back of the house, the sound of a door closing. David was out of his office, then; she could ask him if he was planning to join her for dinner. And for that matter, if he was going to attend the neighborhood meeting, or if he was leaving her to handle it as usual. The neighbors had almost stopped asking, but it would be nice to know.

Who was she kidding? He hadn't been to a neighborhood meeting in at least three years.

She got up, but before she was even in the hallway, she heard the garage door open, and then the sound of his car's engine starting.

Oh well, then.

As long as she was up, she went to the kitchen and stared at the shelf of cookbooks. Was it in the *Best of the West*? No, she was sure it was from her magazine collection.

Well, it didn't matter. She would just invent something, starting with the idea of chimichurri, and bright, strong flavors. She grabbed her favorite knife and a head of garlic and got busy.

As she chopped, she thought about the rest of the meal. If this worked out, she could ask Sharon to bring her famous potatoes—that would make her happy. And Lynne was a master of salads. Maybe something with crunchy romaine lettuce, and bleu cheese? But no; Ernest didn't like bleu cheese. People were so strange!

She wondered idly where her husband had gone—just to town for an errand, or off to work in his rented office? Well, she'd make enough food so there would be leftovers when he got back, whenever that might be. He lived so much in his own world. Usually, he worked from before six in the morning, when the markets opened in New York, until well into the evening. He hadn't worked such long hours when he'd started his remote job for Iron Core Investments; they'd followed the New York Stock Exchange's schedule, so he'd log off in the early afternoon.

But then he'd gotten into his own trading, and had done very well at it. So well that Steph hadn't had to find another job nine years ago when they'd decided to remodel and upgrade their Orcas Island vacation home in order to live here full-time. She felt very lucky to be able to indulge her interest in cooking, especially in the magnificent kitchen she'd overseen the creation of here; but she also felt a little guilty, and a little…well, unsure, maybe. Was it truly healthy, to be so disconnected from one's spouse? Was it wrong to feel so happy doing her own thing?

Was she happy? Truly?

She had her own social life, her own hobbies (well, hobby), and of course the Sunday soup club, which was a *great* group of folks. And David greatly enjoyed playing the markets: it was a game to him. He was very good at it, and he assured her that he never put their core assets at risk. He was an introvert, maybe even a little bit on the spectrum. She'd known all this when she'd married him—though words like "introvert" and "spectrum" weren't in her vocabulary back then. He'd merely been painfully shy, socially awkward.

So was there anything to worry about? If they were both content and fulfilled with their lives, should she just leave well enough alone? Every marriage was different, after all. At least theirs wasn't like Ron and Alicia's. Now *there* was an argument for separate lives if ever Steph saw one.

She pushed that thought away quickly as she finished chopping the garlic and scraped it off the edge of the knife into a small pyrex bowl, setting it aside as she went to the fridge. Something green…not parsley, though: too dull. Not cilantro: too strong, and too many people didn't like it. What about basil? Basil might work—and what could be more summery? She pulled out a reasonably fresh bunch she'd harvested from her greenhouse a few days ago and gave it a quick rinse, spreading the leaves out on a paper towel to dry.

Still. It was the way people glanced around the room when

they came over, or when Steph showed up alone somewhere. They looked for David; she could tell. No one said anything. They just noticed.

Or was she over-interpreting?

The thought continued to nag at her, roaming around in the back of her mind as she considered what else to try in her sauce.

Maybe chives. Chives would bring a gentle onion note without being overpowering. She headed out to the greenhouse to snip a few spiky leaves.

She dined alone that evening, as she had pretty much guessed that she would. Then she read in bed for a while, but turned off the light before David returned.

Not that he would disturb her when he came in. He'd been sleeping on the daybed in his study for years now.

Chapter 2

JULIE

On Thursday, Julie was locking the shop door for the evening when Matt walked up. "Hey, how are you doing?" she asked him, searching his face.

"Okay," he said. "I mean, terrible, off and on, but I'm mostly hanging in there."

She nodded, resisting the urge to ask if he'd heard from Heather. He'd tell her if he wanted to. "You do look okay," she told him. "I can see the strain, but you seem pretty solid." He seemed to be waiting for something, so she added, "Do you want to come back to the house for a glass of wine?"

"No thanks—I'm on my way to this thing at the library and I thought I'd stop and see if you wanted to head over together?"

It took her a moment to remember. "Oh! Right, the parking meters." She supposed she should go, just to show that twerpy Gavin Jones that *Yes, I do in fact care.* She glanced at the jewelry shop next door. "Should we see if Karen wants to walk over with us?"

"Sure."

They found Karen also preparing to close up shop. "Sorry, I can't!" she said, running a hand through her spiky fire-engine-red hair. "I'm already committed—and not in the way you think." She winked at them. "It's open mic night at the Barnacle, and I'm the host."

Julie had forgotten that event as well. This whole *getting older* thing was for the birds. "Okay, have fun tonight!"

"Will do! Stop by after the meeting if you want."

"We will."

On their way back to Julie's shop, she told Matt, "I should feed the cat before we go, if you don't mind waiting."

"No problem."

Back in her house, Matt watched with quiet amusement as she rinsed and refilled the water bowl, then set down a food bowl filled with fresh kibble. "I'm still not convinced you actually have a cat," he said. "Have you seen someone about this delusion of yours?"

"Ha, ha, very funny." She straightened up and washed her hands. "Okay, I'm ready."

There was a short path leading from her door to Prune Alley, a continuation of the trail that cut through from her shop. The library was across Prune Alley and up a stairway. Gavin greeted them at the door, his tousled curls picking up the lights from the lobby. *Why am I suddenly noticing his hair?* Julie asked herself. "We're in the Community Room," he told them. Matt nodded politely at him as they went in.

The Community Room was packed. Every seat around the large table was taken, and people had brought in extra chairs, cramming them in wherever they would fit. At least a dozen people were standing. *Good thing Karen didn't come*, Julie thought. She and Matt squeezed in, sidling along the back wall, trying to make room for more people. "Gosh, maybe they should move the meeting to one of the more open spaces," Julie whispered to Matt.

He looked out the glass-windowed doors to the stacks. "Probably they don't want to do that while the library's open. Disturb the clientele, you know."

"Hm."

"All right, let's get started," said a gray-haired woman at the head of the table. Julie could hardly see her through the crowd. "All right!" the woman said, more loudly. "Can we get started please!" The conversation in the room slowly began quieting down.

"Thank you," the woman said, once she had everyone's attention. "Thank you all for coming tonight. I'm Leslie Magnas, owner of Island Cottages."

Huh, Julie thought. Island Cottages was a very exclusive, high-end vacation spot. They were well outside of town, though; why would Leslie care about parking meters on Main Street and North Beach Road?

"I'm so pleased that this vitally important issue has brought so many concerned citizens out," Leslie continued. "As you all know, Orcas Island is a special, unique place. Visitors come from all over the world to experience our rural environment, our natural beauty, our quiet and serene town. Many of us in this room own businesses that rely on these visitors for our livelihood, and have for many, many years—generations, even. I, for one, have run Island Cottages for my whole working life, after my parents passed. I have raised my own children here; I hope and expect that they will run the cottages after I am gone. As I look around this table, I see many other business owners of similar long standing. Fred Farmer, who owns the feed store; Lauren and Willem Grant, from Solstice Realty…"

She went on in this vein for several more minutes. She clearly cared about the issue, and about the island itself, but she was not the world's most engaging speaker. The crowd began shifting impatiently. Julie began to wish she'd grabbed a snack before heading over.

Eventually, at the back of the room, Gavin cleared his throat and raised his hand, his broad shoulders straining his dark shirt. "Excuse me? Leslie?"

Startled, the gray-haired woman blinked at him. "Yes, Gavin?"

"I'm sorry, but—we have a lot to cover tonight, so maybe, ah, we could get to the discussion part?"

She gave him a sharp look, then nodded curtly. "Yes. Of course. I was merely trying to make the point that this absurd and short-sighted proposal which has been made by a group of…" She shook her head as a look of disgust crossed over her face. "A group of *newcomers*, people who have no understanding of our ways, our history, our traditions, who threaten to destroy the very character of our island—"

Gavin cleared his throat again.

"Right," Leslie said. "Anyway, I know you all are as concerned as I am. Even those of you whose tenure here does *not* go back generations." Did her steely gaze meet Julie's as she said this? There were so many people in the room, would Leslie even know who Julie was? Likely not; she was probably only looking at her because she *didn't* know her. *Don't worry, lady*, Julie thought. *I'm on your team.* "So," Leslie went on, "as Gavin would have us do, let us begin the discussion. Let us decide how we are going to quash this outrageous measure once and for all. We are not Seattle!"

My thoughts exactly! Julie thought. *That's the long and the short of it.*

Sadly, particularly for the many attendees who were standing, there was not a whole lot of "short of it." The meeting went on for several hours, even though clearly everyone was in agreement—about the basic issue, that is. Where the discussion grew long was about what exactly to do about it.

After the first hour, during which time it seemed that people just felt the need to make themselves heard, two factions appeared to emerge: those in favor of simply educating the electorate about the "correct" position so that they would vote down the measure (which looked likely to make an upcoming ballot, either the April special election or the August primary; it was easy enough to gather signatures, and the Help Our County's Coffers crowd had been flooding the streets with fresh-faced young canvassers with clipboards), and those who wanted to propose a counter-measure to forever ban parking meters anywhere on Orcas Island. This faction in turn was divided between those who wanted to include all the San Juan islands in the forever-ban and those who felt it was better strategy to keep their efforts focused on Orcas.

Eventually, Matt raised his hand, and Leslie recognized him. "Voter turnout goes down measurably with every additional item on a ballot," he told the crowd. "Especially when there are dueling items—it confuses the voters. It's been proven; I can share articles with anyone who's interested." A quiet murmur went around the room. "I think we should concentrate on defeating the measure, should it make the ballot," Matt went on, "and then we can brainstorm about how to protect the island's character more permanently after this current threat has been handled."

There were more murmurs of agreement, though a few hold-outs still wanted to fight fire with fire.

After some more argument, a vote was held, and those who agreed with Matt carried the day. Then discussion turned to methods, which proved equally controversial. And it began to seem as though something wasn't being said…or, rather, that someone's name wasn't being mentioned, though clearly the majority of the people in the room knew who they were talking about. One of the *newcomers* Leslie had scornfully mentioned, it seemed. Whoever this was, they had not made themselves popular among the old guard.

Julie shifted on her feet, feeling weary, and not enjoying feeling out of the loop. Could she sneak out? No, not in such a crowded room, and she'd have to squeeze right by Gavin, who was effectively, if unintentionally, barring the doorway.

Had his shoulders always been this broad? And what in the world was the matter with her lately? Was this one of those post-menopausal rebound effects she'd read about? Because, ew, no thank you. Not with Gavin Jones, of all people.

Forcing her attention back to the meeting, she listened for a few minutes more and then raised her hand. When Leslie called on her, Julie said, "Thank you. For those of you who don't know me, I'm Julie Pessel, and I'm the owner of Paper Magic. I don't want parking meters in front of my shop any more than anyone else does. So I'll help in any way I can, but we don't have to solve the entire problem tonight—we have time. The deadline for even the special election isn't until late February. Before then, I can put up signs in my shop, which is right on North Beach Road. I'll talk to everyone I know, and ask them to do the same. I'll be happy to speak at a community meeting—maybe we can get the Grange, or the Odd Fellows Hall, if we're going to have this great a turnout? But right now, I want to go home! I think we've done all we can tonight—we're starting to talk in circles, and I'm starving and my feet are killing me."

"Hear, hear!" someone cried, near the head of the table. The room erupted into acclaim and echoes, and then applause. Several people pushed their chairs back.

"I think you touched a nerve there," Matt murmured in her ear.

"One moment, everyone!" Leslie shouted over the din. "One moment!"

The crowd reluctantly quieted down.

The gray-haired woman smiled at them all. "Thank you. I have just one final request."

Someone groaned.

Leslie cracked a small smile. "And that request is, please leave your names and contact information on your way out—particularly if you are willing to help, as Ms. Pessel has so generously offered. Gavin, there at the back door, has a signup sheet." She motioned at Gavin, who lifted a clipboard. "Thank you, everyone!"

Julie was glad that she and Matt were close enough to the door to be some of the first few people to leave their names and cell phone numbers, and then they were out into the night.

"Whew," Julie said, as her stomach growled. "That went right through dinner—do you want to check out that open mic night?" The Barnacle was Orcas Island's cutest, tiniest bar, not a restaurant, but they did have decent nibbles.

"I have to get back home," Matt said apologetically. "I promised Ramona I'd be back by eight—I can just make it if I head up now."

"Of course," Julie said, and pulled him into a quick hug. "Say hi to your dad for me."

"I will. He likes you."

Julie smiled. The old man liked all women, as far as she could tell.

After Matt headed to his car, Julie walked up toward the Barnacle, but even before she got there, she could tell it was packed. The windows were steamed up, and she heard the sound of laughter. As she got closer, the door opened and she could see inside. It was even more crowded than the library meeting had been—twice as many people packed into half the space.

I don't think I have another standing-room-only crowd in me tonight, Julie thought, turning around and heading back to her little path. She would have gone in to support Karen if it had looked like she'd needed it, but clearly the event was a resounding success.

Back in the quiet sanctuary of her home, she heated up a bowl of leftover black bean soup and thought about the evening. The meeting itself hadn't been much of a surprise: it was the way of small-town community meetings the world over.

But what had that all been about, noticing Gavin Jones? Of all people?

The microwave dinged, and Julie carried her bowl to the table. She stirred the soup as Fergie wandered into the kitchen, examining her own bowl critically. There was still at least half the kibble in it, even if Fergie had pushed it around to make it appear nearly empty.

Cats, honestly.

Why am I so unsettled all of a sudden? Julie asked herself as she took a fragrant, hearty bite. *I like my life—no, I love my life. Nothing is missing.*

Probably it was what had happened to Matt, she decided. From what he'd told them all, he hadn't seen Heather's decision coming. He had thought he was happy in his life. Yes, it was challenging taking care of a parent with dementia, but his and Heather's relationship had seemed solid. They had seemed up to the challenge.

And who just *left* someone when things got a little challenging, anyway? Maybe Heather had had deeper issues that none of the group had known about—maybe even Matt hadn't known about them, entirely.

Many years ago, when Julie had finally realized it was very likely over with Michael, it had still taken them the better part of two years to completely untangle. Part of that was because of divorce lawyers, of course; once they got involved, they managed to drag the timeline out considerably. But before it got to that point, Julie had felt strongly that she owed it to Michael, to their daughters, and to everything that they'd once been to each other to give it every chance she could. They'd gone to couples therapy and Julie at least had worked honestly and hard; it seemed as though Michael put in real effort as well, though he did never fully understand her core complaints.

Therapy hadn't made the ultimate separation any less painful, for either of them, but at least they could both tell themselves they hadn't just given up without trying. And Michael hadn't been left like Matt was now: blindsided, in shock.

She finished her soup and carried her bowl to the sink. Fergie brushed against her ankles; she reached down to pet her. It was strange to think about being so deeply affected by what happened in someone *else's* relationship. Julie hadn't given much thought at the time to how her and Michael's friends were taking their split. She'd been too busy navigating her own emotions, and those of Megan and Lori.

The girls had been fifteen and twelve when Julie first admitted to herself that something needed to be done. Difficult ages, both of them, but for different reasons. Megan, the older, had been a nearly straight-A student, very independent, a little high-strung. Julie had imagined that Megan would be worried about what the divorce might do to her parents' ability to pay for her college, but the girl had surprised her by going out and winning an impressive pile of scholarships, and then applying to a state school. Admittedly, it was the best state school: UC Berkeley. But that had meant she'd needed very little in the way of financial help from her and Michael.

Lori, the younger, had always been more of a dreamer, an artist, and less of an academic—certainly not a poor student, but far less focused on her grades. As an artist and creative person herself, Julie felt a soft spot in her heart for her sweet girl, though she worked hard not to show favoritism. Lori had also been the more gentle and expressive of the two girls, showering both parents with hugs and *I love you*'s that made her older sister's eyes roll. It was ironic, Julie thought now, that Megan was the one who phoned her mother far more regularly—probably that "good girl" persona in action.

Lori had taken their parents' separation harder—well, more noticeably hard, anyway—weeping unconsolably when Julie and Michael had sat the two girls down and told them he was moving out. And she had pushed both parents to stay friends, to an almost ridiculous degree. "Gina's parents do holidays together, even though they're divorced and married to other people," she'd said.

"Gina's parents have been divorced a long time," Julie had pointed out. "Did they always all get along so well?"

"I dunno." A teenage shrug.

Julie had pulled her sad girl into a hug. "I bet not. Maybe someday we will, honey, but everyone's feelings are a little raw right now. I think we need some distance so we can all heal. But your father and I do still love each other, even if we have agreed it's best that we not stay married. And we both love you girls more than anything else in the whole wide world."

Lori's tears had drenched Julie's shoulder.

Julie sighed at the memory as she settled at her desk under the bookshelves in the multi-purpose front room and pulled out her notebook. Things were much better now, though she still couldn't imagine doing holidays with Michael and his new wife Cindy. No, not "new"—they'd been married nearly ten years. Cindy was fine, she was great; a bit younger than Michael, stable and good-hearted, loving to the girls, and she and Michael seemed very well suited to each other.

Julie opened the notebook and read over the last few pages. She needed at least thirty more pithy quotes before her newest book would feel full enough to produce. This one was a themed volume: love and romance, as it happened.

After a half hour, and crossing out at least as much as she composed, she conceded the inevitable and closed the notebook. The community meeting had exhausted her, and her thoughts were all over the place.

And, most annoyingly of all, she couldn't get Gavin Jones's broad shoulders out of her mind.

ON MONDAY MORNING, Alicia texted Julie. *Looks like sun today; can you make a fourth for PB? Logan's off island.*

Julie thought about it, then flipped over to her weather app to confirm. Yes: though it was overcast and felt like rain now, the sun was supposed to come out by one o'clock. *Sure*, she typed back. *The usual time?*

Yep 3. See ya!

It had been a while since Julie had played pickleball: her friends usually played in the afternoons when her shop was open. As a result, she wasn't all that good at the game, but you didn't have to be in order to have a fun time.

When she got out to the courts, she saw Alicia and Lynne warming up, dinking the ball back and forth to each other across the net. "Hey, there you are," Alicia said. "Thanks for coming—we want to get as much play in as we can before the season ends."

"I thought they had indoor pickleball somewhere?" Julie asked, setting her bag down and getting out her paddle. She joined Lynne; Alicia dinked to both of them.

Alicia snorted. "Yeah, sort of. It's at the high school, in the gym, so it has to be in the evenings. Seven thirty or something. I'm on the sofa with a glass of wine by then, if not already full of dinner."

"Ugh!" Julie said, swinging too hard and hitting the ball past Alicia. "Sorry."

"No problem." She pulled another bright yellow whiffleball out of her oversized skort pocket and batted it across to Lynne. "I mean, if we get desperate, maybe we'll try. But it's not the same as being outside."

"Outside is a huge part of the appeal for me," Lynne agreed. "Oh, here's Robin."

After the fourth woman parked and joined them, they sorted into teams, warmed up a little longer, then played. After each game, they shifted the composition of the teams, so everyone got to partner with everyone else—and everybody got a chance to have to squint into the sun. Robin was the strongest player, followed by Alicia. Lynne had a good backhand, and a strong serve, but she also didn't move around very well.

After they had played for forty-five minutes or so, two men showed up and started playing a vigorous game of singles in the adjacent court. *Show-offs*, Julie thought, and didn't pay them much attention until a familiar voice caught her ear. She nearly missed a shot when she glanced over and saw telltale salt-and-pepper curls.

Is he stalking me? she wondered, shaking her head and refocusing on her play.

For this game, she and Alicia were partnered; Lynne and Robin made them work for it, taking the game to a ten-to-ten tie. Julie and Alicia pulled it out, though, finally winning twelve-to-ten. "Woohoo!" Alicia cried, after the traditional across-the-net paddle-tap. "Orcas Island Grand Champions Alicia and Julie carry the day!"

On the next court, Gavin and his friend had also just finished a game, and he had walked over to the sideline to grab his water bottle. "Hey," Gavin said, noticing Julie.

"Hi," she said, deeply annoyed as she felt a flush rise on her cheeks.

He took a long drink of water and then wiped an elbow across his forehead. "Thanks for coming to the meeting last week, and for volunteering to help," he said.

"Of course," she said. "Just let me know what I can do."

"I'm still collating all the names and notes," he told her. Was that a flash of irritation? Did he feel like she was pushing him, being impatient? "A lot of people wrote down things they'd be willing to do, and people they'd be willing to work with—or *un*willing to work with," he added with a smile, making Julie wonder if she'd imagined his annoyance a moment ago, or misattributed its cause.

"Ah." She smiled back. "Island life."

"You know it." His grin seemed entirely comfortable now.

Alicia and Lynne had been chatting; now Lynne said, "Are we ready?"

"I'm going to have to take off," Robin told them. "Sorry, gals; I have to pick up Greg at the ferry."

"Aww," Alicia said, sounding disappointed. Then she perked up. "Hey guys," she said to Gavin and his friend. "Do you want to rotate in with us?"

"Sure," said Gavin, and the next thing Julie knew, she was partnered with the man himself. Playing across from them were Alicia and his friend, an older man with a neatly trimmed silver beard who had been introduced as Will. Lynne sat out, mopping her own forehead and acting as line judge.

Julie flubbed three shots in a row, and then served into the net, before she settled down enough to play at something resembling her usual mediocre level. Fortunately, if embarrassingly, Gavin was a skilled player, both fast and accurate, and he largely carried them to a win. Before they rotated teams again, he pulled off his T-shirt, showing off a well-toned chest and a suspicious absence of love handles for a man of his age.

Librarians should not be this sexy, Julie thought before forcing her mind to focus somewhere, anywhere else. "I'll sit out this one," she said, taking the folding chair that Lynne vacated.

After three more games, everyone agreed they were exhausted; the sun, which had been surprisingly warm for this late in the year, had now sunk below the west hills and the temperature was plummeting steadily. "Do you ladies want to come out to Island Hoppin' for a beer?" Will asked. Gavin nodded eager agreement, and looked right at Julie.

"I've got to get home and start dinner," Alicia said, shaking her head and frowning. "Ron turns into an ogre if I don't feed him on the regular."

"Yeah, I need to get home too," Julie said quickly. Did Gavin's face fall? If it did, he covered it quickly.

Lynne shrugged. "A beer sounds great to me—I'm in."

As she drove home, Julie fought the strong urge to follow them to the brewery after all. Beer *did* sound great, and it had been a fun afternoon, and she didn't really have to get home for any reason, and Gavin looked…

No, she told herself. *Whatever is going on there, it's not for me.* She told herself again what an annoying prig he'd been when she'd dealt with him before, how unhelpful, how clearly judgmental. *If I'm having hormonal issues, I can find someone more suitable to date.*

Or a vibrator.

Alicia stopped by the shop the next afternoon. "Have you had lunch yet?"

"Do you mean have I eaten anything?" Julie asked her. "I don't have any employees who could give me a lunch break, if that's what you're asking."

Alicia laughed. "Yep: hangry. That answers my question. I'll be back in ten minutes."

She returned in more like twenty minutes, but she had a paper bag filled with something that smelled amazing. Julie just about swooned. "Quiche from Brown Bear," Alicia announced as she set the bag on the counter and pulled out two small boxes. "Do you want smoked salmon or ham and leek?"

"Ooh, ham and leek."

Alicia handed her a box, and then found plastic cutlery in the bag for them both. "Dig in."

Julie opened her box, inhaling the incredible aroma, and then took a big bite. "Mmm, still warm. This is so much better than a granola bar."

Alicia laughed. "I know, right?"

They ate in silence for a few minutes, while Julie kept an eye on the door. The day had been slow so far; the switch to winter hours would be coming at the right time. It didn't help that it was raining today. Sometimes rainy days sent all the tourists to town, rather than the hiking trails or whale-watching tours; other days it seemed to keep them away altogether, snug in their hotels or Airbnbs.

"You should have gone to Island Hoppin' yesterday with those guys," Alicia said suddenly.

"What? Why?"

"It was a total double-date waiting to happen. Lynne and Mr.

Silver Fox, and you and that library fellow…" Alicia grinned at Julie.

"Ew, him? No way."

Alicia just laughed. "I saw how you looked at him—and how he looked at you. Didn't you guys used to be friends?"

Julie shook her head. "No way, what are you talking about? We were never friends. I needed his help when I was getting my book project started, and he was—" She cut herself off before she could say *a total ass about it.* "Not very helpful," she amended.

"Huh." Alicia took another bite of her quiche and chewed thoughtfully. "Anyway, he's quite a hunk, isn't he?"

"I didn't notice," Julie lied. "And I'm not looking to date anyone." That, at least, was the truth. Was Alicia trying to live vicariously through her single friends? People in unhappy marriages sometimes did such things. "I'm sure Lynne had fun with them."

"I bet she did," Alicia said. "We should call her and ask how it went."

"It probably went nowhere—beyond three people having beers together after a fun afternoon of pickleball," Julie said primly.

"I wonder if Mr. Silver Fox is too old for Lynne, though," Alicia mused.

"His name was Will."

"Will, yes. Because Mr. Library Hunk is clearly too young for her."

"How old do you think he is?" Julie asked, despite herself.

Alicia grinned. "Aha, I knew you were interested. I don't know—early fifties? Fifty-five tops?"

"Lynne's just over sixty. He's not too young for her."

"We're not talking about Lynne, Julie. We're talking about *you.*"

"We're not, though," Julie said patiently, "because, as I may have *just* mentioned, I'm happily single, and I don't like the man."

"Mmm-hmm," Alicia drawled, setting her fork down. Half her quiche was uneaten. "So, what are you going to bring to the next soup group?" She cocked her head, then widened her eyes as if a brilliant idea had just occurred to her. "A *date?*"

"Alicia, seriously!"

Alicia shrugged, giggling. "Okay, I'll stop. But think about it, that's all. I know you're happy, and that's awesome: happy people make the best partners. The fact that you're *not* looking for someone means you're that much better of a catch. And there aren't a lot of interesting, eligible men our age on this island, you know."

How do you know that? Julie didn't ask. She merely said, "All right, I'll think about it. And I'm going to bring a frosted lemon pound cake. You'll love it."

Alicia patted her hard-won flat belly. "I hate you."

"I hate you too."

The friends grinned at each other.

"Thanks for lunch," Julie added. "I hadn't realized how hungry I was." Only crumbs remained in her box; Alicia was closing her own box, her half-slice still inside.

"I know, you never do. You just sit here and starve all day."

"Oh, I'm a long way from starving," Julie chuckled.

Alicia got up and picked up her oversized handbag, tucking the box in it. "All right, I've got to get back to work. It was good seeing you." Alicia was a freelance children's book editor, so she got to work from home and set her own hours. Sometimes Julie envied her this, but the freelancer's life was too uncertain for her, as a single person. Being a small business owner was scary enough.

She supposed that was one thing marriage, or at least partnership, was good for: increased financial security. Julie knew Ron collected a pension from the state college in California where he'd been an English professor, and he'd also inherited something from his parents—enough that he and Alicia did not have to worry, Julie was pretty sure. He did always seem to have a good supply of excellent wine at hand.

After closing up the shop and suffering through her lengthy commute home (all seventeen steps of it), Julie was pouring herself a glass of wine when her phone buzzed with a text. It was

Megan: *Is this a good time for a chat?*

Sure, Julie answered, taking the wine to the sofa and getting comfortable.

"Hey Mom," Megan's cheerful voice came over the line. "How's island life?"

"It's fine—how's city life?"

Megan chuckled. "Same as ever! I got another parking ticket; I hate my job; and they're gonna raise my rent again in the new year."

"Can they do that?" Julie sat up, all her Mom-instincts swinging into action. "It hasn't been twelve months since the last increase."

"It will be in January." She made a dismissive sound. "But it's fine, really—only going up three percent. Small price to pay for life in the fast lane."

"And what about your job? I thought things were getting better there." Megan worked for an environmental nonprofit start-up with an excellent reputation and a mission that was above reproach. Unfortunately, it also featured a staff of incompetent nincompoops and a deeply ineffectual boss who utterly failed to appreciate Megan's value to the enterprise.

In Julie's humble opinion, of course.

"Oh, it's not that bad either. I just wanted to complain."

"Complain away!"

Megan laughed. "I'm done now, that's all I needed. So what's new up there, anything?"

Julie started to say *Nothing*, but then thoughts of Gavin snuck into her traitorous mind. To banish them, she told Megan about the meeting at the library, and her volunteering to help.

"Whoah!" Megan said appreciatively. "My mom, the community activist."

"Not hardly. Just lending a hand." There was a brief pause, then Julie asked, "Any news on the dating front?"

"Mo-o-om," Megan moaned dramatically, channeling her inner teenage self. "Don't you realize that every time you ask me this, I push all thoughts of nice young men that much further away?" More seriously, she added, "Plus, you know I would tell you. You don't have to ask."

"You know I always will ask, though," Julie said, unperturbed. "It's what mothers do."

"If you say so."

They chatted a few minutes more before Megan said, "Oops—I gotta run, meeting a friend for drinks. A *girl* friend," she emphasized.

"I'd be happy with whomever you wanted to date," Julie said, deadpan. "You know that."

Megan giggled. "Love you, Mom."

"Love you, my dear."

Later that evening, as Julie cleaned up her few dishes after dinner, she found herself thinking about her earlier conversation with Alicia. Specifically, about Gavin. Had Alicia noticed a spark, or was she just projecting?

And what if she had noticed something between them? Julie hadn't been lying: she didn't want a relationship. They were a lot of work. Men, especially men their age, expected to be taken care of—just look at "Ron the ogre" when Alicia didn't feed him on time, for crying out loud. What was it the research said, that older men are happier when they're partnered, while older women are happier single? That was certainly Julie's experience.

Not that she was *older*, mind you. Fifty-eight was solidly middle-aged.

She washed the pan she'd stir-fried her veggies in and set it on the stove to dry. Had Gavin ever been married? Maybe he knew how to take care of himself. Maybe he…

How would *she* know? Julie chided herself. And why should she care?

Idle curiosity, her mind answered.

She slept restlessly that night.

Chapter 3

JULIE

The next morning, the sound of a jackhammer woke Julie. *What the heck?*

She got up, pulled on her bathrobe, and headed to the front door. When she opened it, the noise grew much louder; it was coming from in front of the store. Which of course she could not see from the house.

She went back to her bedroom and changed into a pair of jeans and a sweatshirt before going to investigate.

When she got to the small stretch of sidewalk before her store, she found two men in hardhats. One was manning the jackhammer, pounding directly in front of the steps leading to the shop's small porch. The other was measuring something out against a set of blueprints and spray-painting red squares at regular intervals on the concrete—there was one right in front of Karen's jewelry shop—and on the dirt path after the concrete ended halfway up the block. A county public works truck was parked in the spot in front of her store, with orange cones set around the empty spaces on either side of it.

"Excuse me!" Julie shouted to the jackhammer-wielding man. He did not hear her. She stepped into what she hoped would be his line of vision, but he was entirely focused on his task—making a horrible mess of the entire approach to her store. Nobody would be able to get by him. "Excuse me!"

He didn't look up, so she stomped over to the second man, who was nearly up to the restaurant on the corner by now. "Excuse me, what are you guys doing?" Julie asked him.

Startled, the man looked up, spraying a stream of red paint dangerously close to her feet before letting go of the nozzle. "Oh! Sorry, ma'am, I didn't see you."

"Right. Can you tell me what you guys are doing? That's my shop right there," she said, pointing at the jackhammer-man.

"Job from the county." He waved the blueprints at her, as though that explained everything. Or anything.

"Yes, I can see that. Doing *what?*"

"We're just putting poles in. I don't know what the whole project is for."

"Let me see that," Julie snapped, reaching for the blueprints.

He must have been further surprised by her forthrightness, because he handed them over. She scanned the first page, then swore. "Those bastards!" She flung the blueprints to the ground and started stalking back to the first man.

"Hey! Hey, stop!" the blueprint man called after her. She ignored him, and this time got right up close to jackhammer-man, so that he had to see her.

It was only when he jumped and loosened his grip on the noisy machine that she gave a thought to the potential danger involved. But he held onto the thing as its motor cut off. "Excuse me?" he asked her, looking puzzled, then reached up and pulled his ear protecters down, to hang around his neck. "Is something wrong?"

"Yes, it certainly is. You need to stop this at once. This is an illegal operation, and you are destroying county property—and completely obliterating access to my place of business, and that of every other shop on this street."

His puzzled look deepened to bewilderment. "I'm sorry, ma'am, but our work orders were pretty clear…"

Blueprint Guy had hurried up to them by this point. "Hey, whoah, let's all calm down here, okay? There seems to be some sort of misunderstanding—"

"There certainly is!" Julie felt her voice going shrill. "I was just at a community meeting about this issue last week. There is a *proposal* to add parking meters to Eastsound, not an order. In fact, the original, very unpopular proposal was not approved, so the folks behind it are trying to get it onto the ballot—next year. There should be no tearing up the streets now! You guys need to just pack it up and leave."

Jackhammer Guy looked to Blueprint Guy; then they both got that look on their faces. The one that said they were digging in their heels, and that no *lady* was going to tell them how, or whether, to do their jobs. "Says here it's all signed off on," Blueprint Guy said with a shrug. "The materials have been here since August, and today's the start date. So if you don't mind..."

"I do mind!" She took a deep breath, willing herself to calm down. Yelling at these guys was not going to help anything. "Who's your boss, who's in charge of this?" she asked, controlling her tone with some effort. "Can I speak to him or her?"

"Harlan Hicksman," said Blueprint Guy. "But he's over in Friday Harbor," he added with a smirk.

"Give me his number. I'll call him."

Blueprint Guy shrugged again, then fumbled around in his pocket and produced a cell phone, which he scrolled through a bit before saying, "Okay, it's 360..."

Julie entered the number on her phone as he rattled it off. "You said Harlan?"

"Yep. Harlan Hicksman."

"Good. Wait right here. Don't start that thing up again," she added to Jackhammer Guy, pointing at the noisy abomination.

Not waiting for his response, she strode a few steps away from the men as she placed the call. Naturally, it rang three times and went to voicemail. Schooling her voice as calm as possible, Julie left as clear and direct a message as she could, explaining who she was and asking Mr. Hicksman to call her at his earliest convenience. "Your men seem to think this is a misunderstanding," she finished. "I certainly hope that is true."

She ended the call and turned back to face the two workmen. "I left him a message," she said.

Again, they exchanged a glance before Blueprint Guy said, "Well, we're gonna have to keep on with our job, then. We've got our work orders, and until we hear otherwise from the higher-ups..."

She stifled a curse and nodded at him. "Fine. But be ready to stop again when I hear back from your *higher-ups.*"

Still fuming, she turned and went back to her house, texting Karen as she went: *Get down here as soon as you can, they're tearing up the whole street in front of our shops.*

What???!!?? came Karen's response a minute later. *Who???*

Julie sat on her sofa, just breathing, trying to get to where she could think again. The sound of the jackhammer resumed as she texted Karen back. *The sidewalk, I mean. Which is bad enough. It's the parking meter thing. Are you coming in today?*

I'll be there in fifteen minutes.

What could have happened? Clearly it was a mistake. The county council hadn't even taken up the proposal; it couldn't have been approved any other way. That's why the pro-parking-meter forces were working so hard to get it on the ballot. Probably some plans had been drawn up, and then—what?—gotten filed in the wrong place, under "approved projects" rather than "forget-about-it projects"?

She stared at her phone, which was not lighting up with a return call from Harlan Hicksman. She tried his number again, hanging up on the voicemail message.

She had to talk to someone. Maybe the county planning department? Who approved such things? She went over to her desk to research the county government.

Ironically, as soon as she opened up her laptop, she found an email from Gavin. It was all formal and official, thanking her for volunteering to help with the no-parking-meters effort (ha!), and asking for more information on what specific things she might want to do, with a list of a bunch of action items to choose from—clearly a mailing-list sort of email, and indeed, it was signed by both Gavin and by Leslie Magnas.

But Julie had been written directly, not bcc'd; and at the bottom of the form letter Gavin had appended a personal note:

Julie, it's been great seeing you recently. Pickleball was a blast—we should do it more often. Hope to hear from you soon. –G.

Well, she thought. *Guess what? You're going to hear from me* right away.

She double-checked that the email address he'd sent from was a personal one, and then typed out a reply:

Gavin, thanks for this—yes, pickleball was fun; I don't get out to the courts often enough.

I need to talk to you as soon as possible, though: the county has for some reason started jackhammering up the street in front of my shop, saying they have a work order to put in parking meters! We have to stop them. I don't have your number, so please call me as soon as you get this.

She added her phone number and hit *send.*

Back on the county website, she searched around, trying to figure out who even to call. After leaving several more voicemails with several more people in three different departments, she grumbled, "Doesn't anyone answer their phones anymore?"

Should she call the Sheriff's Department? Would that be escalating it too far? The workmen clearly believed that they were doing legitimate work. Well, maybe she'd give it a little longer; someone was bound to get back in touch with her sooner or later, and she didn't want to look hysterical. Besides, the damage was already done; the sound of the jackhammer was getting fainter as the workmen clearly moved up the block away from her store.

She sighed before closing the computer and getting up from the desk.

Fergie glanced up from her perch in the doorway. She could keep an eye on both the kitchen and the living room from here, without excess trouble or undue exertion. Julie reached down and ruffled her ears on her way into the kitchen, where she started coffee brewing.

What a morning, and all before coffee!

As the machine started to gurgle, there was a knock on her door. Julie opened it to find Karen, looking stricken.

"It's awful!" she said. "Why are they doing this?"

"They say they have a work order from the county," Julie said. "Come on in—coffee's almost ready."

"I don't think I can drink any more coffee right now, I'm too upset." Karen paced Julie's small living room. "You can't get into either of our shops, the sidewalk is totally in ruins."

"We should, I don't know, get some pallets from the grocery store to make ramps," Julie said. "I should go see—they were in the middle of it when I texted you."

"Well it's pretty thorough." Karen sighed and ran a hand through her spiked hair. "God! I shouldn't have missed that meeting."

"I don't know what good it would have done if you'd been there," Julie said. "Everyone was in agreement, but apparently, nobody told these clowns!"

"So, pallets: good idea. I'll go with you."

"Hang on," Julie said, and ducked into the kitchen, pouring herself a cup of coffee. "I'm ready."

Karen looked at her askance. "You're going to carry pallets in one hand and a mug in the other?" She shook her head. "Just drink that, and then we'll go."

Between the two of them, they managed to rig up reasonably stable access to their shops. The workmen, further up the street by now, studiously ignored them. In their wake, as well as down the street from Julie's store, other shopkeepers were showing up, reacting with alarm to the destruction.

"We should clear out of here before they realize we took all the store's pallets," Karen said, glancing down at the kayak rental place.

"They can get some at Girl Meets Dirt," Julie said. "They always have a pile of them out by the road."

"That's true. Well, anyway, good luck today." She headed for her shop, keys in hand.

"You too."

It was still over an hour before Julie normally opened, and she was in no mood to face the public, so she walked back home. *I need a distraction*, she thought. *And not just avocado toast*, she added, as her stomach rumbled. *Though that would be a good start.*

After eating, she went to her desk and pulled out her notebook. An hour was plenty of time to try to scribble out a few pithies. That might be just what she needed, as the entire County of San Juan continued to not return her phone calls.

Something must have broken loose in her creative mind when the men from the county broke up the sidewalk in front of her shop, because the clever, snarky quotes veritably flooded out of her. She credited most of them to her favorite purveyor of wisdom: the Countess Lucinda Devonryshireton, whom she had invented early on. The good Countess was acerbic and witty, yet always entirely socially correct: a Dorothy Parker of Edwardian England, if Ms. Parker had been an impeccably proper aristocrat.

Ooh, this is good, Julie told herself, closing up the notebook after filling several pages. *Maybe I can do a second book of love and romance—for the older set this time.* Of course if they were to be in keeping with the Countess's character, the "older set" would have to be widows and widowers; any unmarried girls older than about twenty, or men over twenty-five or so, would have been considered quite suspect, potentially damaged goods. So she might have to tweak some of the pithies…

Before heading out to the shop, she checked her email again: no answer from Gavin. And no one from the county had called back.

At least the sound of the jackhammer was growing more distant all the time.

Lynne

Lynne Daniels drove into town from Deer Harbor, on the west side of the island, admiring the ever-changing scenery as she passed through Crow Valley. She loved this time of year, when the shadows lengthened and the days shortened, but before the cold winter had fully set in. This part of the world didn't get the brilliant fall colors that the East Coast did, but enough people had planted enough non-native maples and other deciduous trees that provided a pop of bright red or gold here and there. Just enough to punctuate the lush, lovely green of the fields, and the cedars and firs that surrounded them.

Today was her day to volunteer at the senior center. Once a week, she gave a lecture, followed by a Q and A, on medical issues, particularly those relevant to older folks. Lynne was a retired doctor, though she'd kept her license active so that she could provide concrete advice and care to folks who needed it and couldn't afford things that Medicare didn't cover—or who didn't trust the government and avoided "socialized medicine."

She also kept her license active so she could continue to see patients at Orcas Island's health clinic. In theory, this was only as-needed, filling in during extra busy times, but she seemed to be called in at least once a week. It was hard to attract doctors out here to the islands; the cost of living was so high, even on a doctor's salary it was a hardship to live here. The clinic was chronically short-staffed, as promising young docs came and went. Lynne had lost track of how many she'd worked with over the years.

She felt lucky to live here herself. Her late husband, Charles, had also been a physician. She'd lost him far too early, to pancreatic cancer; during the most intense period of her grieving, she'd also lost her mind a little bit, and uprooted herself and their teenage son, Ethan, from their lives, selling their house and buying a plot of land on an island hundreds of miles away, a place she'd never even visited, had barely even heard of until she'd seen the clinic's job posting. The land she bought had had a one-room cabin on it, with no running water or electricity; it barely had a driveway from Deer Harbor Road.

Somehow, it had worked. She and Ethan had managed to improve and expand that cabin into the modest but comfortable home it was today. Lots of sweat equity, and lots of shouting at each other, but they'd gotten through it, and come out the other side closer than ever. *Our joint grief project*, she sometimes thought, looking at the lovely little house, now surrounded by actual neighbors, including her dear friend Steph.

Times did change, even out here.

Ethan had moved off-island for college and then settled in Seattle for work, but he still visited often, and even talked about moving back someday. So maybe she'd done something right. She wasn't sure how hard she should encourage him to move back. She missed him, of course; and there were young people here; but it was really a community of older folks.

Such as the people she helped at the senior center. *Crowded today*, she thought, pulling into the parking lot. She almost didn't find a space.

Her talks this month had all been about helping folks navigate open enrollment with Medicare supplements and Advantage plans. *Insurance*, she thought, as she headed to the small meeting room where she usually spoke. The chairs that had been set up were all occupied, and there was a line of people waiting in the hallway, who looked up and brightened as she walked in.

Sue, the receptionist, hurried after her and pulled her aside.

"We're going to move your talk to the dining room today," she said. "Not nearly enough room in here, and more folks are walking in as we speak."

They both turned to look at the doorway. Lynne could see cars in the lot beyond, circling, looking for spaces that weren't there.

"Always a popular topic," Lynne said. "How can I help?"

"George is already moving the tables and chairs around," Sue said. "It'll just be a few minutes."

"I can move furniture as well." Lynne nodded at the people waiting as she approached them on her way to the big dining room. "We'll just be a few minutes," she told the crowd.

"Need any help?" asked a frail older man.

"No, we've got it!" she said cheerfully. "Thanks!"

Medicare was supposed to be the answer to greedy, grabby insurance companies, she thought, her heart going out to all these anxious folks waiting for her words of wisdom. *Instead, the insurance companies just put their hands out for slices of the government pie, and leave the public out in the cold, as ever.*

If she hadn't already left a big-city medical practice due to grief, she'd have left it due to insurance companies.

Lynne put her shoulders back, stepped into the dining room, and began rearranging chairs.

JULIE

IT HAD BEEN a busy day at the shop, for which Julie was grateful, and also a bit surprised. Customers had had no trouble getting to her front door, walking across the sturdy bridge of pallets surrounded by yellow caution tape. Thankfully, many of her customers had asked about the work being done, so Julie was able to tell them exactly what she thought about it, and how they could help (if they were local).

She was totting up the receipts for the day—yes, the electronic cash register did it automatically, but Julie was old-fashioned and still wanted to review the individual sales—when there was a jingle over the door. Dang it, she hadn't locked it. She looked up with an apologetic smile, ready to send the late customers on their way, only to see Gavin walking in.

"There you are!" she exclaimed. "I've been trying to get hold of you all day!"

"I'm so sorry," he said, with a shy smile. "I just got your messages—and I saw the mess out front."

"I know! It's awful! And I feel like I've been shouting into an abyss all day. Those guys have drilled holes in the sidewalk all the way up this whole side of the street by now, I can't get hold of anyone from the county, and I couldn't reach you, or Leslie Magnas—"

"I'm sorry, I'm sorry," he said again, his voice gentle, soothing. "We need to talk about this, but you probably don't want to do it here." He glanced around the empty shop. "Can you leave, put a note on the door or something?"

"I'm closed—I was just cashing out, I forgot to lock the door. We can go somewhere else, sure." *I'll ask him to the house, and*—

His smile returned. "Can I buy you a drink at the Barnacle?"

Julie stared at him for a moment. That sort of sounded like… "Yeah," she finally managed. "That sounds great, actually." She gave him what she hoped was a friendly smile.

He looked relieved. "Wonderful. Shall we go now?"

"Yes, let's. I just need to finish up here—it shouldn't take more than five minutes."

On their way out, she glanced over at Karen's shop. It was dark; Karen usually closed at five, sometimes even earlier, if business was slow. Julie felt a small, guilty relief as she led Gavin down the path beside her house and up to the tiny bar. If Karen had been there, it would only be right to include her: this affected her business as much as Julie's.

"Good thing we're early," Gavin said, opening the Barnacle's door for her. "We stand a chance at getting a table." And indeed, the two-top under the window was free. No open mic event tonight, thank goodness.

She took a deep breath as they sat down across from each other. "I don't know what's going on," she blurted out. "I asked the county guys, and they said they had a work order, that it was all signed and official and everything—they had blueprints—but none of this makes any sense—I didn't know if I should call the sheriffs or not—"

Without interrupting her, Gavin somehow gently got her attention, stopped her flow of words. Redirected her. He picked up the leather-clad menu, and when she ran out of words, he said, "I want to hear everything. But let's order a drink first."

She picked up her own menu, though she knew what she wanted: same thing she always got here. She glanced through the small booklet just in case, and because Gavin was looking through his. After a minute, a young man came out from behind the bar. "What can I get you two?"

"A Vesper Twist, please," Julie told him.

Gavin nodded at her. "Is that good? It looks good, but I'm not much of a drinker."

"It's delicious, if you like gin."

He shrugged, and gave her that shy smile again. "I like it as much as any other alcohol. Okay, one for me too," he said to the bartender, and turned back to Julie. "Should we get some chips and dip to go with them?"

Julie's stomach rumbled aloud. She laughed, her tension ratcheting down another notch. "I guess so!"

The bartender said, "I'll be back in a minute."

After he left, Gavin leaned forward. "Okay. Tell me everything."

She went through what had happened today, though unfortunately she had more questions than answers. In any event, it didn't take long. He frowned and shook his head throughout.

"It's crazy," he said, when she was finished. "It's got to be some kind of misunderstanding, though why you couldn't get hold of anyone at the county…" He thought a moment. "Did you call or text Leslie?"

"No, I just emailed her—that's the only contact I had for her."

"Ah, she never checks her email. Do you mind if I text her right now? She may know something—and if not, she'll certainly want to be told sooner rather than later."

"Of course, please: go ahead."

He pulled out his phone and typed out a few lines, then set the phone on the table after sending. "I'll put it away if she doesn't respond quickly—"

"It's all right," Julie assured him. "This is a business meeting, you can keep your phone out."

Did his face fall just the smallest bit when she said *business meeting*, or was it just her overheated imagination? Or projection? Julie wasn't sure, and here came the bartender with their drinks and chips. They toasted and sipped. Her Vesper Twist was as delicious as ever: crisp and bracing, the citrus and the gin (and vodka!) just worked perfectly together. And the immediate rush of alcohol did help Julie unclench a little further.

"Ooh, this is good," Gavin said. "I wasn't sure if I'd like it, but I felt that I could trust you."

They smiled at each other for another long moment, long enough that it almost grew awkward. "You're not much of a drinker, you said," Julie said, to break the spell. "Why is that? If you don't mind my asking."

"Oh, not at all!" His smile was still relaxed, unguarded. "I just never got much of a taste for most alcohol, and it's expensive, and full of calories, and—you know." He shrugged. "Just never really became my thing." His eyes widened slightly as he watched her take another sip. "Not that I'm judgmental about anyone else's drinking!"

She laughed. "Don't worry, I'm not that sensitive." She held his eye. "I am remembering that it was your suggestion to come here, though."

He shrugged. "You got me there. It just seemed…like the thing to do."

"Because of my desperate messages, or how I looked when you walked into the shop?" she teased. "You thought I needed a drink, and fast?"

"I figured it couldn't hurt!" he said, laughing. "But no, you looked just—"

Beside him on the table, his phone lit up with a text, and buzzed.

"Ah, here's Leslie." He turned the phone so they could both see the screen.

Oh my god. I need to see, and we need to strategize. I'm heading straight to town.

Gavin looked up at Julie. "Should I tell her to meet us here?"

She thought a moment. "No, like she says, she needs to see the damage—and I'm going to need dinner, as delicious as these chips are."

"Me too."

"My house is right behind the shop. I can cook something…" She cast her mind's eye home, to her fridge. Not much in there; she was due for another off-island big-box shopping trip soon, with maybe even an expedition up to Bellingham for more specialized items. Of course there was always pasta in the pantry…

"Let's go to Mijitas," he said. "I'll see if I can get us a table."

"Sounds good."

He made a quick phone call, then texted Leslie back. They would meet in front of Julie's shop in forty-five minutes, and go to dinner from there.

"Okay," Gavin said, setting his phone down and leaning back to smile at Julie. His drink was still nearly full, while she'd already drunk half of hers. "Thank you for reaching out, Julie," he went on. "I'm sorry, again, that I missed your messages all day."

Her heart gave a little flutter as she smiled back at him. "That's all right. I'm not usually glued to my email either."

"Let's exchange phone numbers so this doesn't happen again. I can give you Leslie's as well."

"Good idea."

After they took care of this business, he put his phone entirely away. "We should probably wait till Leslie gets here to talk any more strategy or anything," Gavin said.

"True." She chuckled. "I guess we'll just have to chat and enjoy our drinks."

"Oh no!"

They exchanged another grin.

"I'm glad you came to find me at the shop," Julie said. "I was going a little crazy, not able to get hold of anyone."

"Your shop is really cool. You must love your work." It was more of a statement than a question.

"I do. Oh, I sometimes get tired of being on my feet all day, but I love meeting visitors to the island, and I especially love making my books."

He took a small sip, then set his glass on the table and gave Julie an earnest look. "Your books. I…think we may have gotten off on the wrong foot about them."

"Oh?" This was interesting. So he did remember their interactions at the library? She hadn't used any of their reference books in several years. She hadn't needed to.

He looked embarrassed, which somehow made him even more attractive. "Yes. I was, well, a little judgmental. When you told me what you were doing. I thought…well, never mind what I thought. I was clearly wrong."

"No, tell me what you thought," Julie said, leaning forward with a challenging smile. She took another sip of her drink, and then another potato chip. "I'm curious. I won't hold it against you." *Since you're being so nice and admitting your snobbery, all unprompted.*

Gavin laughed, still looking abashed. "I thought it sounded, um, kitschy? Not serious? But I've seen your books, and they're really quite astonishing. Lovely, and well put together—both in their construction, and in their contents."

Had he spent that much time in her shop? Julie didn't remember seeing him there before he'd dropped off the flier last week. He certainly hadn't stuck around and browsed then.

He must have read the confusion on her face. "I have some friends who are fans of yours—they've got quite a collection. I saw a stack of your books at their house, and I was really struck."

"Oh, that's nice," Julie said, flattered. Should she ask who the friends were? But she felt suddenly shy. "Well, I appreciate your telling me this. I really enjoy making them."

"Is the paper all handmade too? I mean, by you?"

"Yes, and most of the covers as well—the decorated cardboard ones, anyway. I get the leather covers from Orcas Island Leather Goods."

"Ah, that makes sense. They do a good job."

"They do."

Then they gazed at each other for a long moment, giving each other goofy smiles. *What are we, teenagers?* Julie thought. But this felt good.

She hadn't been interested in a man in a really, really long time. Was she interested in Gavin? It certainly seemed so.

Or maybe it was just nice to be complimented for her work. It could be that.

"So," she said, just as he was opening his mouth to say something. They both laughed, and then there was the ritual of *No, you*. He won, so she went on: "So how is it going, working at the library? Are you in charge of events now, or were you just helping out with the parking meter meeting?"

"Ah," he said, his eyes lighting up. "I'm not entirely in charge of events—Rich still likes to keep his hand in—but he's planning on retiring next year, and they're asking me to do more and more of them, which is great. I have some ideas about community outreach. The library is such a great resource, and it's woefully underutilized. Getting the business meeting in there last week was a good start, but we need to get younger folks involved."

He went on to tell her about a program he had started for teens, and then another one that was still in the planning stages: a lecture series, focusing on current events. Something to take advantage of all the retired intellectual talent living on Orcas Island. Julie sipped her drink and watched him, appreciating his enthusiasm, and the play of the Barnacle's dim light on his handsome features.

"Jeez, I'm doing it again," Gavin suddenly said, setting his empty glass down after telling her about his third new program idea. "Now you see why I don't drink—I get one cocktail in me and then I *cannot* shut up."

Julie laughed. "You're fine! I was enjoying listening—and I did ask, you didn't just take over the conversation."

"I hope not!"

"Not at all. And I think a writing mentorship for youth is a great idea. I'd be happy to help out, if you need more mentors. I mean," she added hastily, "I'm not a professional published writer or anything—"

"No, you'd be great!" he said, looking delighted. "Your books are just the sort of creative endeavor that would be great to show the kids. They need to see that 'books' doesn't just mean writing traditional books, like novels and textbooks and stuff. I'd love to have you help out, if you've got the time."

"I have a little time, and I'll have even more starting in November, when I go to winter hours with the shop." Of course, she'd been planning to spend the extra time reading, relaxing, and creating more of her own books…not to mention that off-island shopping day she really should schedule soon…but she could mentor teens once or twice a week. Especially if it meant spending more time with Gavin, who was just seeming more charming and interesting by the moment.

She looked at his empty glass (hers had been done for a while), and then her watch. "I guess we should settle up here; Leslie should be in town in a few minutes."

"Right!" He pulled out his wallet, as Julie reached for her purse. "Hey, none of that—I invited you here, as you reminded me earlier," he told her with a smile.

She relented. "So you did. Thank you."

After he paid, they walked back over to the front of her shop. In the darkness, it was harder to see the holes, but the streetlights did pick up the caution tape. "I still can't believe this happened," Julie said, remembering her fury of this morning. A little of it rose up again now, though the drink helped blunt its edge.

The drink and the company, perhaps.

"I can't believe it either," Gavin said.

"We really need to get to the bottom of this."

"We will."

Chapter 4

JULIE

As Julie and Gavin stood in front of her shop in the chilly evening air, a car pulled over and parked, and Leslie Magnas got out. "Is this it? My god!" she cried, hurrying over to join them on the sidewalk. She examined the mess. "This is terrible. I knew it was bad, but seeing it is another thing altogether." She walked up and down the whole area, past Karen's shop and all the way up to the corner, looking closely at each hole. When she returned, she said, "All right, let's go to dinner—I need a margarita."

At Mijitas, they were seated at a colorfully tiled table in the second room. Julie ordered her favorite: the pork verde, which always looked like too much food, and yet she always managed to eat it all, even after demolishing a basket of warm house-made corn chips with salsa and guacamole. Leslie asked for a prawn enchilada and a double margarita on the rocks; Gavin got fish tacos. "I'm boring, but I love fish tacos," he said.

"Fish tacos are not boring," Julie hastened to assure him.

"All right, I made some phone calls on my drive in, and here's what I found out," Leslie said, after the waiter had taken their orders.

"You managed to get hold of someone?" Gavin asked. Julie was surprised too.

Leslie gave them both a wry smile. "Give me some credit. I've lived here all my life; I have numbers that aren't published anywhere."

Julie felt better already. With this formidable woman on their team, surely the "misunderstanding" would be cleared up quickly.

But Leslie's smile fell away as she went on. "It's not good news, I'm afraid. Apparently, while it's true that the larger project would need voter or county council approval, a 'pilot project' can be approved by a smaller contingent of councilors—only two, in this case."

"What?" Gavin asked, appalled. "Who?"

"Brinkman and Lovado."

Gavin rolled his eyes, as Julie tried to remember what she knew about those two council members. Very little, as it happened.

"I know," Leslie was saying.

"I've never been sure whether those two were in someone's pocket, or just ineffectual," Gavin said with disgust. "I guess this answers that question."

"Well, but even so, how did the people behind the parking meter project sneak this in?" Julie asked. "Shouldn't even a pilot project be something where public notice is given and all that?"

"Technically, yes," Leslie said, "but in this case, speaking of someone's pocket…"

"Let me guess," Gavin said, darkly, as the waiter arrived with everyone's drinks. Water for Gavin; Leslie's huge margarita; and a normal-sized blended margarita, with a salted rim, for Julie. "A certain vacation-rental developer, fairly new to the island?"

"The very one," Leslie said bitterly, "and those pockets are quite deep." She took a big swig of her drink. "Ahh, that helps." She glanced at Julie, then leaned forward and lowered her voice. "We want to be careful about naming names out in public—one never knows who might be listening in."

Julie looked around the busy, noisy room. Nobody appeared to be paying them any attention, and it was hard to hear even each other. But, as she had pointed out, Leslie had lived on the island all her life; she knew how things worked here.

Leslie leaned even closer to Julie. "It's Sam McLeod," she said, in just over a whisper.

"Oh," Julie said. She'd heard the name before—or had seen it on signs around town, anyway.

"Exactly." Leslie nodded. "You see the problem."

Julie didn't, exactly, but she was pretty sure Leslie and Gavin would fill her in.

Leslie didn't disappoint. "After the council rejected the initial proposal and the ballot efforts began, our developer *friend*," she pronounced the final word with heavy sarcasm, "apparently, went to his two pet council members and convinced them that the ballot measure would stand a much better chance of passing if he could demonstrate the viability of the plan. And the only way to do that, or so he insisted, was to test it on the ground here. 'No other small community, even a small tourist destination, is like Orcas,' he told them."

"That's true," Gavin broke in, "and that's the exact reason *not* to go through with this!"

Leslie shook her head. "You don't have to convince me. But those two are his faithful puppets. They don't wipe their own asses without running to him for permission first. I wonder what he has on them."

"Did he help get them elected?" Julie asked.

"No," Leslie said. "That's the worst part: they're longtime county councilors, and Brinkman's from an old islander family, going back generations. I really don't understand why they're falling all over themselves to serve Himself."

"Like you said," Gavin said, "maybe he's got something on them."

"Or maybe they're just greedy. Or getting older and losing their marbles. I don't know. But I do know that they not only suggested this pilot project, they helped him draw it up so that it would go through without any review—and they even managed to sidestep public notice. I'm not sure how they did that; my source didn't know, but we should be looking into that.

"Meanwhile," she went on, "they made a big show of marching their signature-gatherers all around town and hiring an elections consultant who specializes in small communities. Diverting attention from what they were really doing, which was just going ahead with the entire project. They mean it to be a fait accompli. A 'better to ask forgiveness than permission' kind of thing, and they're counting on the county's unwillingness to spend even more money undoing something that's already in place."

"They *are* just about doing the whole project, too," Julie said, leaning forward. "I looked at those blueprints—from what I could tell, they're putting meters up the whole stretch of North Beach Road! That's half the town!"

"Exactly," Leslie agreed. "And Main Street is on their plans as well—which leaves only Prune Alley."

"That's so dishonest!"

Both Leslie and Gavin gave Julie sympathetic looks.

She shrugged. "I mean, yes, clearly it's wrong, that's why we're here talking about this. And I suppose I shouldn't be so surprised, but I am. I'm not from an old islander family—I haven't even lived here ten years—so maybe I'm naïve, but it has always felt like such a straightforward, honest place."

"It is," Leslie said. "For the most part. And we're going to keep it that way."

The waiter arrived with three large plates. "Careful, these are hot!" he said cheerfully, sliding everyone's meals in front of them. An intoxicating aroma rose up; Julie took a deep, grateful sniff. "And here's tortillas," the waiter added, setting a small dish in the middle of the table. "Does anyone need anything else?"

A time machine to go back and prevent this Sam McLeod villain from tearing up my street, Julie thought, but just shook her head and smiled.

They dug in with enthusiasm; conversation stopped in the face of these more important developments. Once everyone's appetites were sated, they resumed.

"First thing tomorrow morning," Leslie told them, pushing a corn chip around the sauce on her plate, "according to my sources who will remain nameless so don't ask me again, Gavin, a temporary injunction will be filed in Friday Harbor. That should stop any more work being done, at least until it gets ruled on."

"What are our chances there?" Gavin asked. "I'm not asking for any names, but…there's more sympathetic judges and less sympathetic judges."

"Our friends will do what they can. No guarantees. In any event, it might buy us some time."

Gavin nodded. "We need to mobilize immediately, then. Another community meeting?"

"I can help with that!" Julie put in. "Should we try for the Odd Fellows Hall this time? The library is great," she gave Gavin a quick smile, "but even that big room was pretty crowded. I imagine even more people are going to want to turn out once they hear about what happened—once they see the mess the county has made of the public walkways. Everyone I talked to today was pretty upset."

"Yes, you're right," Leslie said. "Odd Fellows or the Grange, though the Grange is rather chilly this time of year—not heated, you know."

"I wonder if we shouldn't also try for more targeted, smaller meetings," Gavin put in thoughtfully. "In private homes."

"You mean like fancy fundraisers?" Leslie asked, frowning.

"Yes, but without the fundraising part." Gavin flushed as he went on. "I'm thinking of the psychology of the thing—a smaller gathering feels more intimate and exclusive, and even if the people aren't any more influential, it *feels* that way. So it might be more motivating. You know—garden club meetings, book groups, things like that. Places where people can talk to each other."

"I have a soup group," Julie said, before she could stop herself. Both Leslie and Gavin looked at her, puzzled. "It was a book group, but the books somehow turned into...soup."

Leslie chuckled. "Sounds yummy."

"It is, actually. We have some really good cooks in the group. Anyway, we meet twice a month. I could see..." She stopped herself, realizing who was hosting next; Ron and Alicia would never agree to inviting a bunch of strangers into their house, even though it was the biggest space. (Well, *Ron* wouldn't.) Steph would be all over it, but her next meeting wasn't till December. Matt, however, was hosting the one after Ron and Alicia. Matt was clearly concerned about the issue; he'd likely be delighted to add some friends and neighbors to his evening. "I'll look into the Odd Fellows too, but for a private thing, I can ask at my next meeting, this Sunday, and see what the group thinks. Then we could do an event two weeks after that maybe? Mid-November?"

"Perfect," Gavin said, looking at her gratefully. "That would be ideal."

Leslie still didn't look entirely convinced, but she nodded anyway. "We'll need to try any number of approaches, I think. Especially since time is short—we'll need to reach as many people as possible, and ask them to reach out to their friends as well." She gave them both a grim smile. "These turkeys will see what they've stepped into before too long. Thinking they can outflank us just because they've moved here with their big-city ideas and big-city dollars!"

Gavin snorted. "You know, probably half the local business owners originally moved here from somewhere else...as did I..."

She shook her head and lifted her nearly empty margarita glass. "Doesn't matter; you're all honorary locals now, so long as you respect the island and its history. *Those* people fail to recognize the uniqueness of our little slice of paradise. They will learn: never mess with Orcas Island."

"Because we're not Seattle!" Julie said, lifting her glass and clinking it against Leslie's. Gavin raised his water glass and did the same.

"Hear, hear!"

After Leslie drove off, Gavin offered to walk Julie home.

She laughed softly. "It's not very far. In fact, you can almost see it from here—well, you could if it weren't hidden behind the shop and the trees."

"Well, exactly," he pointed out. "What if there are crazed weirdos hiding in the bushes? I'd never be able to forgive myself if you were kidnapped and sold to human traffickers when I could have prevented it. Besides," he added while she giggled, "it's on my way. I'm still parked at the library, and the quickest way to get there is up that path."

"All right, I will permit you to escort me safely to my door, Sir Galahad."

He proffered an arm; she took it, and they strolled down the sidewalk, avoiding the ugly holes every few feet. Julie concentrated on the warmth of his arm, and of his body beside hers, even through their jackets. It was kind of nice, she thought, walking down the street on a man's arm.

"I suppose the town could plant flowers in those holes, once the parking meter boondoggle has been defeated," Julie said, glancing down at their feet.

"Not a bad idea," Gavin said. "It could be like an extension of the museum garden."

"Ooh, yeah, the hollyhocks," Julie said. "I love the hollyhocks—I wish I could grow some, but I have a black thumb. And no garden to speak of anyway—which is a good thing, trust me."

"Hollyhocks are easy, and they love this climate," he said.

She shook her head. "Nothing is easy, and nothing but cedars loves this climate!"

"The trick is a greenhouse."

She glanced up at him. He was smiling happily. "You have a greenhouse?" she asked.

He nodded, smiling. "Yes, actually two greenhouses. One for starts and overwintering, and the other for things that don't even like our summers."

She realized she didn't know where on the island he lived. And she further realized that, while she would like to find out—and to see what kind of garden needed two separate greenhouses to support it—she also felt a certain deliciousness in the anticipation. If this went anywhere, she would see his house, his garden.

If this didn't go anywhere…well, it was still lovely, walking home on his arm. Laughing together. Who would have believed that a day that had started so horribly could have ended this nicely?

The walk was over far too soon. She had to let go of his arm to lead him onto the public path, and then past the "private home" sign, through the gate, and down the tiny side path that led to her front door, nearly hidden under a carefully placed arbor.

"Wow, you weren't kidding," he said, looking around. "You're right in the middle of town and yet completely invisible."

"Just how I like it," Julie said with a laugh.

"Is there some sort of metaphor there?"

Still smiling, she said, "If there is, I'd rather not look too closely at it."

He followed her up onto her front porch, where they stood before her door. Should she invite him in?

Would there be a…?

Gavin reached out a hand; Julie took it. It was warm, even warmer than the body heat she'd felt through his jacket, and just the right amount of firmness. He gave her hand a tender squeeze, gazed into her eyes, and said, "Thank you so much for a wonderful evening—despite the reason."

"It was my pleasure—and, same," she said. "Best great ending to an awful start-of-the-day I've had in a long time." She still held his hand. "I'll let you know what I find out about the Odd Fellows."

"Wonderful. We'll talk soon."

And then he squeezed her hand once more before letting it go and walking away.

Inside her house, Julie wandered around aimlessly, from the front room to the kitchen and back. Fergie followed her at first, then settled on the back of the sofa, watching her, puzzled.

Had she wanted a kiss? Well, yes! But...speaking of the delicious anticipation, maybe that was something worth waiting for? The walking arm in arm was certainly nice, and the handshake, but...a handshake, really? *How* old *are we?* she thought, chagrined.

Then she flopped down onto her sofa and laughed at herself. "How old are we indeed," she said to the cat. "Wondering whether a boy likes us or not."

Fergie purred, and stepped down to make her way into Julie's lap.

"You're right, as usual," Julie said, petting her. "He does seem to like us. And weren't you just telling me I needed to fall in love? You're not some kind of witch's familiar, are you?"

Fergie kneaded Julie's thighs.

LYNNE

SHE'D WORKED AT the clinic three days already this week, filling in for one of the young docs. This one was out with covid; Lynne expected she'd be subbing for him for the rest of the week and probably at least the first part of next week too. The medical clinic on Orcas Island was nothing like a big-city hospital, of course, but eight hours of seeing patients, one after another all day long, day after day, was still exhausting.

Aren't I supposed to be retired? she thought as she stepped into her small house, looking around with tired satisfaction. Her little sanctuary, full of bright colors and soft textiles. "You should have been a surgeon, not a g.p.," her husband had frequently told her. "The precise and careful way you work with your hands."

But she would laugh and tell him, "No, surgeons are technicians; I'm an artist. And nobody dies if I drop a stitch."

She had sewed, knitted, and crocheted through a large part of her younger years, keeping her hands busy while her mind focused on conversations, television, or radio programs. Then she had made a brief venture into lace-tatting, but found the threadwork just a bit too fussy. From there she'd found weaving; her large loom was still on the property here, though now banished to the storage shed out back.

Her current handiwork obsession was embroidering, particularly on silk. She'd resisted embroidery for so long, envisioning the long hippie dresses and colorful men's shirts of her youth, thick thread on cheap cotton fabric, rainbows and peacock tails. Then a pillow in a home decorating store in Seattle had caught her eye, and she hadn't looked back since.

"Jeez, Mom," Ethan had said, laughing, the last time he'd come home for a visit. "Is it time to build that extra room on the house after all?"

"Don't be silly," she'd told him. "There's plenty of room for you to sleep in here."

"I always knew someday I wouldn't have a room in my own mom's house..." he'd lamented. "I just never dreamed I'd be displaced by a bunch of fancy pillows."

"They're not displacing you! They're on the bed, where pillows belong. Soft, comfortable pillows."

"Forty of them!"

She'd laughed. "How you exaggerate. Surely there can't be more than, er, thirty-five or so."

He was already counting. "Forty-three! And that doesn't even include the blankets, or whatever these are." He'd lifted several pieces off the bed. "Is a princess supposed to sleep on top of this all, and not feel the pea underneath her?"

"Those are wall hangings," she'd said.

He'd looked them over appraisingly. "These are very nice, actually. You could probably sell them for real money in some gallery somewhere."

Lynne had stopped herself from scoffing aloud. "Yes, maybe."

"But we both know you never will."

She smiled now at the memory, as she stood gazing into Ethan's room/the guest bedroom/the craft room. *Should* she add onto the house? It would be nice to have a little more room—she loved spending time in Steph's spacious home next door—and she could certainly afford it. But ugh, she didn't want to deal with finding a contractor, making building plans, getting permits; and she most certainly didn't want to live with construction.

Too bad she was too old to do the work herself. If Ethan would be willing to come up and help…

But no, he wouldn't be able to leave his job, and his life, for the length of time it would take even to just put one room onto the house. He worked in the tech industry—in computer games, of all things—"pushing pixels" as he called it. Lynne freely admitted that she didn't entirely understand what he did, but it was lucrative, and he enjoyed it. Yes, he could work remotely; but Marie, his live-in girlfriend, could not—she was the hostess at a high-end restaurant on Capitol Hill. Lynne did not see Marie being eager to let Ethan vanish on her for months on end.

And it really wouldn't make sense to just add one room, honestly. If they were going to go to the trouble to open outside walls, they ought to expand the kitchen, and they *really* ought to add a second bathroom. What kind of house in this day and age had only one bathroom? It had seemed perfectly reasonable when they'd done their original remodeling, and it was still quite workable for a woman who lived alone.

It was only a pain when she had overnight guests. Which was

seldom enough indeed.

She'd been planning a complicated protein-heavy salad for her dinner—one of her favorite kinds of meal, which always left her satisfyingly full yet also energized—but she just felt too wiped out right now to do all the washing and chopping, not to mention inventing just the right dressing. So she opened the freezer, staring in at all the healthy frozen meals. Frozen food had certainly improved since the Salisbury steak and tater-tots offerings of her younger days.

But nothing in her freezer sang to her tonight. *What I really want…* she thought, moving to the cupboard.

I shouldn't.

Hell, I worked hard all day.

Retired general practitioner Lynne Daniels, advocate of healthy eating and an active lifestyle at every age, pulled a package of ramen noodles off the shelf. During the three minutes that her dinner spent in the microwave, she opened a bottle of beer and poured it into a tall frosty glass.

"Now there we go," she said, smiling as she carried the steaming bowl of carbs, fat, and a full day's recommended allowance of sodium, to the kitchen table.

Julie

Thursday was Halloween, and Halloween on the island was nothing like Halloween in the California town Julie had grown up in—or the suburb where she'd raised her daughters. For one thing, kids didn't trick-or-treat from house to house: the island was too rural, with no streetlights outside of town. Many houses were on big plots of land, with a half-mile walk just to reach the next-door neighbor's place.

So the business community had organized daytime trick-or-treating in Eastsound, and the sheriff's deputies closed down the town's three main streets—Prune Alley, North Beach Road, and

Main Street itself—for a few hours in the afternoon. Hundreds of adorably costumed kids went from store to store, filling their bags with the bounty provided by poor suffering business owners. And thankfully, the hole-digging had had to stop for the day.

"I need to apply for a grant from the county council to help fund this next year," Julie said to Alicia and Steph with a laugh as she tore open what had to be her fortieth mega-bag of fun-sized M&Ms.

Her friends had offered to help her with the deluge. Steph looked great dressed as a witch, while Alicia was Catwoman—or at least a cat woman. Julie herself had run out of time—too busy dealing with the parking meter crisis—and was going to be a ghost until Steph had run home and brought her a goblin costume. "David is never going to wear it," she said. "He never has; it's completely unused."

Julie felt a little self-conscious in the green suit with the big rubber ears and nose, but she had to admit, it was a pretty effective disguise. Especially once she pulled back her long dark hair and tucked it under the odd little hat.

Kids shrieked with delight when they saw the three friends, hopping up and down in sugar-fueled glee. "I'm sure glad I don't have to take that gang home tonight," Alicia said, after a particularly large and over-the-top group had scampered off to Karen's shop next door, screaming anew as they took in her vampire get-up. "I don't know how parents do it."

"In my day, we didn't go around with them," Julie said, smiling as she thought about Megan and Lori venturing off into the fun-scary night, carrying hollow plastic pumpkins to fill to the brim with candy. "I think they burnt most of that excess energy before they even came back home. Or maybe I just don't remember, it's been so long."

"Hard to imagine parents letting kids just run wild," Steph said, shaking her head. "I mean, we did it ourselves when we were kids, but the world is so different now."

"Even on Orcas Island," Alicia said sadly.

"It probably isn't," Julie said. "I'm sure it's perfectly safe to send the kids around alone—to the stores and restaurants, in broad daylight. But it would look so weird, I can't see anyone being willing to give it a try."

"It would look criminal," Steph said. "Remember that story a few years ago, about the Scandinavian woman who left her baby in a stroller outside a store here in the U.S. because that's what they do in her country? And she got arrested?"

Julie and Alicia nodded as another troupe of little monsters swarmed up to the shop door. "Eek, you're so scary!" Julie said to the lead monster, who was so covered in shaggy brown fur that she couldn't tell if it was a boy or a girl.

"You are too!" the child shrieked. "Trick or treat!"

The invasion wore down after a few hours, and the deputies went up the street, ushering stragglers along and removing the barriers to traffic. "Whew," Julie said, after she glanced out, ensuring that it was really over. She pulled off her hat and rubber nose, and wiped her forehead. "That was a marathon."

Alicia was consolidating the last few pieces of candy into one bag. "They just about cleaned you out."

"We should take that to the meeting Sunday," Julie said, nodding at the bag. "In fact, that can be my contribution—I'm signed up for dessert, but this week has been insane."

Steph laughed. "Sure, but you're not going to *not* also bake something. I know you, Julie Pessel."

Julie put her hands up in a gesture that said *I surrender*. "Guilty as charged."

"Didn't I hear some sort of a rumor about frosted lemon pound cake?" Lynne asked.

"Ugh!" Julie said. "That's a ton of work, and I realized it's more of a summer thing anyway. Maybe I'll just make brownies." She reached for the bag and peered inside. "What's left?"

"Mostly Junior Mints and some Almond Joys," Alicia told her.

"Those won't survive long enough to bring to the meeting—you're right, I'll bake. Do you know what soup you're going to make?"

"I don't," Alicia said. "Something cozy for winter, though. Do you think anyone would mind if I did something with beans again? I know you just did black beans."

"I can't imagine anyone would protest," Julie said, and Steph nodded agreement.

"All right, we'll leave you to it," Steph added, to Julie. "See you Sunday."

Chapter 5

MATT

Matt *really* didn't want to go to the Sunday Soup Social. Everyone had been so kind and understanding two weeks ago, right after Heather had left him. When he was still numb, still raw. (And then drunk.) He knew they'd be just as kind this time—and forever, if he needed it.

He just…didn't want to face anybody. Kind or otherwise. The numbness was fading. The heartbreak underneath it was much worse.

The trouble was, he didn't really have much choice about staying home tonight. Ramona was already on her way to come and stay with Gordon, his dad; she relied on the regular schedule of visits that Matt had arranged with her. And frankly, Gordon relied on them too, if for different reasons. It was important, when caring for someone with dementia, to keep as much routine as possible. As much familiar, regular, ordinary stuff to anchor to.

Plus, his dad really liked Ramona.

Of course, Matt could always just go out and *not* go to the soup group. Drive around aimlessly. Take himself out to dinner. Go drink somewhere.

But no.

He knew, somewhere in the remaining rational part of his mind, that seeing his friends, being among people who cared about him, eating homemade soup: this was the best thing for him right now. He knew he would heal. Someday.

Certainly not tonight.

"Hey Dad," Matt said, heading into the living room where his father sat in his recliner, reading last month's *AARP Magazine* (again). "You know Ramona will be here in a few minutes, right?"

"Oh yes, of course," his dad said with a big smile.

Matt believed him, too. Not only did Gordon look forward to her visits, but Matt knew his dad checked the little calendar on his bureau many times a day, circling important events, and crossing off each day on his way to bed every night. Another familiar anchor: the calendar.

But then Gordon followed this with a puzzled frown. "Didn't she move out, though?"

Matt forced himself to smile bravely back at his dad. "That was Heather, Dad. My girlfriend. Ramona is our friend on the island who comes and stays with you when I have to go out somewhere."

"Oh. I knew that."

You did, thought Matt. *It's all in there somewhere...*

"Anyway," Matt said, "I've left dinner for both of you in the oven—I got pizzas at that new place that you both like so much."

"Pizza! Pepperoni, I hope."

"Yes, pepperoni. And also a veggie one; Ramona doesn't like to eat so much meat, remember?"

"That's just silly of her," his dad said. "She could use a little more meat on her bones."

He was still thinking of Heather; Ramona was comfortably proportioned. "Well, you go right ahead and tell her that, then."

His dad guffawed. "Not me! She'd feed me the veggie one just to punish me!"

Matt's smile became more genuine, even as his sorrow deepened. His dad was such a sweetheart. How could Heather have just walked away from him? Whatever her issues with Matt might have been—of course they weren't perfect together, no relationship is ever perfect—but how could she have left Gordon? Gordon had adored her, and she'd seemed to be fond of him in return.

She hadn't even called, or sent an email, asking how Gordon was doing.

The sound of the front door opening echoed in from the front hall; Ramona, as practically a member of the household, just let herself in when she arrived. Matt headed out to greet her.

"Hi, how are you doing?" she asked, giving him a worried look. Her white hair was pulled back in a low ponytail, and she was wearing a long black coat—probably just for the weather, but the effect was elegant and sophisticated.

"I'm hanging in there." He shrugged. "You know."

She reached up and ruffled his hair. "I do know. Your friends will cheer you up."

"They'll try."

"They will. They love you." Ramona gave him another searching gaze, then shook her head. "And how is Gordon today?"

"Come on into the kitchen," Matt said. "I've got to finish putting my potluck dish together before I head out."

Behind the closed kitchen door, as he took the popovers from the cooling rack and wrapped them in a clean kitchen towel before nestling them into a large basket, he updated Ramona. "He's been pretty clear these last few days, though he still loses track of who's who, and of which month we're in—keeps thinking it's spring, and that we're headed into summer."

"I don't blame him for that," Ramona said, with an exaggerated shiver. "It's gotten awfully cold in quite a hurry. I'd rather head into summer as well."

"Yeah. Also, he's getting a bit more stubborn about movement, and of course about drinking water. I tell him he needs to stay hydrated and to keep moving so often, I feel like a broken record. But he'd rather sit in that lazy-boy chair and watch TV. He says he's never thirsty, and that he's afraid of falling, no matter how many times I point out that he needs to use those leg muscles to keep any strength in them."

She cocked an ear. "Is he watching TV now?"

"No, he's reading, which is great. But see if you can get him to at least go into the dining room for dinner, and drink a full glass of water."

She nodded. "If he wants to eat, he has to come and get it! And I'll give him a tumbler of water with his evening pills, and watch him drink it all." Then she sniffed. "Is that pizza I smell?"

"Indeed it is. I got everyone's favorite kind."

Ramona leaned forward and pulled him into a sudden hug. "You are a good man, Matthew Richards. And a good woman will find you sooner than you think, take my word for it."

"If you say so."

She squeezed him and then let him go. "Remind me: how many lovely single women are in this soup society of yours?"

"Ah, Ramona, give it up. They're my friends. And they're all too old for me."

"Even that nice lady who owns the gift shop? With the pretty books?"

"Julie? She's great, but—yeah, she's a friend, that's all, honest." Julie was probably less than ten years older than him, and he liked her a ton, but still: not his type.

Whatever that was.

"I think she's a nice one," Ramona said firmly.

"I do too," Matt agreed. "And if I don't head out now, I'll miss the appetizers-and-wine part of the proceedings."

Ramona laughed. "Don't do that! And don't worry about us here, we'll eat pizza in the dining room. Maybe I'll make Gordon take several laps around the house first. Or run back to the kitchen for this and that and the other."

"Sounds like a plan, except for the 'running' part."

"Has he been using his cane?"

Matt rolled his eyes. "He keeps leaving it places—his bedroom, the bathroom, the car. I should get a dozen of them and leave one in every room, like his reading glasses."

"Good idea!"

Matt said goodbye to his dad, made sure the ringer on his cell phone was on and turned all the way up, and headed out.

Ron and Alicia lived in a large, sort of discombobulated house out in Rosario. However many times Matt visited them there— five or six times a year at least, in all the years the soup group had been going on—he had never quite internalized exactly how to get there. So many little twisty-turny roads; so many houses up so many little driveways that started looking so much alike, at least from the road.

This time, he found it more easily than usual, as he was the last one to arrive. He had to park down on the road; the other soup-eaters had filled up the small driveway.

"There you are!" Alicia cried, from the open-plan kitchen. Her cheeks were vividly flushed; he could see the steam rising from the pot of soup before her on the stove. "Get this man a glass of wine, stat!"

Ron, at the other end of the huge kitchen island/guest bar, shot his wife a look of such naked hostility that Matt froze in place, only stopping himself from taking a step backwards at the last moment. It was there and gone in a flash, the glare, and Alicia clearly didn't see it; then Ron smiled mildly and lifted an open bottle of red. "How's about it, Matt? Pinot okay?"

"Of course," Matt said, toeing his shoes off and then setting the basket of popovers on the island next to the stove. "Sounds perfect."

Over in front of the large fireplace, Julie, Steph, and Lynne were deep in conversation about something, all holding glasses with varying levels of wine in them. Julie was in the oversized easy chair, her legs tucked up under her; Steph perched on the chair's ample arm, and Lynne sat on the stone hearth, her back to the roaring fire. Their heads were close together, and Julie had a small, almost private smile on her face. It all looked very cozy, and like he shouldn't impose himself upon it.

Ron poured Matt a generous glass of wine and handed it to him, then raised his own, with that same mild, genial smile on his face. Had Matt imagined the look he'd given Alicia? He shrugged internally and toasted with Ron, then raised his glass in Alicia's direction—her hands were full, but she smiled back at him. "Thanks," Matt said, to them both. He sipped. "This is fantastic."

Ron's smile grew. "Yeah, I got a case of it when we were down in the Willamette Valley last summer. Oregon Pinots are the best."

Matt didn't know a whole lot about wine, but he did know that in the finished-out crawl space beneath this odd house was a large wine cellar, and that Ron was a very knowledgeable collector. You could never go wrong accepting a glass from the man. "I love it, I'll have to get a photo of the label."

"Sure, sure." Ron scooted the bottle forward, so Matt dug out his phone and snapped a photo.

"Oh Matt!" cried Steph, from the arm of Julie's easy chair. "I didn't see you come in."

The other two women looked up as well, and beckoned him over. "Here, there's an extra cushion," Lynne said, scooting over and placing said cushion right in front of the blazing fire. "Cure for whatever ails you."

"I thought that was this," Matt said with a smile, holding up his wine glass.

"That too," Julie agreed, chuckling.

What was up with her? He wasn't imagining the small, private smile she wore, as he settled onto his cushion and the women exchanged glances. "I'd ask if I was interrupting something, but you did invite me over," he said pointedly.

"I was just updating them on the situation with the parking meters—which I need to tell you about too," Julie said.

"I saw the holes and the caution tape in town," he said. "What's going on?"

"It's awful," Julie said, shaking her head. "Sam McLeod, of the expanding vacation-rental business, has apparently bribed a couple of county council members—"

"You don't know that, Julie," Ron called over from the end of the island. He walked toward the grouping by the fire, carrying the bottle of wine and topping up the women's glasses, emptying it. "They're business owners too; they may have just made common cause."

"Whatever." Julie tossed her head dismissively. "Well, in any event, they've authorized a 'pilot study' to bolster their cause, which involves installing parking meters in only just over *half* the town. If you can believe such sneaky, underhanded…"

"That's terrible," Matt said. "Can we stop them?"

"Leslie Magnas managed to get a temporary injunction approved by Judge Varela, on the day after Halloween," Julie said. "But it's only a ten-day hold on the work, so we don't have much time to organize."

"So, November tenth?" Matt asked.

"No, ten business days—so, two weeks, basically. But still. There'll be another meeting next week, on Wednesday—at the Odd Fellows Hall this time. I've been going around to all the local businesses spreading the word. Everyone is appalled, so we should have a good turnout."

"I'll be there," Matt said. "And what else can I do?"

"I'm glad you asked," Julie said, giving him a suspiciously cheery smile. "You're hosting the next Sunday Soup meeting."

"Ye-es," he said slowly.

Her grin widened. "How would you feel about inviting a few extra folks to it? Friends, sympathetic neighbors—anything we can do to spread the word."

Matt forced himself to think about it, rather than rejecting the idea out of hand. He hadn't even wanted to come here tonight;

he really didn't want to host a bigger gathering, of people he knew less well than these dear friends—and liked far worse. But his dad didn't get out of the house nearly enough, and he did enjoy social gatherings; they were good for him, too. "How many extra people are we talking about?" he asked.

"I don't know—half a dozen, whatever you're comfortable with. We're thinking small enough groups to facilitate actual conversation, get people talking with each other about the issue. Brainstorming. The idea would be, they then go out and talk to other people, either hosting their own meetings or just when they run into each other at the grocery store or on the ferry. Spreading the word however we can."

"I...suppose I could do that," he said.

"Great!" Julie beamed at him, then turned to Lynne and Steph. "You guys can help spread the word as well, about the meeting at the Odd Fellows Hall, okay?"

They both nodded. "Do you need anything else for the meeting?" Lynne asked.

"I might be able to use a little help setting up chairs and stuff," Julie told her. "I'll call you Monday, all right?"

"Of course."

Ron had drifted back to the kitchen with the empty wine bottle. Matt heard him say something to Alicia in a low voice, but he couldn't make it out.

Lynne gazed at Matt, studying him like a mother would look over her injured son. "It's good to see you, Matt. It really is. I'm glad you're here, and I'm glad to see you looking rather more... together than you did two weeks ago."

"Actually," Julie said, also giving him an assessing look, "you sound a little more sorrowful than you did at first, and also than you were the night we went to the meeting at the library."

"I do?" How could she tell? They were talking about community drama, not his heartbreak.

She nodded. "It's in your voice, and on your face. But I think this is a good sign; it means the shock is passing, and you're letting more of what's really happening manifest."

Hmm, she was in kind of a new-agey mood tonight. "I think you're probably right," he said. "I definitely miss Heather, and I do feel sad a lot, though I'm also starting to feel super pissed at her every now and then." *Mostly about my dad, but hey. It counts.*

"Excellent progress!" Lynne said, patting his knee. "Anger is a very important emotion. We've all been so worried that you went straight to depression without doing the earlier 'grief and loss' stages."

"No, I went straight to whiskey. Which stage is that?"

Everyone chuckled.

Alicia came over with a platter of cheese and crackers and set it on the low table between the chair and the hearth. "Dig in, but not too much—tonight's soup has an entire pint of heavy cream in it."

"Ooh," Julie said. "Just the thing to wash down all the extra Halloween candy."

"Which I notice you didn't bring," Alicia said with a laugh.

"You told me not to! I made brownies—a much more grown-up option."

"I like Halloween candy," Steph said with a fake pout.

"*I* like frosted lemon pound cake," Lynne teased.

Alicia took a few crackers and slices of cheese, and sat beside Lynne on the hearth. Matt glanced over at the island—was Ron tending the soup? Surely not—but nobody was there. "Where did Ron go?" he asked.

Around a mouthful, Alicia said, "Getting another bottle from the cellar, I think."

The conversation soon found its way back to the parking meter situation.

"It's so ridiculous, we're not Seattle," Lynne said disgustedly. "I thought it was going to be on this coming ballot."

"No, too late—we vote in just a couple of days," Julie said.

"But they could have a special election in the spring."

"So a waste of money on top of everything else!" Steph said, shaking her head. "Well, let me know if there's any other way I can help, besides coming to Wednesday's meeting. Do you want me to organize a meeting of neighbors too?"

"Yes please, the more the merrier," Julie said.

"I can come early and help set up at the Odd Fellows too, by the way."

"Thanks," Julie said. "I was just talking to Gavin Jones from the library; he's coordinating the tasks and collecting contact information—as well as getting names of folks who might be interested in hosting smaller gatherings in their homes, to reach more people and strategize in breakout sessions. So if anyone else is willing…"

Did Julie's cheeks glow when she mentioned Gavin's name? Matt's gaze sharpened, and that's when he noticed Julie glancing furtively at Steph and Lynne before leaning over and grabbing a handful of crackers. *Interesting…*

"I can do one too," Lynne said. "A small one, of course."

Steph looked at her. "Or we can work together, since we have the same neighbors."

Julie gave them both an absurdly grateful look. "Great! I'm *so* glad, you guys. Oh gosh, what a thing, what a crazy thing…"

JULIE

JULIE FELT HER cheeks blaze with heat. Dang it! She hadn't want-ed to say anything about Gavin to the group, because there was nothing to say—it hadn't even been a date, it had been *one drink* and a nice little walk home (with a handshake!) after basically a business dinner with another person along; and though it had gone very nicely and she had gotten some promising hints, she didn't actually know if there would be a real date, if she even wanted there to be a real date, if Gavin wanted…

Oh, who was she kidding? She wanted one, and she was fairly sure Gavin did too.

But it was too soon! Definitely too soon to tell her friends anything at all about it, so why had she let Steph and Lynne drag the whole story out of her—including that she would likely not say no if he asked her out? And then she'd no sooner promised herself to shut her dang mouth about it when she blurted Gavin's name out to nearly the whole soup group.

What was it her daughter Megan called it? "Mentionitis"? When you had such a terrible crush on someone that their name kept finding its way onto your tongue, no matter how hard you tried to stop it?

Okay, fine, she had a crush on Gavin, and now most of her friends had at least some inkling about it. Thank goodness Ron was down in the wine cellar; she didn't know how a retired English professor from a decent university would feel about a small-town librarian, and she really didn't want to find out. Not tonight, anyway. Not until she knew a whole lot more about where this thing was going—if it was going anywhere at all. If it was even a thing.

Matt was giving her a quizzical look, but he didn't ask any questions. Lynne and Steph were still talking about how absurd it was that new transplants to the island seemed to want to move in and change everything. "I know we haven't even been here ten years," Steph said, "but we've always been very respectful of the way things have been done."

It was strange to hear Steph refer to "we", Julie realized. As if she and her husband actually made decisions together, did things together. Thought of themselves as a couple. Did they even talk? As good a friend as she was, Julie wasn't sure she knew the answer to that.

Julie kept her eyes from Matt's, concentrating on her wine and these delicious crackers. Eventually, the conversation moved on, and then Ron emerged from the stairs leading to the wine cellar.

"Alicia?" he said, frowning across the room at her as he headed to the kitchen island. "Is the soup supposed to be bubbling so much?"

"It's fine!" she cried, but sprang to her feet and hurried over. She grabbed a spoon and stirred. "It's fine," she reassured everyone again. "In fact, it's probably ready. Ron, can you get everyone to the table and make sure everything we need is there?"

"After I open this," he said grumpily, wielding a dusty bottle. "Took me forever to find it, and it's going to want to breathe a minute."

Matt got up and went to the kitchen island. "Can my popovers get a few minutes in the oven? What have you got in there?"

"My brownies!" Julie cried, leaping up and rushing over after Matt. "Oh, my goodness, did I set a timer?"

"I did, hon," Alicia assured her. "On the stove. See? They've got thirty more seconds."

"Oh, thank goodness. I forgot all about them."

Matt gave her another odd glance as she dug around Alicia's cupboards for a cooling rack. *Right, I did just mention the brownies like ten minutes ago, so obviously I didn't forget* all *about them. Just…mostly.*

Did having a crush on someone make you lose your brain entirely? Ugh, Julie was not looking forward to that.

Wasn't menopause supposed to have cured all this? Apparently not.

The timer dinged; Alicia handed Julie a set of hot pads. "There's a rack right there." She pointed.

Julie pulled out the brownies. They did indeed look perfect, and smelled pretty great as well. "Mmm," Matt said approvingly as he unpacked a bunch of yummy-looking popovers and arranged them on a baking sheet.

"What temperature do you want?" Alicia asked him.

"You can turn the oven off, actually; they're fully baked, they just need to warm up a bit while we all get to the table."

Within ten minutes, the party was settled at the dinner table, facing steaming bowls of creamy white bean soup flecked with cubes of ham. In the middle of the table was a big bowl of sauteed green beans and radishes, a huge green salad studded with brightly colored chopped peppers and several kinds of olives, Matt's basket of popovers, and a loaf of French bread. A truly ridiculous number of wine glasses were present; Ron had switched to a Cabernet, and refused to let anyone use the same glass as the Pinot Noir had been in, so most everyone had two glasses.

Wine snob, Julie thought, as she raised her new glass to the general toast. *Damn, this is good, though.* Maybe there was something to this wine-snobbishness.

Conversation flew around the table, growing louder and more exuberant as the wine flowed. Ron vanished downstairs again for another bottle; Julie wondered why he didn't just bring up a few before an evening like this. It always went this way.

Maybe he needed his moments away from the table, the group. He never did seem to enjoy being a part of the scene. So why not just excuse himself entirely, as Steph's husband did?

I guess I never did understand marriage, Julie thought. *Even when I was in one.*

Then she wondered again if Gavin had ever been married… and then she practically had to shake her head, trying to shake his name out of it. She turned to Lynne beside her and said, "Jeez, I'm distractable this evening."

Lynne patted her arm. "Don't worry, I understand. Nobody's noticing."

But across the table, Matt gave her another questioning glance.

"I'll tell you later," she mouthed to him. He smiled and went back to his soup.

After dinner, the party gathered around the fireplace for port and brownies. Several more comfy chairs were dragged over from their usual spot in front of the water view (or what would be the water view if it weren't dark outside); and everyone moaned happily about how full they were, and how they couldn't eat another bite, and how wonderful these brownies were, maybe just a small half-piece more?

"I love this group," Alicia sighed, still glowing with pride over the success of her soup, which had been simply astonishing—and *very* hearty. "I'm glad we gave up that book group idea and found our true calling."

I still miss talking about books, Julie thought, sipping her port. *I wonder if Gavin wants to form a book group? He's a librarian, after all...*

Only the tiny jeweled glass in her hand kept her from smacking her own forehead with her palm.

STEPH

IT WAS A long drive, from Rosario all the way back to Deer Harbor. Steph was glad that Lynne was willing to drive to the Sunday Soup Symposium evenings together—and willing to do the driving herself. Ron's wines, and then the port... Steph leaned her head back against the headrest and sighed with the pleasure of a full belly, and a happy buzz.

"That's fun, about Julie and Gavin, isn't it?" Lynne asked, after they'd passed through Eastsound and turned onto Crow Valley Road. "Too bad it took having her sidewalk destroyed to bring them together."

"Hmm? Oh, yes," Steph said, bringing her mind back to the earlier part of the evening. "Yeah, he seems like a nice guy. I don't know him that well, though, do you?"

"No, I don't. I've seen him at the library a few times is all. I wonder what he does for fun?"

"Besides being a total lightweight about drinks?" They both giggled. Steph went on, "I don't know. I guess Julie will find out. If this actually does go somewhere."

"If that's what she wants, I hope it does."

They drove on in silence for another minute or so before Steph said, "Do you ever think of dating again, Lynne?"

"Oh, sometimes," she said, easily. "I enjoyed being married, and Charles passed far too young. But my life is also just fine how it is—no one to have to negotiate with or work around. Except when Ethan visits, I'm entirely my own companion. You know?"

"Maybe," Steph said, not quite managing as carefree a tone as Lynne had.

Lynne instantly picked up on it. "Oh, gosh, I'm sorry. I didn't mean it like that."

"No worries! David and I are fine—we have a really good arrangement. He just craves so much more alone time than I do, and he doesn't mind at all that I have a more active social life than he does. I think," she added, "that Ron and Alicia could benefit from something more like our arrangement, and I've been wondering how—and if—I could bring that up with her."

"Hmm," Lynne said, slowing down for the stop sign at Nordstroms Lane. "That's a dicey one. He doesn't seem the type to let fun things happen without his direct supervision, does he?"

"No. It's a wonder he even lets her go play pickleball."

"Men." Lynne sighed. "It's when I see marriages like that that I think, Nah, I'm fine. But if the right man came along? I wouldn't say no—at least to a dinner date, or a drink like Julie did. And then see where it went from there."

"But you're not going out looking for one?"

Lynne laughed. "I am *not* going out looking for one, no."

They passed the rest of the trip in companionable silence. And when Lynne pulled into Steph's driveway, the porch light was on but the rest of the house was in darkness.

"Thanks again for driving," she said, as she opened the door.

Lynne nodded. "It's my pleasure."

She waited until Steph had opened the front door, and turned around and waved, before pulling out. City habits were still a thing, though Lynne had lived here forever, and Steph assured her again and again that she didn't need to wait.

To be fair, though, it had taken Steph a while to get used to not locking her doors. Now she wasn't even sure she knew where her house key was. She set her purse down on the entry table and peered down the long hallway, looking for light coming from under David's study door. She didn't see any, so she flipped on the hall light and headed to her bedroom.

Well, "their" bedroom, technically, though she couldn't remember the last time David had set foot in the room. He even kept all his clothes in his office now.

Steph sighed as she sat down on the bed and pulled her shoes off. Was she really okay with this? Was there anything that could be done? She did like her life, and she did get much better sleep when she was alone in the bed—especially when she was having hot flashes. And it was nice not having an alarm going off at his ungodly East-Coast-rising time.

When had this stopped being a temporary measure, though, and become their way of life?

And why was she suddenly questioning everything? Maybe it was the abrupt changes in their friend group: Heather leaving Matt, Julie maybe-dating Gavin. For years, everything had just gone along comfortably the same with them all—even while the outside world faced upheavals, politics and pandemics and all. It had been easy to assume, at least after the initial shake-down period, that the soup group folks and their regular dinners were the steady, unchanging center of her world.

Maybe it was good to question everything. Maybe what had happened, or almost happened, during that first dinner at Ron and Alicia's, in that early time when they were all just getting to know each other, hadn't just been an anomalous thing...

But she wasn't going to question everything—*anything*—tonight. It was late, and she was full and tipsy. She'd think about what it all meant...later.

Ron

Ron Alderson rinsed the wine bottles and set them on the sideboard. The dishwasher hummed quietly; Alicia had gone to bed after her part of the cleanup was done. She had just about dislocated her arm, patting herself on the back for that overly heavy soup. What was so impressive about following a damn recipe?

Steph's green beans and radishes, now: that had been a stroke of genius. With pine nuts, for added richness, which was nice. But it was the thinly sliced cooked radishes that were the standout flavor. Who had ever heard of cooking radishes? Steph had, obviously—and that was crazy, fantastic. Ron could still taste the dish, at least in his mind's palate.

Steph was such an amazing cook. She really should open her own restaurant or catering business or something. She was always trying out new things in that clever kitchen of hers, and acting like it was no big deal. Acting like everyone had her deft hand with flavors.

Maybe Julie had started the group, but Steph was the heart and soul who held it all together.

Ron smiled absently, the smile fading as he pulled the wine cellar notebook out of its drawer and updated his inventory list. That Cab had been on entirely the wrong shelf; had Alicia been down there, messing with his system? She'd sworn she never went to the basement, that it was full of spiders and mold, which was simply untrue, just something she said to hurt him.

The cellar was Ron's pride and joy. Well, one of them. His library was another. Though Alicia had pushed hard for them to downsize considerably before moving from California to Orcas Island, he had insisted on bringing his entire library, and having bookcases custom-built in both the great room and in his office to house them all. His books were like old friends. He remembered when he first read nearly all of them, and where.

He'd liked teaching, but he'd *loved* being a scholar. "Professor Alderson." Sure, he'd only managed tenure at a state college, not an Ivy or even a good state university like Berkeley; but he'd been respected by his colleagues, and he'd published several well-regarded books of his own.

Even if nobody read them, outside the tiny world of Coleridge scholars. Early on, Ron had sworn to never be one of those professors who assigned his own books, though he understood why others did it. Even if they were wrong. It was simply greedy, and felt like double-dipping. He'd been adequately paid, with a gentle workload and regular sabbaticals, and he had a fine retirement income; so it wasn't the money. It was just...it would be nice to feel as though one mattered, perhaps, just a little.

He finished updating the cellar notebook and left it out on the counter, to remind himself to go down tomorrow and see if anything else was out of place. With nearly a thousand bottles, of so many different varietals, and of so many vintages, from so many different regions of the world, it was crucial to keep it all straight. If he hadn't remembered that particular Cab (well aged and mellow, but with enough acidity to counterbalance the cloying creaminess of Alicia's soup), it might well have stayed on the shelf with random Zinfandels and red blends until long past its ideal age of drinking. It had been delightfully robust tonight; another few years and it would start to fall flat, lose its depth, take on too much of the cork.

The dishwasher clunked and sighed. Ron sighed as well, and went around the great room turning off lights, before going to their large master bathroom and brushing his teeth.

In the bedroom, Alicia snored softly, curled up on her side of the king size bed. She'd left his reading light on, and had donned her sleeping mask against its glare. Thoughtful, he supposed. But he didn't feel like reading tonight. It was fairly late, and the book he was reading was a little dense for this time of night. So he just eased into the bed, switched off the light, and tried to still his mind.

Cooked radishes...and Steph's proud smile as everyone complimented them.

But not *too* proud. Humble, as well; Steph was a woman who knew her worth but didn't go around boasting about it. Making a big deal of every little thing.

Beside him, in the dark, Alicia snored on.

Chapter 6

MATT

Ramona wanted to attend the meeting at the Odd Fellows, so Matt had brought Gordon along as well. It was indeed good to get him out of the house—and for more things than just lunch or Spite and Malice at the senior center. Gordon hadn't entirely understood the meeting or all the back-and-forth of everyone's ideas, but he certainly grasped the central issue.

"We're not *Seattle*," he'd said, more than once.

He said it again as Matt drove them up the hill. "No, we're not, Dad," Matt said easily. "Or Bellingham, or even Anacortes. It was nice to see such a big turnout, wasn't it?"

"It was! Did I see Libby Swarthmore over by the window? I thought I did."

"Hmm, I don't think so," Matt said. He knew for a fact Gordon hadn't; Libby, who had also frequented the senior center lunches and would always sit at their table, had died last year.

So much of Gordon's life now was loss, Matt thought. Perhaps that was one of the blessings of dementia: he mostly did live in the moment, forgetting how many loved ones he'd lost along the way.

It was better than the flip side, of having to be reminded of the losses repeatedly. Like with Heather.

Matt stifled a sigh and tried to focus on being upbeat. "So

Dad, you know the parties that my friends and I have every couple of weeks, with the soup?"

"Yes, yes," Gordon said, smiling. "I like soup."

"So do we. Do you remember we're hosting the next one, next Sunday?"

His dad cocked his head. "Sure," he said, the way he did when he didn't actually remember but was willing to go along with it. "What soup are we doing this time? I like that macaroni and meatballs one."

Matt smiled. "I don't know—maybe we'll do that one. We can talk about it. But what I wanted to ask was, how would you feel if we added a few folks to the gathering this time?"

"More people who like soup? Fine with me!"

"Soup, yes," Matt said, "but these people wouldn't be joining the group. This would be a one-time thing, specifically related to the problem—kind of like a focus group, to work on individual parts of it."

"The problem? What problem?"

"You know. The parking meters. The thing we just talked about at the meeting this evening."

"Right, right," Gordon said, confidently.

"Remember when Julie mentioned that folks could sign up for gatherings in their homes, to strategize and plan? This would be one of those, at an already scheduled time."

"I like that Julie. She's so pretty."

"I like her too. So, you're okay with me adding a few extra people to the meeting next Sunday?"

Gordon gazed out the window for a minute, at the darkness. He pulled a crumpled kleenex out of his breast pocket and wiped his nose, then returned the kleenex. "I like having people over," he said finally. "But sometimes I lose track of them all, you know?"

"I know, Dad. But don't worry. I'll be there, and we'll see if Ramona wants to come over and help out. You won't have to do a thing except be your usual social, friendly self."

"What if I don't remember everyone's names?"

"You won't have to. Everyone I'd be inviting already knows that you have a little memory problem."

"They do?" Gordon sounded as surprised as he always did whenever he and Matt had this conversation.

"Yes, they do," Matt said, patiently.

"Who told them?"

Matt smiled, and signaled to turn onto their little lane near the top of the hill. "You and I did, together. Don't worry, Dad—I'll run the guest list by you before I invite anyone. You can just let me know if there's someone you'd rather I not include."

"Oh, I like all your friends."

"And they like you too. I think it'll be fun."

"What will we feed all those people?" Gordon frowned, looking worried. "Where will they all sit?"

"Well, we'll feed them soup, and we can ask folks to bring a dish, just like we do with the regular soup meetings."

"Right! Soup."

"And we have enough seating to add six or seven people, I think. It doesn't have to be formal. You don't have to worry about that part, Dad."

"All right."

As they pulled up to the house, Gordon said, "Did I see Libby Swarthmore this evening?"

"Maybe you did, I don't know."

"I like her."

"Me too."

JULIE

JULIE AND GAVIN had been in frequent communication, of course, though it was largely to do with the business at hand. Yet his emails always managed to have some personal content, however small. She liked that, and found herself looking forward to checking her email, something that had always been a bit of a chore.

On Wednesday, after she got home from the very successful planning meeting at the Odd Fellows Hall, she pulled up the email he'd sent earlier that day. She hadn't had time to respond to it in the moment—she'd spent the first part of the day in her paper-making studio (a lean-to shed behind her kitchen), beginning the process of making a big batch of her favorite off-white sheets, and then had to hurry over to the hall to coordinate setup. This note, unusually, was only business. No personal touch. She'd had to double-check to make sure it wasn't a group email, but no, he'd sent it only to her. Was he not really interested? Did he think *she* wasn't interested? Granted, it was most important to focus on the urgent work they were doing together, but couldn't he just…? Ugh, now she remembered the rest of what dating was all about. The uncertainty, the second-guessing, the dance of "act interested but not *too* interested." Couldn't come on too strong and frighten the man off, after all.

"The hell with that," she said aloud, and hit *reply*. She was too old for such adolescent nonsense. If Gavin couldn't handle a woman who asked for what she wanted, then he wasn't worth her time.

She started typing out an invitation to go out to dinner, together, just the two of them, and then paused as an even better idea occurred to her. Why not have him over here? She loved to cook—she was no Steph, but she knew her way around her little kitchen. And this would be another way to find out if she and Gavin were compatible. If he liked her cooking, if they were relaxed and comfortable together in her home…well, that would be a very good sign.

She deleted everything she'd typed and started again.

Great meeting tonight! I'm really happy with how things are going.

On another matter, I was wondering if you would like to come for dinner here on Friday? I have a new recipe I'd like to try—baked chicken thighs with garam masala and lots of other good stuff—I think you might enjoy it. Let me know.

She hit *send* and leaned back, satisfied.

Well, satisfied for about a minute, anyway.

"Oh, now comes the part of waiting for the phone to ring!" she said, laughing at herself. He probably wouldn't answer until tomorrow; she didn't even know if he checked his messages in the evenings, and it was getting late. He hadn't even left the hall yet when she did this evening. He might still be there. He might live far from town—she knew he didn't live right in town, but she wasn't sure how far out of it he did live. He might be grabbing dinner with someone. He might...

"Stop it!" she said aloud.

He'd better let her know tomorrow, though—she'd need to shop for the meal.

She went into the kitchen and poured herself a glass of Sauvignon Blanc as she thought about what to have for dinner tonight. It was late, but she hadn't had a chance to eat anything before the meeting. Now that she was thinking about the chicken thighs, she wanted them now. Too bad she didn't have the makings. Tomorrow she could shop for them; she'd make them Friday night whether he came over or not. They'd be good left over, if she ended up making them just for herself.

Speaking of leftovers...she poked through the fridge, seeing what she could find. Some brownies Alicia had insisted she bring home, and the last cup or so of that amazing rich and hearty white bean soup. That, plus a green salad, would make a perfect light dinner.

She pulled out the soup and poured it into a small pot and set it on the stove.

And then somehow she found herself back out in the living room, at her desk, opening her laptop. *What am I doing?* she asked, even as she opened her email.

It refreshed, and... Yes!

She clicked on the message. *I would be honored and delighted to have dinner at your home on Friday evening. What time should I arrive, and what may I bring?*

Her grin widened as her fingers hovered over the *reply* button. Should she not write back so fast? His message had come in barely five minutes ago. "Rules are for other people," she said. "I'm not twenty-two." She typed, *Wonderful! Six-thirty, and you can bring a good bottle of dry white wine and a healthy appetite.*

There.

She hummed to herself for the rest of the evening.

FRIDAY SEEMED TO take forever to arrive, and then the day itself meandered along, each minute seeming like ten. It didn't help that business was starting to get awfully slow. Even though she'd moved to her winter hours—Fridays through Sundays—she'd had hardly any customers, and the ones who did venture in bought very little. It was that weird time of year, too early for Christmas shoppers, too late for general tourists looking for a souvenir of their trip. Julie sometimes wondered if she should shut down altogether in November, and then just open up for a few weeks in December—or actually, for Small Business Saturday—or maybe just get a table at the holiday crafts fair and call it good.

Well, perhaps it would pick up closer to Thanksgiving. But as it was, the long, idle day gave her plenty of time to think about the evening ahead...to question her choice of meal, her forthrightness in asking a man over—was it wise to invite him into her home so soon? What did she really know about Gavin Jones, anyway?

Oh, for crying out loud, she told herself. *He's lived on the island for years; he works at the library. If he were a deranged serial killer, the whole community would know about it by now.*

At last, six o'clock arrived. She closed up and cashed out in record time, then locked the doors behind her and hurried back to her cottage.

It was chilly in here; did she have time to build a fire? Why had she told him to bring *white* wine? Never mind that it supposedly went with chicken; it was way too cold to drink chilled wine. A nice rich red would be so much more warming on a cold November evening…

"Stop it," she told herself, and turned on the oven, then washed her hands and gathered her ingredients.

The chicken had just gone in when there was a knock on her door. She hadn't even had time to change! Well, too late now: what he saw was what he'd get. Julie took a deep breath, put a smile on her face, and opened the door.

"I know you said white," he said, holding out a bottle of the same Marlborough district Sauvignon Blanc she still had an open bottle of in her fridge, "but it was so chilly out, I thought we might want this instead. Or in addition. Or, at least, maybe you would, because I'm such a lightweight." He produced an interesting-looking bottle of something red.

Julie laughed heartily. "Oh, perfect! I was just second-guessing white—but you brought my favorite, so now I don't know what to do. I do know I won't be drinking two entire bottles by myself!" He laughed as well, and her nerves unclenched another degree. "Well, come in," she continued, "we'll figure it out." She stepped aside and ushered him in.

"I love your house. It's so much bigger than I realized!" he exclaimed, standing in the entryway and looking all around. "Ooh, so many books."

"Thanks," she said, smiling. Of course he would notice the bookshelves first thing. "It's not a huge place, but it works." He had dressed up: nice slacks and a dark shirt, from what she could tell under his wool coat. Even his shoes looked shiny. And, mmm, he smelled good. Like clean man, with maybe a hint of sandalwood, faintly spicy.

"I had no idea it was even back here before I walked you home the other night. And even then, from the porch, I figured it would be the size of a toolshed. Or one of those tiny houses that are springing up all over like mushrooms."

Julie took both bottles of wine from him. "It's clever, isn't it? I feel so lucky to have found it."

"Do you own both it and the shop building?"

"I do. Well, technically the bank does."

He chuckled, and started to shrug out of his coat. "I know that one."

"I think most of us do." She nodded toward the coat rack by the door. "You can hang that there—I'll take these to the kitchen. Do you want a glass, and if so, which one?"

"I will drink whatever you pour for me. I like those both, so you can't go wrong."

"All right. Have a seat and I'll be right back."

In the kitchen, she studied the bottle of red. Meadowcroft, a Cabernet from Mt. Veeder in the Napa Valley. It had a somewhat stylized picture, in gold, of a bee heading toward a scruffy-looking flower—a dandelion? No, but a weed of some kind. It was the bee and flower that decided her. She just wanted to keep looking at the bottle.

She opened it quickly, poured a small measure into two glasses, and sniffed. Mmm, lovely. She carried the glasses and bottle back into the living room.

Gavin leaped up from the sofa and rushed to take one of the glasses from her. "Oh gosh! I should have come to help you carry all that."

She smiled as she took the easy chair catty-corner from the sofa, and set the bottle on the coffee table. "I had it; and I did tell you to have a seat. I'll get us some munchies in a minute, but for now," she held up her glass, "cheers."

"Cheers!" He clinked, and they both sipped.

"This is really nice," she said. "I haven't had it before."

Gavin looked a little abashed. "I've only had it once—my sister brought it to a family gathering, and everyone raved over it. I thought you might enjoy it."

"I do." She took another sip. "So, just to be clear, before we go any further: I know we're working on the parking meter situation together, and I'm happy to talk about it if there's anything new to share, but this isn't a business meeting. I invited you here tonight because I'd like to get to know you better. As a person."

"Uh." He grinned, awkwardly, and swallowed. "That sounds… nice."

She gave him an encouraging nod. "So, tell me about yourself, Gavin Jones."

He fidgeted a little, looking like he was trying to hold still. Julie stifled a smile. "Well, I work at the library…"

"I know *that*," she said, with a gentle emphasis. "Tell me what I don't know. Have you ever been married? Any kids?"

"Wow, you, uh, went right there," he stammered, and then his face grew as red as the wine. "I mean, that's good! I just…" He visibly gathered himself. "No, no marriages, no kids. I came close a couple of times—to getting married, I mean—but never made it all the way to the altar."

Hmm, she thought. Not necessarily a deal-breaker, though definitely something to follow up on. But she wanted this to be a comfortable evening, not to give him the third degree. Despite how she'd started. "I have," she said, instead of waiting for him to ask. "We divorced over fifteen years ago. I have two grown daughters, who are lovely and perfect in every way. You might meet them someday."

"I'd like that," he said, now with very little visible unease. So, he got a grip on himself readily enough. "Where do they live?"

"They're both in the Portland area; Megan is in Beaverton, and Lori, the younger, is in Portland proper."

"I love Portland. What do they do there?"

Julie smiled. *Good, he's not scared off by my having children.* "Megan works for an environmental nonprofit that she helped start up. Lori is an artist, and she also temps downtown. To 'support her art habit,' as she puts it."

Gavin looked genuinely interested. "What kind of art?"

"Big kinetic sculptures, these days. Whenever I visit her, we walk over to this huge salvage place on Mississippi. Then I have to help her get the big pieces of whatever she's fallen in love with back home."

"Mississippi—North Portland, then. The fifth quarter."

She laughed. "Right! How silly is that—Northeast and Southeast and Northwest and Southwest—and North. Why call them quarters if there are five of them?" She shook her head.

"North Portland is fun, though. I know that salvage store—it's this great massive place with everything you'd need for any house project ever. And art project too, I guess! And then of course there's Hippo Hardware…" Gavin got a dreamy look in his eyes, as if he were exploring all three floors of the magical place right now.

"I gather you used to live in Portland, then?" Julie asked.

"I did—for about five years not long after college. It was a wonderful city. It's…well, bigger now. I still visit every now and then, and always try to get to Powell's when I do—"

"Powell's!" Julie cried. "Of course, Powell's is the best. Which branch?"

"Downtown, of course—the city of books. I can spend all day in the Rare Book Room without even realizing it."

They gazed fondly at each other. Of course a librarian would be enamored of Powell's. Not that she spent much time in the Rare Book Room, general fiction being more her thing. "I love the downtown store," she said, "but since Megan is in Beaverton, I'm familiar with that one too. It's not bad."

"None of them are bad."

"Oh, I promised munchies," Julie said, after another sip of wine. "I'll be right back."

"Can I help?"

She almost told him no, but she hadn't had a chance to assemble a plate of appetizers either. "Sure—come on in."

In the kitchen, she got several cheeses out of the fridge and set them on the counter. "You can unwrap those and put them on a platter—maybe that yellow one on the high shelf over the sink." She pointed. "I'll get the crackers out, and then those grapes need washing, if you finish with the cheese."

Within minutes, they were back in the living room noshing happily. Julie topped up their wine glasses, careful not to give him too much. "How long have you lived on Orcas?" she asked him.

"About twelve years. After Portland, I moved to southern California for a job, but I hated it. It paid well, though, so it took me a while to extract myself."

"Also as a librarian?" Julie asked.

He shifted on the couch. "Oh, I'm not a librarian, actually; I don't have an MLIS."

"MLIS?"

"Master's in library and information science—a library school degree. I just work in the library. The so-Cal job was in finance."

"Finance!" she blurted, then laughed. "I'm sorry, that just doesn't seem like you."

"It wasn't, and don't apologize, you're right. I was a poor fit, but the money was hard to turn down. I mostly saved it, though, knowing I would want out before too long. That's how I was able to buy up here when the time came."

"Had you known about the island before moving here? I mean, obviously right before, but—"

He laughed. "Yes, I'd vacationed here when I lived in Portland, a couple times, and do I get to ask you questions?"

She blushed and sipped her wine. "Of course you do! I'm sorry, I'm just curious. I always like to know how people find Orcas Island, and what makes them tick in general." Then she realized how that must sound and added, "And I'm specifically interested in your story, as I mentioned earlier."

Was he blushing as well? Oh nice. "You can ask me anything you like," he said, "but I do want to know more about you as well. How long have you lived here, and where did you move from?"

"San Francisco, and about eight years ago."

"Was that when you and your ex divorced?"

"Oh no—we'd been divorced for many years before that. I lived in a nice condo between Cole Valley and the Haight—basically a flat, the whole first floor of one of those giant Victorian houses. I loved it, and I thought I was going to live there forever. But then...city life sort of started getting to me. It seemed to get more crowded and noisy all the time, and the parking started to drive me nuts. And I stopped liking my job so much. Our company reorganized, and I got put into a division with an awful boss."

"What did you do?" he asked. "What was your company?"

"Real estate—I wasn't a realtor, though, I was back office. Paperwork and compliance, mostly, and helping with staging sometimes, but after the reorg, they were talking about everyone having to take shifts of 'floor time' and even sit open houses, which—well, some people loved it, but it was just not me. I'm not a sales person."

"I would think you'd like selling, interacting with the public. You run a shop now."

She considered this a moment. "True, but now I sell *my* things. Stuff I make, or at least hand-select. Real estate selling is completely different."

"I can see that."

"Anyway," she went on, "I had just turned fifty, and both the girls had recently moved north. I missed them, and I was questioning everything. I visited my girls, of course, but even Portland felt too big, too bustling; I already felt too old to enjoy living there. Eventually, the three of us took a long weekend up here, at a bed-and-breakfast, and I knew immediately that it was home."

He beamed at her story. His smile lit up his whole face, and made her stomach flutter a little bit. A nice flutter. "It's like that, isn't it? I knew at once that I wanted to live here as well. I didn't think I'd be able to until I retired, but I always kept my eye on job openings. When the library position came up, I sent in an application that very day."

"Did they wonder why you wanted to leave finance to come work in a small-town library?"

"Sort of, but also, they knew. When the island calls…"

She nodded enthusiastically. "Exactly."

"Which bed-and-breakfast?" he asked. "The one you and your daughters stayed in when you visited."

"Ah." She smiled wistfully. "It's not there anymore—it was the Blue Heron Inn out in West Sound. It was such a charming place—only three guest rooms. We splurged, each taking a room of our own, so we had the place to ourselves. Two of the rooms looked out over the water; the whole place was just cozy and so sweet. The innkeepers were fantastic, but eventually they retired, and the place sold. It's a private house now." She was surprised at the pang of emotion she felt as she told him this. It had been a special weekend, a wonderful time with her girls; and, of course, it had begun her love affair with the island. But she could never revisit the inn.

He nodded. "The Blue Heron, I think I remember that, though I never stayed there." He took a cracker and put a slice of cheddar on it. "So many things that were here when I moved here aren't there anymore. Half the shops I loved, the restaurants…nothing stays the same."

"No, it doesn't, and the pandemic didn't help any of that along either."

"No." They sat in silence a moment, each in their own thoughts. Yet it was a comfortable, easy silence.

The smell of the chicken cooking wafted in from the kitchen. "I should probably go and take a look at the dinner," she said.

"I can't wait to taste it," he said. "The aroma is making me crazy."

She stifled a flirtatious comment—too soon, she thought, though this was going well—and went to check on the chicken. It did indeed smell amazing, and looked even better. She quickly rinsed a cup of white rice and set it going in the rice cooker, then returned to the living room. "Should be ready in about thirty minutes," she told him.

"Are you sure there isn't anything I can do to help?"

"Nope—it's all under control. It's almost a one-dish wonder."

Thirty minutes flew by, as they continued chatting comfortably; Julie nearly jumped when her phone alarm went off. "My goodness," she said, getting up. "I didn't even hear the rice cooker click off."

"Oh, is that what that was? I didn't want to interrupt you—it went off about fifteen minutes ago."

"Shall we move this party to the table?"

The chicken was as delicious as it smelled. Julie felt very proud of herself—for pulling it off, as well as for having the courage to try a new dish on a man she was interested in getting to know better. Not 'trying to impress,' as she would have put it when she was younger; this was far more mutual. Wanting to find him impressive—and doing so. Wanting to see her attraction to him reflected back from him—which it was.

He cleaned his plate and sat there looking so shy and adorable that she laughed as she offered him a second chicken thigh, on its bed of sliced onions and Bosc pears. He looked like he wanted to refuse, to be polite or something, but then she could almost see him decide to be himself. To be honest, to say what he wanted. "Yes, I would love another one, thank you." He gave her that radiant smile again.

"My pleasure. No greater compliment to a cook than someone

cleaning their plate and asking for more."

"I've just never had anything quite like this. I wasn't even a hundred percent sure what garam masala was, to be honest."

"I haven't cooked with it a lot," she told him, "but I do like what it's doing here. This recipe is definitely a keeper."

"A keeper," he said, his smile somehow growing even warmer. "I like the sound of that."

Suddenly, it was as though the temperature in her kitchen had raised by twenty degrees. *A hot flash, now, really?* she thought. But no…it was just the sparks passing between them. They gazed at each other across her small table. His eyes were really interesting, she realized. At first glance, they had seemed light brown, but now she saw that they were more hazel, amber—almost green in some lights—full of color and life and warmth.

"I'd really love to kiss you right now," he blurted, and then looked suddenly mortified.

She was up and out of her chair, crossing around the table to his side before he could second-guess himself. "I would like that too," she said, her voice husky as she reached a hand down to him.

He took it and rose to his feet, pulling her into his arms. He was tall, but not too tall; just right. Their bodies fit together as though they'd been designed for it. She tilted her head up as he leaned down and brushed her lips gently with his.

That spark from a moment ago flared hotter; she gave an unexpected moan against his lips, then kissed him less gently. He seemed to sigh into her, his arms pulling her closer, one hand dropping to her waist, and then a little lower. She kissed him greedily, and let her own hands run up his back, to his strong shoulders, his firm muscles.

A minute or ten later, he broke the kiss but did not let go of her. "Whew," he said, still grinning down at her. "Wow."

"Yeah." She blinked up at him. "Very nice. Wow indeed."

"I…want to kiss you some more, but I also don't want my

chicken to get cold. After just asking for seconds…"

She burst out laughing and released him. "I feel like we can probably figure out a way to have both chicken and kissing in our lives."

It was an amazing evening, Julie thought as she cleaned up the dishes. There had indeed been both more kissing and more chicken (she had even had another half-piece herself, though usually one thigh was plenty for her). He had not pressured her into anything more than she was happily willing to give—of either the chicken or of herself, she thought with a secret wicked smile—but had made it clear that he was on board for whatever she was ready for, whenever she was ready for it.

"Call me old-fashioned," she'd told him, "but I will not be asking you to stay over tonight."

"Of course," he'd said, not seeming surprised or offended. "That doesn't seem old-fashioned to me."

He had offered to help her with cleanup, but her kitchen was so small, they would only get in each others' way. Besides, her resolve was not quite as firm as she might like it to be…she could imagine the "getting in each others' way" leading to all sorts of non-dishwashing activities, and she really did want to take this at a sensible pace.

"Sensible!" she said aloud, laughing at herself as Fergie tiptoed back out from where she'd been hiding under the bed. "What about any of this is sensible? I'm an old woman, with grown daughters—ready to be a grandmother—and I'm suddenly giddy over a boy!"

The cat sniffed thoroughly around the kitchen, whether exploring the delicious aroma of the chicken or the alarming smell of a strange man in her sanctuary, Julie wasn't sure.

"You might want to consider becoming slightly less spooky, Fergs," Julie said to her. "It's entirely possible that that man will visit here again." She set the serving platter in the dishwasher, then turned her attention to the skillet she'd cooked the thighs in. If it weren't cast iron, she'd soak it…too bad.

Fergie gave the blank space next to her water bowl a pointed look, then looked up at Julie to underscore her message, in case it wasn't clear. Julie got her food bowl out of the cabinet and set it on the floor.

"And if things go like I think they might go, I will be inviting that man into the bedroom," Julie went on, running hot water into the pan and then gently scrubbing the stuck-on bits. "So, if you're unwilling to reconsider your stance on people who are not me, you might at least consider finding a few new hiding places."

The cat pretended that Julie had put an empty bowl on the floor, continuing to stare up at her. Julie ignored her. Eventually Fergie, receiving no satisfaction from her bid for fresh food, reluctantly took a bite of the clearly disgusting, probably even poisonous, hours-old kibble. She chewed, dropping a few pieces on the floor.

"Or maybe he'll invite me to his place. I wonder what it's like. If there's two greenhouses, maybe the house itself is spacious! He did buy it with investment banker money, after all. Or finance, or whatever." She got the last piece of stuck chicken off the bottom of the pan, then gave it all a good rinse before setting it on the stove.

Fergie pulled out another piece of kibble and dropped it onto the floor without even bothering to chew it this time.

"Yeah, that's a good idea. We should spend our time at his house. He probably doesn't have an annoying cat who distributes her food all over the kitchen when she's mad about something." Julie wiped the cast iron pan dry with her dishtowel, and then added a drop of olive oil to the center, rubbing it in with a paper towel.

Fergie looked up at her and meowed pitifully.

Julie chuckled. "All right, you spoiled little thing. Only because I am feeling *so* happy about how tonight went…" She sliced a small piece of meat off one of the leftover thighs, careful to avoid the seasoned skin, then chopped it into tinier chunks before arranging them on a little dish and setting it on the floor next to Fergie's bowl. "Don't say I never did anything for you."

The cat fell upon the chicken as if she hadn't eaten in a week.

Julie was so wonderfully wound up, she thought she'd have a hard time falling asleep that night. But she was under in minutes, and had marvelous dreams all night.

Chapter 7

ALICIA

Alicia Alderson finished her yoga workout, including three minutes of savasana. She knew you were supposed to lie in corpse pose for much longer than three minutes—she'd been to classes where the last fifteen minutes were spent flat on your back, a towel over your eyes, motionless!—but that was the beauty of practicing at home, wasn't it? She knew the poses, and she could spend as much or as little time in them as felt right.

Because that was the other thing about yoga: you were supposed to listen to your body, right? And Alicia's body just could *not* lie still. She had so much to do, so many places to go, so much life to live!

Or, rather, so much energy. To be honest, she really didn't have that much to do. The nature of freelance work was basically feast or famine, and she was in a sort of famine phase right now—not that she and Ron were in any danger of starvation, ha. Truthfully, they could have survived quite well on Ron's retirement income and his inheritance, which was well invested...but Alicia didn't want to cede yet another piece of herself. She liked her work, even loved it sometimes. Occasionally clients were surprised when they learned that a children's book editor had no children of her own, but Alicia always explained that she was acquainted with a vast universe of children—both kids she knew in person, and the many multitudes of kids she knew through their literature—and that this made her a better judge of their books, not a worse one. If she'd had kids, they would have been particular and specific, and they would have liked *these* books and not *those* books, and Alicia would have found it impossible to set aside their unique tastes and desires when considering her work.

Of course, this argument had been more relevant when she had been an acquiring editor for Pacific Playground Press, not the freelance editor she was now, working on whoever wanted to hire her and was willing to pay her fee. But still. She knew her stuff, she loved her work, and at the moment, she had an extra span of free time. Things always slowed down a bit toward the end of the year. Writers who were trying to get books out for Christmas already had them done; others were spending time with their families, planning to refocus on their writing after the new year.

So Alicia really needed to figure out what to do with all this excess energy. Because lying flat on her back on her yoga mat was not it.

Ron was busy with one of his own projects in his study—working on a new book, maybe, though he was at the stage where he wasn't telling her about it, and would get annoyed when she would ask. After seventeen, nearly eighteen years of marriage, she'd learned his moods by now. He got extra-prickly when he was in the first phases of a project, as if sharing any part of it was stealing a bit of its soul, or something.

She supposed he'd been like this from the start, but she hadn't seen it as clearly then. Back when they lived in California, and both had busy professional lives. They had met when his divorce from Gena was still fresh and raw—so fresh, in fact, that Alicia hadn't taken their thing seriously, for quite a bit longer than Ron had been happy with, it turned out. Alicia had figured she was a rebound romance for him, and she was perfectly happy with that. Ron was intelligent, interesting, and certainly knew his way around a wine list. Alicia, a bit younger than him, had had a few serious relationships but none that had made it all the way to marriage. She was focused on her career, on figuring out who she was, on being a fully developed, well-rounded person, accomplished in her field, fit and healthy, busy and engaged. Happy, in other words. Not looking for marriage.

But Ron had wanted it, and he generally got what he wanted.

Alicia had wanted to move to Orcas Island as badly as Ron had, but sometimes now she wondered if it had been the right decision after all. She enjoyed her freelancing, and her friends, and her pickleball, and all the rest; and it was certainly beyond gorgeous here, a true garden spot; but sometimes…sometimes it felt as though she had stepped off the escalator without exactly meaning to. That she had drifted out of the fast lane and coasted to a halt by the side of the road.

She sighed and rolled up her yoga mat, stashing it on its shelf in the hall closet on her way to the shower. Ron's office door was closed, which meant he didn't even want to hear her moving around the house.

Fine, then. She'd go out and do…something…when she was cleaned up.

After her shower, she left a note taped to his office door, and double checked to make sure her phone was on, fully charged, and the ringer was on. Because once he was *done* playing the lone ogre in his cave, if he couldn't find her quickly…she shook her head. That was no fun.

As she drove to town, she mulled over her options. It was sunny, if chilly; she could cruise by the courts and see if any pickleballers needed a fourth. But she'd just showered, and though she was restless, it wasn't exactly for more exercise.

Then she had it. It was Saturday: Julie would be in her shop, and undoubtedly too busy to get herself lunch again. That had been fun, when they'd eaten together a few weeks ago. And Alicia could find out more about how things were going with that cute librarian, Gavin.

She parked in front of the shop, shaking her head at the torn-up sidewalk with the ugly holes surrounded by yellow tape. What a stupid thing—who in the world thought parking meters here were a good idea? Did they *want* to annoy the tourists? The island's whole economy depended on tourism. It made no sense.

She climbed the few stairs and opened the shop door, the little bell ringing cheerily.

Julie looked up from behind the counter and gave Alicia a warm smile. "Hi! What brings you to town? Doing a little early Christmas shopping?"

"No, though that's not a bad idea. I just wondered if you needed another lunch delivery, my poor granola-bar-eating friend."

Julie laughed. "You'll spoil me! But no—I actually have a real lunch today, delicious leftovers from last night." Her eyes sparkled with mischief and joy as she said this.

"Oh?" Alicia asked, intrigued. "And what was last night?"

"Garam masala chicken thighs on a bed of sliced onions and Bosc pears…"

Alicia made a *go on* gesture; yummy as that sounded, that was clearly not the reason Julie looked so pleased with herself.

"…which I cooked for Gavin Jones."

"Aha! I thought so! My instincts are spot-on as ever." Alicia stepped behind the small counter and pulled up one of the metal stools Julie kept back there, parking herself on it. "Tell me *everything*. When is the wedding?"

Julie laughed heartily, and her cheeks colored. "Well, we're not quite there yet, but it did go very well…"

ALICIA WAS ABLE to hear the whole story, *and* share some of the astonishingly delicious leftover garam masala chicken, before Ron called in a grouchy huff, wondering where she was, in spite of the note she'd left. "I can't find the Carmelita coffee beans. Didn't we get another bag?"

All in all, she thought, driving back down Olga Road, it had been a nice outing. Maybe she would work on updating her web-site this afternoon.

JULIE

GAVIN CALLED JULIE on Monday afternoon. Well, he'd called her Saturday as well, to thank her for the lovely evening and ex-press his desire to spend more time together soon, sentiments she heartily shared. And he'd called her on Sunday, to see if she want-ed to meet him for a cup of coffee at Karma Kafe, but she was working at the shop, so he'd offered to bring her a cup instead, and a slice of their goat cheese strawberry toast, which sounded so strange but which he assured her was the yummiest toast she would ever eat in her life—even better than avocado toast, he swore. He called back a few minutes later with the sad news that the Karma Kafe was closed on Sundays, but offered to bring her an acceptable substitute. She'd laughed. "Of course."

When he did get to the shop, with an egg-and-sausage biscuit sandwich from Olga Rising, he'd only stayed about ten minutes, as she'd become swarmed with customers, which normally she'd be thrilled about (the whole point of running a shop was to sell things to customers, after all), but at this moment, she'd just wished they would all turn around and go away.

When Gavin called on Monday, it was with good news. "I just got off the phone with Leslie. She took several armloads of peti-tions to Judge Varela, and he agreed to extend the ten-day stop-work order until the end of the year."

"Really?" Julie exclaimed, pushing back from the worktable so she wouldn't get paper pulp on her phone. "That's wonderful! But—what petitions?"

Gavin laughed. "That's right, I forgot to tell you. One of the sub-groups that got together after the meeting last week was about a dozen kids from the high school. They were so incensed about the issue that even though they're not old enough to vote, and none of their petitions are official for getting on the ballot or anything, they started taking an 'unofficial survey of opinion' around to everyone they could get hold of, and they got a ton of signatures. I think half the island has signed on in protest of the parking meters by now!"

"Woohoo!" Julie crowed, startling Fergie, who had followed her into the paper-making shed, even though she usually found the space less than perfectly hospitable. "That's amazing! Oh, kids these days. Just when I think this island couldn't get any more amazing..."

"I know, right?"

"So we need to celebrate!" She looked down at her messy work tunic, and at the half-finished batch of paper before her. "I'm in the middle of something right now, but do you want to come over this evening? I think I have a bottle of something bubbly in the back of my fridge." If she didn't, she could pop over to the market and grab one.

"Well..." he said, sounding dismayed.

"What is it?"

He sighed. "I mean, this is great and all, but we haven't actually won anything except a delay. Should we really be celebrating a victory that isn't in hand?"

Was he serious right now? "Gavin," she said patiently, "I understand that, but you don't think it's important to celebrate incremental wins? Or even—and I know this is crazy, but just bear with me—get together and drink bubbly simply for the pleasure of it?"

"I, um," Gavin said, "of course I'd love to come over tonight! Unless another evening this week would be better?"

"It would have to be tonight," she told him. "I'm leaving on the eight forty-five boat tomorrow morning and not back till Saturday."

"Oh? Where are you going? If it's all right for me to ask."

"Of course it is," she assured him. "I would have told you earlier but it just came up. I'm visiting my daughters in Portland for a few days and then doing some big-box-store shopping. I don't get off-island very much during the summer, when the shop is open nearly every day. I was on the phone with Megan last night—to discuss the holidays, actually—and she talked me into coming down."

"Are you up for entertaining? Right before a trip?"

Did he want to see her or not? What was the matter with this fellow? "I am—" she started, but he interrupted.

"Or wait!" he said, sounding suddenly excited. "I have a much better idea. How about you come to my place instead? You could bring that bottle of bubbly, but it's my turn to host you. And then you won't have to cook before you leave town."

Oh good, she thought. It must have just been his social awkwardness rearing its head again. "I would love to. Just let me know where and when."

"I get off work at five, and then I need to get home and, um, figure out what to make for dinner…"

Julie interrupted him with a laugh. "You can feed me instant noodles. I'm not picky."

"Not after you served me delicious homemade gourmet chicken with I can't even remember the name of the exotic spice!"

Still laughing, Julie said, "I'd offer to bring the leftovers of that, but I finished them off with a friend at lunchtime the next day. But Gavin, I'm serious. I'll bring the bubbly and help you throw together a simple dinner. Don't worry about it." *Besides,* she thought, *if it's going to be anything like Friday, we won't much be able to focus on the food anyway…*

He might have been reading her mind, or at least thinking the same way (one could hope!), because he gave a knowing low chuckle. "All right. Come at six and we'll figure it out; I'll text you the address."

"Perfect."

After they hung up, she finished her batch of paper and got

it spread out to dry. Had she rushed the job just the tiniest bit? Maybe? But she wanted time to shower, and to figure out what to wear, and if she *didn't* have any bubbly in the fridge, she would need to budget time to go to the store... Not to mention she hadn't even thought about what to pack for her trip to Portland...

Fergie followed her into the house, and hung around just outside the shower like she always did, because she liked to go in immediately afterwards and lick the shower walls. Julie had long since stopped wondering at the peculiar ways of cats.

By the time she'd gotten dressed, undressed and dressed in something completely different, and was contemplating changing her outfit yet again, she remembered that she still didn't know quite where he lived—he hadn't texted yet when she got into the shower. She grabbed her phone and raised her eyebrows. "Oops!" No time to change: he lived out past Olga, nearly to Doe Bay. If she left right now, she stood a chance of not being late.

"I sure hope I have that bottle," she said to the cat, who voiced no opinion on the matter.

Fortunately, she did have one; she tucked it into a decorative wine bag, gave herself one last look in the mirror (good enough!), and set out.

It was fully dark, of course, for the drive down the east side of the island. Night came so early this far north, this late in the year. She hadn't bothered putting his address into her phone; cell service was spotty most places outside of Eastsound, and his text had included both directions and landmarks to watch for.

She slowed down after making the big turn at Olga, even though she knew she had several more miles to go. After the first landmark, a small house very close to the road with lots of bric-a-brac decorating its yard, she slowed even further, peering at the street signs, looking for his road. Even so, she almost missed it; good thing nobody was behind her.

She turned and drove up the narrow gravel road, counting

three bends and watching the address numbers on their (thankfully) reflective signs. Finally, his number came in view. She drove up his steep driveway and parked in front of his house, which was ablaze with lights.

He came out onto the porch as she was getting out of the car and grabbing the wine bag. "You found it!"

"I did—good directions, thank you."

"I've had practice." She could see the flash of his smile under his porch light. "Come on in—I guess you don't need help with anything."

"No, I can carry a champagne bottle and a purse all by myself," she said lightly.

He ushered her into a small but cozy room, with two short sofas at one end, a nicely set dinner table in the middle, and a narrow galley kitchen at the other end, divided from the main room by a counter with two stools. A crackling fire was going in a wood stove facing the sofas; was that the house's sole heating? It might be. The room was a very pleasant temperature.

"Here, let me take that," he said, reaching for the wine bag.

"I know you're not much of a drinker—" she started, but he grinned and carried the bag to the table, where two champagne flutes were set beside some lovely, obviously hand-thrown dinner plates.

"I'm certainly enough of one to celebrate our stunning, if preliminary, victory—with a stunning woman."

Julie felt her knees go weak as she grinned back at him. "I think that might be one of the sweetest things anyone's said to me in a long, long time."

He pulled the bottle out of the bag and started taking off the foil. "I'm both happy and sad to hear that," he said. "You deserve to have sweet things said to you, on the regular—but it's nice to know I don't have competition."

"You're safe," she said, as he levered the cork out of the bottle with a satisfying *pop*.

He poured the bubbly into the flutes; the right-hand one over-flowed a little, dripping down one side toward the tablecloth. "Oops!" He looked embarrassed. "I'm not all that good at this…"

"You're fine," she said, quickly taking the messy glass and lick-ing the drip off its side before it could make further trouble.

His eyes widened as he watched her.

"Come on," she added, "let's toast."

He set the bottle on the table and picked up his own glass. "I don't have an ice bucket," he said, frowning at the bottle.

"Not a problem," she assured him. "I told you I'm not picky."

"Well then," he said, raising his glass to her, "here's to Judge Varela!"

She clinked with him. "And to Leslie."

"And everyone else! None of this would have happened with-out the whole community getting behind the effort."

They smiled at each other, then Julie drank a sip. Gavin fol-lowed suit. "Shall we sit a minute?" he asked, nodding at the couches.

"Absolutely."

He took the left-hand couch; Julie paused a moment, consider-ing. They were more like love seats, and it would be really, *really* cozy to sit beside him on one; but she also didn't want to throw herself at him, or to rush things along. She deliberately hadn't packed an overnight bag, after all—reservations on the eight for-ty-five boat meant leaving her house at seven forty-five. So she took the right-hand couch, but sat as close to his side of it as possible. The sofas were angled to face each other and also the fire. It was a very welcoming setup; she could see herself curled up on one of these sofas with a book, happily reading away all afternoon, snow falling outside, fire blazing away in here…

"What are you thinking?" he asked, giving her an amused look.

She took another sip, then set her glass down on a low table set conveniently between both sofas. "I was just appreciating how nice and comfy it is in here—the fire, these couches. I love your home."

He shrugged but looked pleased. "It's small, but it works. I'm sorry it's too dark for you to see the grounds—that's where I've spent the most effort since I bought the place. I always thought I'd expand the house someday…maybe I will."

"Yes, I'd love to see your two greenhouses," Julie agreed. "And the garden that goes with them."

"Not much garden happening in November!" he said. "But I'll get you over here in the daytime soon and show you what's what."

"I'd like that."

Then they just grinned at each other for a long, comfortable moment. Julie was relieved to see him seemingly relaxing further. She picked up her glass again and sipped. "I'm not happy that some idiots decided that what Orcas Island really needed was parking meters, but I'm thrilled that the issue brought us to each other's attention."

"I am as well." His eyes sparkled in the firelight, as did the bubbles in his glass. "I…I'm even more glad that you weren't scared off by the fact that I haven't been married before, and don't have any kids."

Julie felt her eyes widen as she looked back at him in surprise. "What makes you say that?"

He chuckled, slightly uncomfortably, but leaned forward, clearly determined to say his piece. "I know how it seems—a man my age, in reasonable health, not apparently monstrous or overly strange, and yet somehow never having managed to get married? I, um, did some online dating for a while, and it became clear that this is kind of a red flag for some women. Plus, I did see your expression, Friday night, when I told you."

Now it was her turn to laugh uncomfortably. "Well, yes, it does seem like most everyone who makes it to our age is either still married or divorced." She smiled at him, and thought of Ron and Alicia. "Or on a second marriage." *Maybe even headed for a third…*

"I know. And I just…well, I don't want to have secrets from you, or things that you feel you can't ask me about. Things we can't talk about. If we're going to, well, if anything, you know…" He sort of stammered to a halt and looked embarrassed enough to fall through the floor. So much for him relaxing.

This might be one reason he never married, Julie thought fondly. *Maybe he couldn't get the proposal all the way out.* "If this goes where it looks like it might be going?" she prompted. "And yes: I appreciate that. Secrets are a terrible idea, nearly as bad as topics that may not be talked about." She sipped her champagne and gave him an encouraging smile. "So I will say the same: please feel free to ask me anything as well. The only topics I may use discretion on are questions about other people—my daughters, for example."

"Oh, of course!" he said quickly. "That's totally understandable, and appropriate." He took a rather larger sip of his own drink, then set the glass on the table slightly farther away from himself than necessary.

He really needed to calm down, and stay there; he was going to make her anxious too if he kept this up. "Gavin," she said, "I like you. We're good. We're figuring this out, and there's nothing to be worried about."

He clearly started to protest, and then gave her a sheepish smile. "Is it that obvious?"

"I'm afraid so." She leaned forward and put a hand on his knee, stopping its jiggling. "I'm out of practice dating as well, so we can just find our way forward together, all right? Dating is for finding out if that early spark of attraction is going to lead somewhere, or is just a false alarm. Dating is for getting to know each other. So," she said, giving his knee a squeeze before letting go and leaning back again, "let's continue getting to know each other."

"Yes. Let's."

A log in the wood stove crackled and half-collapsed, sending up a pretty shower of sparks behind the stove's window.

"So," Julie said, "since you brought it up: you mentioned that you'd come close to marriage a few times but didn't get all the way there. Do you want to talk about what happened? Are there things I should know about you?" Before he could compose a reply, she added, "And just to be clear: I am not looking to get married myself. I was married, it was fine, it ended for good reasons, and my life is quite satisfying now. I have close family and good friends, and interesting, fulfilling work—and, of course, a cat." She gave him a quick grin. "But I get the sense that there's a story or two there, with you, and I'd love to hear them if you're willing."

He shrugged and smiled. "I suppose I asked for that, didn't I?"

"I believe you did."

Oddly, now he finally seemed to relax for real. He held her gaze and started talking, with much less hesitation and stammering than before. "I thought I would marry my first serious girlfriend. I suppose many men do this: their first true love feels so profound, so intense, they just can't imagine not spending the rest of their life with her."

"Not just men," Julie put in.

He nodded. "Fair, yes. Anyway, that's how it was with me and Jennifer—well, how it was with me, anyway, which is probably why I said 'men'." He smiled ruefully. "We were in college, and I fell so hard for her." Now he got a wistful look on his face that Julie was happy to see: he clearly didn't hate Jennifer, wasn't angry with her. At least not anymore, if ever he was. "In retrospect, the signs were there: she and I had such different goals. She wanted to make her first million before the age of twenty-five, and I wanted to go to library school."

Ah. "Is that why you went into finance?"

"Exactly. I followed her into her major—business—and I hated it, but I was really good at it. It's...not rocket science, you know?" He shrugged again. "It probably didn't help our relationship that I was better at it than she was, even. She pretended not to resent me, but eventually, her continual 'jokes' about finance being a man's world, and no wonder it was all so easy for me, and all that…that wore us down. I can see that now.

"But I didn't see it then," he went on. "And I probably didn't take her struggle seriously—she had to work so hard to get the same grades that I just breezed into. I was probably kind of a jerk about it." He looked embarrassed, uncomfortable, but determined to lay it out there. "I was young, but that's no excuse. I did offer to help her study, and all that, but she was determined to do it on her own. She did, and she graduated with honors, but it took a lot out of her.

"When we graduated and were interviewing for jobs, I just assumed we were okay, that we were heading out to spend our lives together. I bought a ring, and started planning a big romantic proposal. For her interviews, she was focused on New York, of course, where all the big bank and brokerage headquarters are. I would have followed her there, even though I'd never been interested in big cities and certainly not *that* big city. But she accepted a job and informed me that she was moving. It was just like that: she told me she was leaving. Not that we should leave, or that she wanted me to think about coming with her…just that that was her plan, and that was that."

Julie gave a soft exhale. The poor man.

"I was so stunned," he said. "At first I was just frozen, I didn't know what to do. Eventually, we talked about it, and she admitted that she just couldn't keep doing this dance anymore. That she loved me, but she couldn't see building a life with me. It wasn't just that I was good at something that I wasn't really interested in, but that she was; it was that I hadn't even tried to live my own life, to do what I wanted to do. 'I can't respect a man who doesn't respect himself,' she told me.

"So I returned the ring to the jewelry store and took the first job I was offered, in Portland." He gave Julie a sad smile. "And that's the story of Jennifer."

"I'm sorry for the pain that caused you," Julie said gently, "but I'm glad you two didn't get married. That would have led to much more pain down the road, I'm sure. For both of you," she added, to be kind, though the story didn't leave her feeling entirely charitable toward Jennifer.

Though it would be interesting, she mused, to hear her side of the story.

"Oh, yes," he said, gratefully. "Like I said: the signs were there from the start. But I was young."

"So you didn't want to go to library school then?"

He looked even more embarrassed. "I can be a slow learner sometimes. And like I said, the money was hard to ignore. Library school would have been several years of expensive tuition and no guarantee of a job at the end. The brokerage was right there, with a sweet offer, and living in an interesting city. It was the path of least resistance." He shook his head. "I'm not proud of it, and I'm trying to make up for my earlier mistakes by listening to what I really want and honoring that now." He gave her a meltingly warm smile.

Julie flushed and looked down, drinking the last of the champagne in her glass. Gavin noticed at once and lifted the bottle, offering; she nodded, and he poured another measure for her.

"Thanks," she said. "For the champagne, and for the story."

"But wait, there's more," he said with a smile. "My second near-miss came six or seven years later, after my company offered me a transfer to Santa Barbara. It was a nice city, pleasant and comfortable, but I was lonely and a little lost, so after I had only been there a few weeks, I asked out a co-worker, having clearly not learned my lesson about women in finance."

Julie chuckled.

"Elizabeth was a lot less driven than Jennifer, or at least she seemed so, outwardly," he went on. "She seemed to be in the field for similar reasons as I was: she'd sort of fallen into it in college, and was good at it, and found the money too hard to say no to, even though her heart wasn't in it. She really wanted to be a writer, but she was convinced there was no money in that. So she worked nights and weekends on a romance novel, though she would never let me read her work."

Julie nodded, understanding *that* one. "Some people make money in writing," she said.

"I know—but it's not nearly the sure thing that working at a brokerage house is. Even entry level staff at our firm made two or three times what I make at the library here; and I make a decent living compared to the working writers I know."

"It's not right and it's not fair," Julie agreed. "Humans need creativity, yet we don't seem to value it. We value money."

He shook his head, but in agreement. "It's terrible. So, anyway, Elizabeth and I saw each other for about two years, casually at first, but it grew serious over time. I really thought we were very compatible, and I thought she felt the same. Eventually, I asked her to move in with me. She hedged a bit, not wanting to give me an answer, saying that she wanted to think about it. After I nudged her about it several times, she finally admitted that she enjoyed her solitude too much; she was afraid of losing her writing time. I promised that I wouldn't interfere with it, that we could set a schedule in stone, I would give her as much space as she wanted, her own room for an office, anything she needed; but she insisted that she wouldn't do that to me. 'I know what will happen,' she said. 'We'll try, and then one little thing will come up, and another little thing—you'll want to have a friend over for dinner, or you'll want to watch a TV show together, and little by little the writing will lose its place in my life. It will fall away—I might even push it away. And I won't want to blame you, but I will. I've seen enough friends go through this. I won't do it to you, or to me.'

"I didn't buy another ring," he said ruefully. "I could see the writing on the wall, if you'll forgive the pun."

Julie smiled at the joke. "Did she ever finish that book?" Somehow, she felt that he would know, that he would have kept in touch with her, or at least kept track of her.

He nodded. "She did, and another one after that. As far as I can tell, she didn't get any big book deal for them or anything; they're not self-published, but they were put out by a small press." Gavin looked a little abashed as he added, "I requested that the library buy copies of them, and I read them. They're okay, I guess. Not bad."

"Do you read a lot of romance?" Julie asked.

"No—not any more than the average man, I suppose." He grinned at her. "But I had to see if I recognized myself in any of the characters, you know?"

"Makes sense to me." Julie wondered if she'd have the nerve to read a book by her ex-husband, if he were to have written one. Would she want to know? Or would she want to hide from any and all revelations? "Though actually I think that was kind of brave of you. So—did you recognize anything?"

His grin grew lopsided. "Sort of. Not in either of the main romantic heroes, funnily enough—or, maybe not funny, given where we ended up. But there was a minor character in the first novel who worked at a bank even though he wanted to be a librarian, and in the second novel the brother of the heroine had, um, kind of a lot in common with me."

"Ouch."

"Yeah."

They gazed at each other for another long, yet comfortable moment. Julie felt the heat of the cozy fire on the side of her face, and the warmth of the light champagne buzz in her bloodstream.

"Anyway!" Gavin said, with theatrical brightness, "those are my sad stories. And I am not forgetting the fact that I lured you over here with a promise of dinner, and thus far have only managed to help you drink up the champagne that you brought."

"Right," Julie said with a smile, taking another sip of her drink.

"For my part, I seem to remembering offering to help figure out that dinner." She glanced over at the kitchen side of the room. "Shall we?"

"Speaking of sad stories!" he said with a laugh, and got to his feet, reaching a hand down to help her up.

She took it, just to feel his hand in hers again. *I could get used to this*, she thought, as he led her across the room.

"So you see," he said, opening the fridge, "not much here."

She peered inside. "I see plenty of veggies, and some good parmesan cheese." She looked up at him. "If you have any pasta at all in your cupboards, we're good to go."

"Ah, so you weren't kidding about instant noodles," he teased.

"Oh honey, these won't be instant," she bantered back.

Cooking with him was a delight. Or maybe it was the constant flirting, the accidentally-on-purpose bumping into each other as they worked together in the small space, their fingers touching as they reached for ingredients or utensils. *I could get used to this too*, she thought, grating a good measure of the cheese to sprinkle over the simple pasta they'd concocted. The smell of garlic filled his house, and she sipped slowly at her champagne. He had clearly stopped after one glass; she wasn't going to drink the rest of the bottle herself, for all sorts of reasons.

Soon they were at the table, and the conversation was bubbling along as easily as any she'd ever had on a date. *I really, really like this man*, Julie thought, watching his eyes sparkle as he talked, as he looked back at her. *Once he gets past tripping over himself*. He'd lit a pair of tall candles, one at either end of the table, making her wonder why she didn't burn candles more often. The light was so…gentle. Romantic, yes, but also just warm, welcoming.

All too soon, their plates were empty and their bellies were full—at least, hers was. "That was wonderful," she said, looking wistfully at the serving bowl.

"Do you want more?" he asked, already lifting the pasta fork.

"No, no—I'm stuffed, and you'll want that for lunch, or for

dinner tomorrow night."

"Or right now," he said with a laugh, forking a big pile onto his plate.

"Hey, it's your pasta! Go for it." She watched him eat, marveling at where he must be putting it all. He was trim and, as far as she could tell from her earlier explorations and that day on the pickleball court, toned and fit.

Men. Honestly, it was so unfair, how they burned up calories just by living in their bodies.

"So you helped me cook," he said, when he was done a few minutes later. "I am *not* going to let you help me clean up as well, so don't even think about it."

She laughed. "Okay, I surrender. I…should actually probably be getting home soon anyway. My cat has probably starved to death by now, but on the off chance that she is somehow miraculously clinging to life, I ought to go and feed her. And I haven't even thought about packing for my trip."

"Who feeds her when you're gone? Do you need someone to do that?"

"Karen, who has the jewelry store next door, takes care of that. Thanks, though."

"Right. Of course you've already arranged that, the night before you leave. Silly me."

"That's all right. You're clearly not a pet owner, so how would you know?"

Gavin shrugged, and gave her a sad smile. "I do know you have to go, and it's fine with me to not rush things…but I also wish you didn't have to leave so soon."

"That's a good sign, isn't it?" She reached out and put a hand on his arm, almost without consciously deciding to. It was just hard to keep her hands off him; she kept just wanting to touch him. "Because I don't really want to leave either."

"When do you get back to the island? Saturday, you said?"

"Yeah, though I'm not sure what time. I haven't decided on

whether to open the shop for a half-day Saturday afternoon, or just close both days and hope to make up all the lost sales on Sunday. Ferries willing, in any case—I haven't made a reservation for coming back."

"At least you can do that this time of year! Show up without a reservation, I mean."

"True. The off season is good for something." She thought a moment. "Say, remember that soup club I told you about?"

"The one with all your closest friends on the island? Yes."

"Our next meeting is this Sunday. Do you want to come along?"

He managed to look hopeful even as he frowned. "That would be—I mean, is that all right with the others? I know it's kind of a special thing."

"Normally, yes, but this one is going to have other extra folks involved—it's a combination of soup group and the small meetings we're planning to talk to friends and neighbors about the parking meter issue. It's going to be at Matt's house. You should come, if you want."

"I do want! I'd love that." He looked amused. "I suppose, even with our spectacular-if-preliminary victory this week, we do still need to organize the community."

Julie laughed. "Yes, there will be more battles before we win the ultimate war."

"Because win it we shall!" he cried, raising a fist triumphantly. Then he looked sheepish. "Ahem. I'll clear the table now." He got up and picked up his plate, and reached for hers.

But Julie was laughing even harder. "Not so fast, you goofball," she said, getting up from her chair, taking the plate out of his hand and setting it back on the table, and pulling him into her arms.

His own arms wrapped tightly around her as his mouth found hers, and suddenly they were kissing hungrily, greedily, as if they needed each other for nourishment. *I think maybe we do*, Julie thought, before losing herself in the deliciousness of him—his taste (some garlic, a little champagne, and a lot of healthy man), his smell (warm and clean and welcoming), the feel of his arms strong around her. Again, their bodies fit together as if they were puzzle pieces. She began to regret not packing an overnight bag, early ferry be damned, as his hand caressed up her back and then into her hair, holding her to him as he kissed her, kissed her, kissed her...

It was twenty or thirty minutes before she painfully extracted herself and somehow made it to her car. He walked her there, of course, after helping her on with her coat (and bestowing more kisses), thanking her again for the wonderful evening, promising to call very soon, wishing her a wonderful and safe trip, saying how much he looked forward to their next meeting...

Whew, she thought, starting the long drive home up the east side of the island. She grinned in the darkness. *Whew and wow and whew again.*

Chapter 8

STEPH

From: Stepher-cat@gmail
To: Sunday Soup Group Email
Subject: Christmas already??!!!

Hey gang,
Looking at the calendar here and can you BELIEVE that Decem-
ber is about five minutes from now? I know we got up to some wonky
schedule stuff last December with everyone's travels, and I want to get
ahead of it this time. I also want to throw a Christmas party (I know,
shocking, right???) ●
My next soup-hosting date is technically mid-December, after
Lynne's at the end of November (and tell me WHY again do Ron &
Alicia get to combine their date, since they're both members of the
group, no fair!) (Just kidding!!!) What if we pushed it out a week and
combined it with a party here? Thoughts?

From: Julie.Pessel@PaperMagic.com
To: Sunday Soup Group Email
Subject: Works For Me

A party at Steph's house? I'm in!
My daughters might be here by then (we're still working out the

exact dates—I'm in Portland right now so I should know soon). May I bring them if so?

From: ProfRon@CSUNapa.edu
To: Sunday Soup Group Email
Subject: With Pleasure

Steph, Alicia and I will be delighted to attend a Christmas party at your house in lieu of a regular meeting of the Sunday Soup Social. Just let us know what you'd like us to bring—in addition to wine, of course.

From: Matthew@WebSolutionsOrcas.com
To: Sunday Soup Group Email
Subject: Christmas already??!!!

Yep, I'm in too—and I have a similar question as Julie: if Dad is up for coming, can I bring him, and maybe Ramona?

From: Stepher-cat@gmail
To: Sunday Soup Group Email
Subject: Christmas already??!!!

Great! That's quorum, nearly (Lynne, will this work for you?). Yes, bring everyone, the more the merrier.
Party!!!!!!

(Three days later)

From: LynneDanielsMD@OrcasHealth.org
To: Sunday Soup Group Email
Subject: yes of course

I don't know why you youngsters insist on emails rather than the far more expedient method of texting. ● *But yes, a party at Steph's house sounds ideal.*

Maybe we should all bring a soup, since there will be so many extra people there? It could even be a friendly competition! Like a chili contest, only better, because soup.

We can discuss this more at my meeting—or this Sunday at Matt's. See you then!

STEPH SMILED AS she read Lynne's email. Great: it was all settled then. She'd been pretty sure her neighbor and friend would have no problem with the schedule change, but she wanted to have full buy-in before nailing it down.

Consistency was the important thing about groups like the soup club, after all. A reliable rotation, clear instructions, something to count on, in a world with so little that was predictable.

At the back of the house, she heard David's office door open, and then his footfalls in the hallway. A moment later, he stepped into the kitchen.

She closed her laptop and looked up at him. "Hey."

"Hey." He gave her a friendly, vague smile on his way to the refrigerator.

"There's some pork tenderloin in there, left over from a day or two ago," she told him. "It would make a nice sandwich with some of that mango chutney, maybe on the fig bread."

"Oh, that sounds good. Thanks." He turned to her. "Are you having one?"

"Sure."

He closed the fridge and went to sit at the bar.

Steph was halfway to the fridge before she realized that he had just assumed she was offering to make them. Well, she was the food person, wasn't she? Pushing down the tiniest flash of annoyance, she kept going, telling herself that if he made them, he'd just do it wrong, and would mess up her kitchen in the process.

It would be better this way.

She got out the meat and the bread and the chutney, and then rummaged around further, looking for what else to add. Some mache greens, maybe? Nah, too delicate. Something spicier, maybe arugula, or some baby bok choy.

She turned around to ask him what he'd prefer, but he was already deep into reading something on his phone.

He wouldn't care anyway—he'd just say, "Whatever you think is best." So she sliced up the bread and put the pieces in the toaster oven, just to take the chill of the fridge off them. She didn't normally refrigerate bread, but this fig bread seemed to benefit from it.

The meat, however, would be best cold, if she made sure to slather a good amount of the chutney on it.

By the time the sandwiches were ready, Steph realized how hungry she was. She hadn't even noticed until David had come in.

She brought the plates to the bar and sat on the stool beside him. He put his phone down and gave her another polite smile, then dug in. "Mmm, good," he said, around his first bite.

"Thanks."

They ate in silence for a few minutes. Beside him, his phone beeped; he glanced at it, then ignored the message.

A minute later, it beeped again. This time, he wiped his hands on a paper towel, then picked it up and typed out a text in answer. He took a final bite of his sandwich, then got up and carried his plate to the sink. "Thanks," he said. "That was great."

"You're welcome."

He started to walk out, shoving his phone in his pocket.

"Oh," Steph said, as he reached the doorway, "I almost forgot: we're going to have a Christmas party on the twenty-first. Of December."

He stopped and stared back at her. "Here?"

"Yeah, here."

"Okay." He turned to go again.

"Will you show up for it, please?" she asked, keeping her voice even.

He nodded. "Okay, sure. If you want."

"I do want." She gave him a smile. "It's important to me—I'd really appreciate it if you could be there."

His brow furrowed. "I said I would."

"You did, yes. But sometimes you forget." She put the slightest emphasis on *forget*.

"If you put it on my calendar, I won't forget."

"I will do that."

"Okay."

"Thank you, David," she said to his back, as he was off down the hall on the way to his office.

JULIE

JULIE HAD A wonderful time in Portland. But then, she pretty much always did.

She stayed with Megan out in Beaverton; Megan had a guest bedroom. Well, technically Lori did too, but Lori's was a foldout couch in an alcove, while Megan's was a real room with a real bed and a door that closed.

She took both daughters out to Bamboo Sushi for dinner on Friday, her last night there; tomorrow she would get up super early, hit Trader Joe's before leaving town and then do her big-box shopping in Burlington, all before throwing herself on the mercy of the ferry system.

Megan picked up a piece of Green Machine maki with her chopsticks and popped it into her mouth. "Ohh," she moaned, as she chewed. "This is the *best*. Mom, you need to visit more often."

"Someone needs to open a sushi restaurant on Orcas," Julie countered, before eating a bite of Ume Shiso roll. "It's unconscionable that we don't have one."

Lori took a sip of sake and grinned at her mom and older sister. "You guys realize we have this exact same conversation every time we eat here, right?"

Julie nodded. "It's important, in such perilous times as these, to have strong family traditions."

"Next she'll be asking, oh-so-carefully, about our love lives," Megan teased, rolling her eyes.

Lori laughed. "No, actually, this time we get to grill her about *hers!*"

"I've already told you everything you need to know," Julie answered primly. "When there's anything more definitive to share, I will."

"Don't get too serious before we've had a chance to vet him," Megan said, with a mock frown.

"La la la la I can't hear you," Julie said, reaching for the sake bottle.

"Yeah," Lori added, "why hasn't he ever been married before? If he's as good-looking and smart and sweet and everything else as you say, but he's still on the shelf, there must be *something* wrong with him."

Julie didn't want to run Gavin down, but she realized her girls did deserve a little more. "Well, he can be a little awkward sometimes," she admitted. "He didn't make the best first impression on me, when I met him a few years ago. I think he has a kind of judgmental streak, especially when he feels insecure."

"Gosh, that *does* sound attractive," Megan said, pushing her long dark hair behind her shoulders. "And what other good qualities does he have? Does he kick puppies? Steal candy from babies?"

Lori laughed, but also swatted her sister's arm. "Be nice, or Mom won't tell us anything."

"That's true," Julie said. "But don't worry about me. I'm being careful, and protecting my heart."

I hope that's true, she thought, and steered the conversation elsewhere.

The next day's driving and shopping went frenetically but successfully. Julie was glad to finally pull into the ferry terminal in Anacortes, and even gladder to score a spot on the 3:40 p.m. boat back to Orcas. She had already told Karen to leave the sign on her shop's door saying that she would reopen on Sunday at eleven. There had really been no way she could have gotten back in time for a half-day Saturday. She knew this, but somehow, she always imagined that time and space might work differently this time.

She just hoped she didn't regret the two lost days of sales. She'd spent a *lot* of money at Costco.

It was a lovely sail home. Julie went upstairs to the passenger deck and enjoyed the colorful sunset. The boat was not very full, which was also nice. She did like the ferry rides; they were an enforced pause in all the rushing-around of the mainland world. An airlock, separating the big chaotic Out There from the peaceful, remote Here.

She was still appreciating the peace and serenity of island life when she pulled up in front of her shop, glad to find a close parking space to unload all her purchases. Except...what was all that mess by her shop's steps?

"Not again," she muttered as she hurried out of her car.

It wasn't new demolition this time—the makeshift pallet bridge was still as it had been when she left. But it looked as though someone had gathered up all the broken concrete and twisted rebar from the whole block's jackhammering and heaped it just past the bridge, on her stairs. An accident, an innocent mistake? Julie didn't think so.

The orange cones arranged around the ugly pile made that point pretty well.

She was on her way back from her car where she'd grabbed her phone when Karen stepped out of her shop next door, keys jangling. "Oh, hey! You're back!" she called over.

"Did you see this?" Julie asked, pointing at the mess.

"What? No!" Karen left her shop unlocked and rushed over. "Holy crap! Who did this?"

"I was hoping you might know. You didn't hear or see anything?"

"No, nothing. It was fine when I got here this morning—and when I went out to grab lunch today, I didn't see anything then either." She frowned, staring at the pile. "Well, let me go get some gloves, I'll help you clean it up."

"Hang on—I think we should report this. And document it."

"Ugh, you're probably right. What a pain." She shook her head. "This is very not-Orcas."

"Very." Julie swiped her phone on and opened the camera app. She took pictures of the mess from every angle, including Karen in one of the photos to help show the scale. Then she phoned the sheriff's non-emergency line, where of course there was nothing to do but leave a message.

Then they donned work gloves and got busy, moving the mess off the stairs and piling it beside the pallet bridge.

"This stuff is heavy," Karen said, after they'd been at it a few minutes. "Someone really put a lot of effort into this."

"Yeah; I wonder who," Julie grumbled. "Can you get the other end of this piece? I can't budge it myself."

Between the two of them, they managed to shift it, but barely.

"Just dump it to the side so people can get by," Julie said. "I can get Gavin over here to help move it farther away, but I want the sheriff's deputies to see it first."

"Gavin, huh?" Karen asked, with a twinkle in her eye. "I thought I've been noticing him around here a lot."

"Yes, well," Julie said, unable to stifle a smile. "We've been working on this very important community project together, you know…"

"I see."

"And how is this fair, come to think of it?" Julie said. "He pulled me into this whole thing, but nobody's dumping a load of crap on *his* steps."

"Do you think this is somehow personal?" Karen looked surprised at the idea. "Not just random?"

Julie shrugged. "I don't know, but as I think about it, I have to wonder."

"That's kind of scary." She tugged on a chunk of concrete, pulling it loose from a larger pile. "Speaking of Gavin, have you talked to him since you got back?"

"No, I came straight here. And found this."

"Well then. Maybe the library is also covered in rebar. Or his house."

Julie thought about Gavin's remote, nearly impossible-to-find house. "I doubt it."

She invited Karen to her house for a thank-you drink when they were finished, but Karen had to rush off to dinner with some friends over in Rosario. "You are the butterfly-est social butterfly I know," Julie told her.

"Says the woman who just got back on-island after visiting another state! I bet you even went out to sushi."

Julie gave an innocent shrug. "Doesn't everyone?" She hugged her friend. "Okay, have fun tonight. And thank you again, for everything!"

"My pleasure, hon."

Once she'd unpacked her car and poured a glass of wine, she sat on her sofa and pulled out her phone. Fergie immediately jumped up onto the couch, purring and rubbing against Julie. She spent a few minutes scratching the cat's ears and telling her how much she'd missed her, then called Gavin, who was, of course, very alarmed to hear of the vandalism. "That's awful! Did you call the sheriff?"

"I left a message on the regular line. I didn't want to call 911— this isn't an emergency. But it's clearly personal."

"Do you think so?" Gavin asked, though he didn't sound quite as surprised by the idea as Karen had.

"It clearly didn't happen to anyone else's shop—I walked most of the way up and down the street, and it was only piled at my place. I've been rather public about my opposition to parking meters. I think someone's trying to send me a message."

"I think you might be right," Gavin said. "I wish you could have made a real police report."

"Oh, I will." Julie sighed in frustration. "This is so stupid. I've never even *met* Sam McLeod."

"It might not be..." Though Gavin didn't even sound convinced enough to finish his own sentence. "Well. Is there anything I can do right now? Do you want me to come over?"

Julie thought a moment. "I do and I don't. I've missed you, but I'm exhausted and overwhelmed right now, and honestly kind of cranky. I'm not sure I'd be very good company."

"You wouldn't need to entertain me. I could even bring dinner."

She hesitated another moment. "Are you still up for coming to soup group tomorrow night?"

"Of course! I'm really looking forward to it."

"Then let's just do that. What I really need right now is to drink this big glass of wine, make a grilled-cheese sandwich for dinner, and then fall into bed. Alone."

Gavin chuckled. "Then that's what you should do. I'll see you tomorrow."

MATT

"REALLY? ITALIAN MEATBALL soup?" Steph said, giving him a mock-horrified look after she peered into the pot. "Ron's gonna turn his nose up at this, you know."

Matt crossed his arms over his chest. "Dad wanted it. It's his favorite."

Steph's gaze softened. "I mean, it looks good to me, and smells even better. But you know I'm no snob."

"Ron's the only snob around here," Matt muttered, frowning. "The one who never cooks anything, I might add."

Steph chuckled. "Well but he brings the *wine*. And we can't have a fine meal without the *wine*, you know."

They laughed together. "We all have our parts to play, I suppose," Matt said, stirring the soup.

Out in the living room, Ramona sat with his dad, keeping him company and out of the way. Steph had come over early to help with the setup, and to bring fresh bread from the bakery—three loaves this time, as Matt was expecting around twenty people.

Steph had just gotten the loaves into the oven to warm up when the doorbell rang. "Is someone early?" she asked.

Matt shook his head. "It's probably Julie and her new boyfriend—I told them they could come up whenever they wanted. We could still use help getting the furniture rearranged out there."

"Good plan." Steph headed out to answer the door, and returned a moment later with Gavin and Julie.

"Hey," Gavin said, smiling at Matt and reaching out a hand to shake.

Matt wiped his hands on a kitchen towel before extending his own hand. "Hey, thanks for coming, and welcome."

"Thanks for having me! I've been so curious to see what this whole soup group is about."

"Besides, well, soup?" Steph asked.

"Well, but this one will be a little different—" Matt started, but Julie laughed.

"He knows," she said. "I've told him if he's really well behaved, he *might* get invited back…someday…but that we'd have to have a secret meeting to consider his candidacy first."

Matt smiled at her, noting how happy she looked, how…fresh, bright. Younger, almost. She'd always been attractive, but now that she had hooked up with Gavin, she was radiant.

Was she in love? Maybe not yet, but she seemed well on her way there.

"I will be on my best behavior, tonight and forevermore!" Gavin declared, grinning at Matt and then at Julie.

"Excuse me while I record this moment for posterity," Julie said with an answering grin. She pulled out her phone. "Would you mind repeating that for the record?"

"You don't need to do that, you have witnesses," Steph put in, getting the cutting board and bread knife out from the cupboard next to the fridge. "Do either of you want anything to drink? The wine snob isn't here yet, but there's a nice six-pack of local ale in the fridge."

"Mm, that sounds good," Julie said. "I'll have an ale."

"Just water for me," Gavin said.

Matt was already moving toward the fridge. "Sparkling, or still?"

"Either one."

Once everyone got their drinks, Gavin and Julie moved out into the main room, working with Ramona to move tables and chairs around to accommodate everyone. Matt watched them for a minute through the kitchen doorway, making sure they didn't need any help or guidance, but they had it well in hand. He went back to check on his soup, stirring it before ladling a small amount into a ramekin. "Want a taste?" he asked Steph.

She winked at him. "Already did, and added some red pepper flakes. Not much!" she added, seeing his look of alarm. "Just the tiniest bit. Your dad won't even notice; he'll just wonder why it's so delicious."

"If you say so." He shook his head but smiled at her as he blew on the spoon, then tasted. "Oh, that is good. I'd have never thought."

"That's why you have me, sweetie." Steph patted his shoulder.

Matt turned down the heat on the soup, covered it, and then

proceeded to sort of roam around the house nervously, checking on everything that his friends were entirely in control of, until the first guests started arriving. Then the evening became a blur of getting people drinks (Ron did indeed turn his nose up at the soup, complaining that if he'd known, he would have brought a bottle of Boone's Farm or Thunderbird), making sure there were enough bowls and plates for everyone, that the chairs were well distributed, and the bread got sliced and served. Oh and also chasing Ramona out of the kitchen every few minutes, as she kept trying to act like the hired help, washing bowls and replenishing serving dishes.

"But I am the hired help," she protested, the third time this happened.

"You're not a maid. You're a companion for my dad."

"Who is right now surrounded by a bevy of beautiful young women. He practically shooed me away himself."

Okay, this he had to see. Matt peered out into the living room, then laughed. "Oh, those are just the neighbor girls. You know the Churches."

"I do, but I don't remember that willowy one. She must be six feet tall! I thought those girls were still in high school."

"Most of them are; that's Genevieve, though, the oldest. She's in college, just here for the weekend."

"Ah." Ramona washed another bowl and set it in the drying rack.

"Stop that!" Matt said, pretending to swat her hand. "Go have another glass of wine and flirt with somebody yourself. There's gotta be some college boys out there too."

Laughing, she dried her hands and headed back out to the party, shaking her head.

It was supposed to be a gathering for political organizing, of course. Gavin did say a few words to the group about some of their tasks ahead, and Julie told them about someone leaving a pile of construction trash in front of her store yesterday, but since the recent ruling by the judge had extended the work ban past the new year, it was much more of a celebration. Which suited Matt just fine. It felt really good to have life, warmth, and laughter in his house again. This was his first time hosting since Heather had left, and he'd been worried about having it be such a big group, but now he realized the genius of it. This crowd was happy, noisy, and entirely not focused on him. Nobody cornered him with a serious look and asked, "So how *are* you doing, *really*?"

It was great.

And the evening was over before he knew it. Lynne and Steph both stayed over to help him clean up (whatever was left after Ramona had snuck back into the kitchen for the fourth time), so it was all handled in a jiffy.

"Thanks for everything!" Steph said with a big smile, pulling him into a hug at the front door.

"No, thank you, honestly," he told her. "You're amazing. You, too," he added to Lynne. "Thank you."

Lynne hugged him as well, then buttoned up her coat. "It's our pleasure, my friend. Now, sleep well tonight, hm?"

"I will."

Fortunately, his dad was a champion sleeper. Matt knew that some dementia patients suffered dysregulated sleep—napping all day, up and agitated at night. So far, Gordon hadn't had any of those issues. He hoped that continued.

Gordon was in bed already; Ramona had seen him through his tooth-brushing and pajama-changing ritual while Matt and his friends had been in the kitchen cleaning. So, once the door closed behind Steph and Lynne, there was nothing to do but go to bed himself.

JULIE

"That went well," Julie said, as Gavin drove down Enchanted Forest.

Gavin nodded. "Yeah—I think? Should we have done more recruitment work, though? Gotten people committed to sign up for tasks? The first of the year will be here before we know it."

She reached across and put her hand on his arm in the darkened car. "There's time enough for that. You did talk about the issue, and everyone listened—I think there were some folks who hadn't even known this was going on. This was supposed to be for spreading the word, and that's what it did."

"I didn't even take contact information..." he fretted.

"Those are all Matt's friends, not strangers off the street," Julie said. "We can get all their names and info from him—I'll call him tomorrow, in fact."

"All right."

"And thank you, seriously, for being fine with not getting together last night. I'd gotten up so early, and had already had a full day before I got home and found the mess—"

"Of course," Gavin said. "You were clearly exhausted. And I did get to see you today."

"Yes."

In a minute, they were at Lover's Lane. Soon, too soon, they'd be back at her house, and Gavin would kiss her goodnight, and then start his long drive out past Olga...

Though she'd had a lovely time in Portland, she'd really missed Gavin. More than she'd imagined she would, and she *had* imagined that she would.

Was it time...?

He parked in front of her shop and turned off the car. He was leaning over, perhaps for that kiss, when Julie said, "Do you want to come in for a minute?"

"A minute?" he asked. She could see the flash of his smile in the darkness.

"A minute...or several minutes. Or more."

He did lean forward and brushed her lips with a soft kiss. "I would like that very much."

At her door, she fumbled with her keys; she often didn't lock up, since her house was so well hidden, but since she knew she was going to be out late tonight, she didn't want to invite any trouble—from lost tourists trying to find their Airbnbs...or asshole developers with a vendetta. Eventually, she found the lock and let them in.

He drew her into his arms the moment she closed the door behind them. She sighed and melted into his touch, then pressed against him hungrily.

I think it is time.

They kissed in the front room for a long while. Julie suddenly felt languid and unhurried, wanting to savor each moment before moving to the next one. *Or am I shy, nervous?*

But no, she didn't think so. She felt ready for this. And unrushed.

I'm a grown woman, with two adult daughters, after all, she reassured herself. *Just...out of practice.*

Gavin, whether out of practice himself, shy, or simply a gentleman, let her set the pace. So eventually she drew him into the kitchen, where they paused another long while, exploring each others in the new environment.

And then, at last, she led him to her tiny bedroom. She heard the softest shuffle of cat-feet as Fergie slipped out of the room to hide elsewhere, and then forgot her cat entirely as she shrugged out of her blouse, somehow still kissing Gavin.

He gasped softly, drawing back just a bit, taking in the sight of her in the faint moonlight coming through the window. "You're...beautiful."

Julie felt goose bumps on her shoulders, throat, and chest as a delicious chill shivered down her spine. No, not a chill—a thrill, a sensation of such tender delight that she wanted nothing more than to drink it up—all night, forever. She pulled him close again, and then leaned back, still holding him tight.

He got the message, his body following hers down onto the

bed.

AFTERWARD, THEY LAY in each others' arms, breathless and replete. Julie had the sudden urge to giggle with happiness, though she wasn't sure how he would take such a thing. "Thank you," she whispered instead.

His eyes widened. "No, thank *you*! That was amazing."

"I thought so too." She snuggled against him. "I never want to let you go."

"Then don't."

She purred a little, holding him close, starting to feel drowsy, amazingly, though still infused with fizzy delight. As though their lovemaking were champagne, and it ran in her veins instead of blood.

"I'm afraid I might fall asleep," she murmured, after another long blissful moment.

"Then do," he said softly.

"Will you stay?"

"I would love nothing better," he said.

AND HE WAS still there in the morning. She blinked over at him in the gray dawn light, admiring the lines of his sleeping face, his well-kissed lips, his relaxed brow. She didn't want to wake him, and she also did want to wake him, and enjoy him again.

He solved the dilemma by waking a minute later, then reaching for her.

Their lovemaking was relaxed and gentle this morning; last night's had begun unhurried but had quickly heated up into a feverish hunger, for both of them. The morning brought not only a slowing of the pace but also the ability to see each other; Julie had not managed to turn on the bedroom light last night before tugging him down to her bed.

He was just one delight after another.

She held him close long after they were spent, then finally released him with a sigh. "I'd invite you to shower with me, but I'm afraid there's no room."

He chuckled. "Then you shower first. I need to get…a few things from my car."

"Ha!" She laughed, surprised. "Did you pack an overnight bag then?"

"Sort of." He looked only a little sheepish. "I just tossed in a clean shirt, change of boxers, socks—you know. Just in case."

"That was very wise of you. And also probably smart not to bring them in."

"One doesn't want to presume."

She leaned forward and kissed him. "I'm glad you semi-presumed, at least. And that you were prepared." For he had also produced a condom, at each appropriate moment. She stretched luxuriously and sat up at the edge of the bed.

"*Ohh*," he sighed.

"What?" She turned to look at him. He looked kind of… stunned? "What's the matter?"

"Nothing is the matter." Now he shook his head and gave her a salacious grin. "Do that again—that stretching thing."

With another laugh, she got out of bed and headed for her petite bathroom. "Not just yet." At the doorway, she turned around and grinned back at him. "Gotta give you something to look forward to, hm?"

When she got out of the shower, she smelled coffee. *This man just gets better and better*, she thought as she toweled herself off. *Why in the world didn't I take up with him sooner?*

It just went to show how wrong first impressions could be.

Chapter 9

JULIE

The second half of November flew by in a giddy, happy blur. Julie had more free time, with the shop on its winter schedule, but Gavin still worked full-time at the library, of course. Even so, they managed to spend most evenings—and nights—together.

With her daytimes largely unscheduled, Julie poured herself into her creative projects, not only making the paper and writing her pithies, but conceiving and drafting preliminary plans for several new lines of products: large sketchbooks, tiny diaries, perhaps a line of chapbooks featuring classic (and, more importantly, public domain) poetry. She felt on fire, in the best possible way: her mind alive, wide awake, ideas cascading in one after another.

"It's the best," she said to Steph and Alicia over lunch at the Lower one Wednesday—the weather being just a bit too terrible for pickleball. She took a big bite of her French dip, a drop of juice dribbling down her chin. "Sorry," she said around the mouthful, grinning at her friends.

"It's all right," Alicia said, laughing. "It makes me happy to see you so, well, happy."

"Me too," Steph said, with a bright smile.

Julie looked at them both as she wiped off her mouth with a

paper napkin. Neither of them were in the best of marriages, she knew; and they in turn knew that they could talk to her, if ever they wanted to. Well, Julie was pretty sure that they both knew that…but now felt like an awkward moment to bring it up. She settled for, "Just let me know if I get annoying, okay?"

Steph patted her arm before taking a bite of her cheeseburger. "You could not possibly be annoying, Julie. We love you, and you've been alone too long."

Alicia picked at her green salad. (Seriously, who came to the Lower for *salad*?) "What she said," she echoed.

"I was happy alone," Julie said. "I think that's part of why this is so wonderful: because I wasn't looking for it. I didn't need it— so it's not filling some sort of hole—"

Both of her friends rolled their eyes at the unintentional pun; Steph actually groaned.

"Sorry! I didn't mean that!" Julie felt her face flame even as she laughed. "Ah, jeez, I *am* obnoxious, aren't I? I'll just shut up and eat my lunch. You two talk amongst yourselves."

"Not a tiny chance," Alicia said. "We want to hear every single, sexy detail."

Now *that* wasn't helping Julie's blush. "Oh, I'm sure you don't."

Steph swirled a fry around in ketchup and ate it. "Or even the non-sexy details then. You're saying Gavin's so great because you didn't need him?"

"Well, exactly," Julie said, leaning forward, reclaiming the thread of her thought. "When I was younger—certainly when I met Michael—I was just desperate to find love, to get married, to have kids. And I'm not sorry I did that, of course; Megan and Lori are the best things that ever happened to me. But I think that very desperation on my part led me to, I don't know, give away parts of myself that I probably shouldn't have. Michael is a decent man and all, but he and I were never all that well suited. We were never going to go the distance, and I was too immature to know that. We both were, but I think women particularly give up a lot in the service of marriage—even a good, fairly equitable marriage. And I think young women especially do this. I know I did."

Steph and Alicia were both nodding. Again, Julie wondered how close this was hitting home for them. Steph had been pretty young when she'd married David, but Alicia had been in her late thirties, maybe even forty, when she married Ron: her first marriage, though not her first serious relationship.

So why did she let Ron run her life so fiercely? Alicia was bright, vibrant, intelligent—yet she bowed to her husband's every whim and cranky mood. Julie wished she could help her friend out of this dynamic.

Or punch Ron in his surly nose. Whichever.

"That makes sense," Steph said, nodding and clearly thinking about it. "A traditional marriage doesn't leave a lot of wiggle room for women—and yet it's what we're supposed to want, above all else. Or at least it's what we *were* supposed to want."

"Definitely, in my generation," Julie agreed.

Steph chuckled. "What do you have, like five years on me, old woman?"

"A very crucial five years."

"She's right, though," Alicia put in. "That whole system only worked when women weren't given any other real choice. The cruel part was making them believe they had chosen it." She shook her head. "I thought I was escaping that, just living with Russ all those years, no marriage involved. Then ole Professor Ron Alderson swept me off my feet." She gave a rueful smile. "Never underestimate the power of an intellectual man with a fancy bottle of wine."

Everyone laughed at this. Alicia reached over and stole one of Steph's fries, and ate it slowly, savoring it.

After a minute of enjoying their meals, Alicia asked Julie, "What are you doing for Thanksgiving—are you going to introduce Gavin to your girls yet?"

"Mm, not yet," Julie said. "They're both coming up for Christmas; I haven't decided if I want to go down to Portland and spend it with them there, or just do something small up here. What are you guys doing?"

Alicia frowned slightly. "Ron doesn't want to do anything. I wish I could go to Portland with you."

"I wish you could too," Julie said, and also wished she could press the point without making Alicia even sadder. "If I do stay here, you guys should come over," she said.

Alicia shrugged. "I'll ask him—or we could cook together at my place if you want. Ron can hardly object to that. And you'll bring Gavin, of course."

"Of course." Julie smiled at her, then turned to Steph.

"I'm flying back East to see my folks," Steph said. "Mom isn't doing as well with travel these days, so I said I'd go there."

"Will you be back in time for the soup group at Lynne's?" Alicia asked her. "I hear she's doing something a bit different."

"Yep—I'm coming back on Saturday, and I'm doing Kenmore Air so I don't have to worry about the ferries."

"Oh, that's smart," Julie said, wishing she could afford the small-plane flights directly from the island to Seattle. Forty minutes versus hours of driving in holiday traffic, *plus* an hour ferry ride (assuming the ferries actually ran).

"I know," Steph said with a chuckle. "I just hope the weather holds!"

Which was the other potential complication, of course, especially in winter. No-pickleball weather was often also no-tiny-planes weather. "Good luck—let me know if you need to be picked up at the ferry or anything," Julie told her.

"Thanks. I should be fine, but…who knows?"

Julie polished off her French dip, savoring the last of the salty dipping sauce, the soft toasted bread, the tender meat. "Mm, what an indulgence," she said, patting her belly. "Good idea coming here—I can't believe either of you were up for it."

Steph laughed. "Even gourmet cooks appreciate a good pub burger."

"And someone else's fries," Alicia said, now stealing one of Julie's. "Hey," she said, at Julie's glance, "be grateful to me: you don't want to get all fat now that you have a new boyfriend, do you?"

"Oh, I don't think Gavin would have any problem if I put on a few pounds," Julie said in a suggestive purr.

"Annnnd that's enough of that!" Steph sang out with a laugh, looking around for their server. "Where's our check?"

THE MEETINGS, BOTH of the small working groups and of the bigger committee, continued despite the brief reprieve. Leslie Magnas and Gavin shared the work of organizing them, with Julie helping as much as she could.

There had been no further vandalism at Julie's shop. A nice young sheriff's deputy had come by to take a report the Monday after she phoned it in, and had promised to inform the county of the need to come and remove the pile of debris. He'd also promised to let Julie know if anything came of the investigation into who had left the pile, yet managed to do so in a way that left Julie certain that this was the last she'd hear of it.

Which was about what she'd expected.

The annual Solstice Parade was scheduled for the second Saturday in December—a few days before the actual solstice itself—culminating in the big tree lighting on the village green. All the local businesses geared up for this important event; some shops in past years had reported sales even better than the immediate post-Thanksgiving days.

Whether she had good sales or not, this was a time that Julie looked forward to even more than Halloween. There was just something about Christmas in a small community: the lights, the festive music, the spiced cider. The joy and togetherness. Occasionally, there was even a dusting of snow on the ground for the parade, which made it all the more memorable.

In the weeks leading up to the parade, Julie kept busy creating a bountiful stock of both blank notebooks and back-of-the-toilet books filled with pithies, and also talking to her fellow business owners about the parking meter issue. It was ironic, in its way: it almost seemed as though this little crisis had brought the whole community together, in a new and deeper way.

With her increased book production and a turn of the weather to a wintry cold and gloominess, Julie decided to skip Portland and stay on Orcas for Thanksgiving after all. She reached out to Alicia, but Ron didn't want to entertain, or even to leave the house—"We'll just see all the same people three days later for the soup group," Alicia told her the old grouch had said—so she roasted a chicken, made stuffing from a mix from the grocery store (where she also bought a pumpkin pie), and had Gavin over for a sweet, cozy, romantic celebration-for-two.

He stayed through the weekend, leaving only on Sunday after-noon as Julie was getting her dish ready to take down to Lynne's.

"Don't feel bad," he said, leaning over and giving her a kiss as she was thinly slicing cucumbers for an Asian salad (Lynne's spe-cific request, and a slightly puzzling one, as Lynne was the queen of salads and usually provided her own, even when she hosted). "This is your thing. You don't need to include me."

"But you came last month and had a great time."

He smiled. "Last month it was also a political meeting. This month it's just you and your friends."

"Your friends too, I hope," she said, then quickly added, "I mean, someday—you know what I mean."

"I do, and it's fine, really," he assured her. "But there's no need to rush into anything. If your group wants to invite me to join, I'll be honored to. I don't want to impose, or step on any toes."

"It's not that formal!" she said, giving him a helpless smile. "Anyway, technically, the group has an opening—Heather and Matt joined as a couple, but she left and now it's just him alone."

"I'm not much of a soup cook either," Gavin said, which was not exactly responsive to her point.

"Soup isn't hard," she started, but then interrupted herself. "Sorry, I'm being ridiculous. You're right: all in good time." She didn't mean to be clingy. She just really, *really* liked having him around.

He stepped up behind her and pulled her into an embrace; she set the knife down and turned in his arms, kissing him back greedily. "I love that you want to spend time with me," he breathed against her lips after a minute. "I want that too, more than anything—I actually hate to go home, but it's where I live. I have responsibilities, and a life, and so do you."

"I know. And it's fine. Truly."

He kissed her again. "That being said, when can I see you next? What are you doing tomorrow night?"

She laughed, heartily, feeling warmth and a sparkle down to her toes.

LYNNE WAS STANDING over a large rice cooker when Julie walked in with her cucumber salad. "Where do you want me to put this?"

Lynne turned around, looking flushed and a little out of sorts. Her brow was damp, and her gray hair was pulled back in a messy ponytail. "Oh, just on the counter—wherever you can find space."

Julie scanned the small kitchen, looking for anywhere large enough to hold the low, flat dish without spilling the rice-vine-gar-and-sugar dressing. Lynne's whole kitchen seemed crammed with bottles of Asian ingredients and concoctions, including a whole row of colorful rice seasonings in oversized spice shakers. She finally managed to squeeze the dish at the edge of the counter closest to the dining room, but only by scooting over four or five jars of sauce. "What on earth are you making?"

"Oh!" Lynne wiped her forehead with her sleeve. "It was supposed to be simple, but I failed to take into account all the 'optional' instructions, and now I got myself so far down a primrose path that I can't find my way back, and I'm not sure if any of it even will make any difference, and everyone's going to be here in a minute, and…" She caught Julie's gaze and laughed. "I know, I know: it'll be great, nobody will know what it was supposed to taste like, and we're all friends here."

Julie laughed with her. "Exactly." She looked at the rice cooker. "Anything I can help with?"

"Not with this—I was just looking to see how much longer it had. You can stir that broth on the stove there, though."

Julie picked up a spoon and gave the delicious-smelling mixture a stir. "Is this miso?"

"It is! With shiitake mushrooms and green onions and seaweed, and some other stuff; then it all goes over rice, with more seasonings; and some flash-cooked salmon flaked over top of that. Oh! I should have been heating up the pan for the salmon…"

THE MISO BROTHY salmon bowls were a great hit, of course; no one needed to ask for the recipe, because part of the deal of the soup club was a shared database of every recipe made for their meetings. Not just the soups, but the entire potluck.

We should put together a cookbook, Julie thought, as she brought a warm, rich spoonful of soup to her lips. Around the table, everyone was tucking in with equal gusto; even Lynne looked relieved and pleased with herself. *Why haven't I thought of a cookbook before?* She could publish it herself, on her fancy paper, and sell them in her shop. Ooh, and Alicia could hand-letter the book—her handwriting was basically calligraphy. What a gorgeous artifact it would be! Julie's book-making mind then immediately took over and started working through the logistics: should it be organized by category (soups; salads; meat dishes; desserts) or meal by meal? One of her favorite cookbooks from years ago was one where a collection of chefs had presented the meals they liked to cook at home, for company; and that would go along with the theme of their meetings. But hmm, what about photographs? Cookbooks needed to have photographs. Maybe the fancy paper idea wasn't quite right for this…

She was so lost in thought that Steph had to elbow her to get her attention.

"Hm?" Julie said, blinking and looking around the table.

Steph laughed. "Earth to Julie—Matt asked if you had a nice Thanksgiving, but by the look on your face, I'd say you probably did."

Julie felt herself blush, but she grinned. "I did, but that's not what I was thinking about. I was wondering if we should publish a cookbook of all these amazing meals we've been sharing these last few years."

Alicia perked up. "Ooh, I like that idea. I could talk to one of my publishers…they all know each other, it's a small world."

"Or we could just do it ourselves," Julie said. "Handmade, individually produced—like my Paper Magic books. Except I was just trying to figure out how to include pictures…"

"You'd have to charge a fortune for a handmade cookbook," Ron said, frowning. "Who's going to want to pay that much for a collection of soup recipes they could just find on the internet?"

From across the table, Steph gave him a look. "You'd be surprised, actually. I think it's a great idea."

Oddly, Ron seemed chastened by this. He shrugged, and poured himself more hot sake, dropping his gaze from Steph's.

The conversation flew along, with nearly everybody throwing in ideas, and within a few minutes, Julie had agreed to come up with a preliminary plan for the contents of the cookbook, while Alicia had promised to handwrite up a few recipes and keep track of how long it took her, to see if this was a viable approach. They would work out the paper and illustration issues after they had the first part figured out.

I love my creative friends, Julie thought, driving home. The miso soup felt warm and nourishing in her belly, and the sake warmed her blood further, though not as much as the comfortable camaraderie of her community. Even grumpy Ron had eventually seemed to come on board with the idea, however grudgingly.

Once she got home, she did miss Gavin, but she also felt happy at being alone in her quiet, cozy space. In bed, she stretched out diagonally, taking all the room (except the part that Fergie perched on, near her feet). As she fell asleep, her last thought was, *Everything is going so well. My life is just grand.*

THE SOLSTICE PARADE was in two days, and Julie's house looked like a book warehouse. Her paper-making shed was crammed so full of inventory that she'd had to resort to piling boxes in her living room and even a stack of them in the kitchen. Only the fact that her bedroom was barely larger than her bed had saved it from becoming a storage shed as well.

"I'm sorry about the mess!" she said to Gavin, laughing, as he tried to find a place to sit. "This is why I kept suggesting we hang out at your house."

"It's fine!" he said, squeezing onto the sofa next to an open box. "And I love having you there, but your place is more convenient to Orcas Center."

"I know, I know." They had tickets to see a new play this evening, and Julie had offered to cook a quick meal before the opening curtain. "I'm almost done in there," she said, nodding toward the kitchen. "Can I get you anything to drink before we eat?"

"No, I'm fine—can I help you at all?"

"I'm good. Just have to dish it up, mostly."

She left him in the cluttered living room while she gave the risotto a last, quick stir before getting out the brick of Parmesan cheese and the grater. In a minute, everything was on the table; she leaned into the doorway to the living room and said, "It's ready!"

He set the book he'd been looking through back into its box

and got up with a smile. "Smells amazing," he said, coming to the table.

"Thanks. Just simple mushroom risotto." She raised her glass of wine to him; he lifted his and toasted. "It was one of the first 'fancy' dishes my girls would eat, so I made it a *lot* when they were growing up. Sort of a self-defense against mac and cheese."

He sipped his wine and set it down, then took a spoonful of the creamy risotto. "Oh, wow. That's delicious."

She smiled at him and took her own bite. Yep: pretty good.

They ate in companionable silence for a few minutes. Julie re-filled her own wine glass but left his alone, setting the bottle on the table.

He was scraping his bowl clean before she was halfway through with hers. "Do you want seconds?"

"I do, but I should probably have some salad first." He pulled the bowl over and dished some out onto his plate.

"Hey, we're adults. You don't even have to have salad if you don't want any."

"I love your salad." He grinned at her. Wow, he was adorable. "I love everything you cook. In fact, I love everything you do—you've clearly put a lot of work into those books."

"I have," she said. "I'm glad you like them. I hope the tourists like them too—I might have kinda gone overboard in my pro-duction, but once I got started, I just kept going."

He nodded. "That newest book of quotes—where did you get them all? They're so perfect."

"What do you mean?" She finished her own risotto and con-templated the salad-versus-seconds question for herself, then opted for just another scoop of the rice. While it was still nice and hot.

"The quotes you use, from those historical figures. How did you find them all? I know you used to use the library's refer-ence collection, but you don't anymore. I've never even heard of Countess Derby-whatever-she-was."

"Oh, that!" Julie laughed and took a bite of risotto. "Yes, I used to use real quotes, but now I write them myself. I invented the countess, and all her cousins and friends and hangers-on who populate the books." She picked up her glass and took a sip of wine to wash down the bite with, savoring the buttery flavor, and how nicely it played with the mushrooms and their own butter. Normally she wasn't a big Chardonnay fan, but with this risotto, it was just perfect.

Gavin was oddly silent. She looked up at him, and he was giving her a…kind of odd look, as well.

"What's the matter?" she asked.

He paused, then shook his head. "Nothing. I—uh, nothing."

Julie set her glass down. "No, something's weird here. Gavin, what's wrong?"

"I…I guess I'm just a little surprised, is all."

"Surprised about what?"

"I. Uh. Thought they were real quotes."

She chuckled. "Is that all? I was afraid it was something big." But at the look on his face, she sobered. "Gavin. Is this something big?"

He shook his head again, but didn't look happy.

She stared back at him. "What difference does it make, whether the quotes are real or not? These aren't research documents— they're books for fun."

"No difference! I'm sure. None at all." Those were the words he said, anyway. His face said just the opposite.

Julie felt an awful sinking in the pit of her stomach, curdling around the risotto she'd eaten. "So…you're 'surprised' that my creative product is actually a creative product?" She hadn't meant it to come out quite so sharply, yet his judgmental air about her work years ago, when they'd first met, came roaring back to her. The very thing that had turned her off about him.

The thing that had happily seemed to be missing when they'd gotten to know each other more recently. He'd even called her books creative, when he'd told her how much he liked them, after seeing them at his friends' house.

Gavin sat there, his mouth open a little, looking like he didn't know what to say. Not looking happy. Finally, he closed his mouth, then opened it again and said, "Uh, yeah. I'm surprised that your books are all...invented, I guess. Fake. Like I said, I thought they were real quotes. I was, um, really impressed that you found so many perfect quotes, and I wondered where they came from. It's the wanna-be librarian in me, I guess."

Julie fought the urge to scoot her chair farther away from him. It would have been impossible in the tight space anyway, and she was *not* going to give ground in her own home. Not even to her exciting, sweet, fantastic new boyfriend who was currently being...not very fantastic at all. She held his gaze with hers and said, levelly, "So the ridiculous name didn't clue you in? *Lucinda Devonryshireton*, really?"

"I...was going to look her up, but I, um..."

She leaned forward. "And the 'wanna-be librarian in you' doesn't value fiction? Acts of *creative* writing?"

He flushed, and raised his hands in a warding-off gesture. "Of course I value fiction. But I thought you valued research! It's what you used to do."

"Well, yes, and of course I value research! But that's not why people buy these books. They buy them because they're fun, and funny, and they look good on a coffee table."

Gavin looked like he wanted to argue back, but suddenly shut his expression down. "I shouldn't have said anything," he said, somewhat woodenly. "Julie, I'm sorry, I just—like I said, I was surprised, is all. I thought I understood something, and I didn't realize that I had been wrong about it." He took a breath. "I didn't mean to hurt your feelings—I can see that I stepped in something here, and I didn't mean to."

She started to automatically tell him "it's fine," and then stopped herself. It was not fine. The sick, sinking feeling in her gut told her that much. If she was understanding what he was saying—and she was pretty sure she was—he was making it clear that he didn't respect her work, her art. He wasn't just "surprised;" he was judgmental. He'd called it fake, as if inventing a whole character, with a sassy personality and a witty tongue and an endless supply of bon mots, was somehow deceitful.

And he didn't even get why this should be hurtful to her.

Now she did push back from the table and got to her feet. "I think I'm not actually up for the theater tonight," she said. "I'd rather stay in...alone."

Gavin sat frozen in his chair, staring up at her in shock. "Wait..." he stammered, after a long moment. "You're...not coming out with me?"

"That's what I said. Gavin, I think you should go now. Go to the play alone, or go home, I don't care. I need to think about what just happened here, and I can't do it with you in my house."

After another frozen minute, he scrambled to his feet, nearly knocking over his chair in his haste. "I said I was sorry!"

Julie shook her head sadly. "I know you did, and I heard you. But I just...need to process this. Now. Please respect what I am asking for here."

The look on his face. It just about broke her heart, and she would have relented right then if she hadn't been so angry—and so hurt herself.

"Okay," he said, in a small voice, hoarse with disbelief, and a little bit of...defensiveness? Julie focused on that, so that she wouldn't relent.

Relenting was what she'd done her whole marriage. Making herself smaller, softer, quieter. Less demanding. Less needful.

Less.

"Thank you," she said, nearly as quietly as his *Okay* had been.

He walked slowly to the front door, picked up his jacket, and turned around. "Can I...call you later? Or tomorrow?"

She bit her lip as she thought about it. "You can call me, but

I won't promise to pick up, if I'm not ready. As I said, I need to think."

"I understand," he said, and opened the door, letting himself out.

I wonder if you do, she thought, as the door closed behind him.

Chapter 10

JULIE

Julie sat in the small comfy chair wedged in the corner of her bedroom, sniffling, after she'd cleaned up the dishes. She hadn't wanted to be in the living room, hadn't wanted to see all the books.

The books she'd been so excited about.

The books she *was* so excited about, so proud of.

The books Gavin had basically crapped all over.

"How *old* am I?" she whispered to herself, only now she wasn't marveling at the flare-up of the fires of passion inside her that she'd thought were banked long ago. Now she was agonizing over an ancient wound, one she'd thought long since healed.

Her ex-husband Michael had been—mostly—a good man and a decent human being, and their separation had been largely amicable. But he, like so many men of his generation and social stature, had had opinions about things, and, also like so many men of his ilk, he had been encouraged by everything he encountered in his life to regard those opinions as unassailable, self-evident truths.

Consequently, when someone tried to challenge one of those opinions, however mildly or gently, Michael had not always been entirely gracious about it.

Julie snorted softly, even as she was wiping away tears. *Not entirely gracious* indeed. Michael could be a supercilious asshole, especially when it came to the idea of his wife, and the mother of his daughters, having creative ambitions of her own.

No, Michael was the creative one in their family, and the breadwinner to boot. He was an architect, he sometimes had to work long hours, he was well-paid and well-regarded in the field. Julie's job had been to be the steady, unwavering presence at home. Not just the housewife, although yes, certainly that—shopping, cooking, cleaning; handling the girls' appointments and activities, meeting with their teachers, knowing their friends and their friends' parents. Buying their school clothes and packing their lunches and soothing their skinned knees and, later, broken hearts. Managing the domestic sphere and all that it contained.

There was no room in such a role for a woman who might want to write something, anything—as Julie had, once, all too briefly. There was hardly room for a woman who wanted to read, though Julie would sooner have perished than to give up her shelves of novels, her volumes of poems. Michael, to his credit she supposed, had recognized the futility of that battle from the start.

When Julie had left Michael, she'd dreamed of moving into a garret somewhere—oh, Paris probably—containing nothing but a mattress on the floor, a writing desk, an espresso pot, and books lining every wall all the way to the ceiling. Of course, with two daughters to take care of, she'd instead stayed in the family home and kept everything as stable for them as possible, though she had redecorated the former master bedroom—now *her* bedroom, her sanctuary—to hint at such dreams. The bookshelves she'd had built had been some of the only things she'd moved here to Orcas Island; they now graced her small living room.

Gavin was not Michael, of course; they were very different men, in so many ways. Yet his "surprise" had brought Michael rushing straight back, to lodge firmly under Julie's skin, where he had lived for so many years. Suddenly, while Gavin had been clearly struggling with how to say "I think your writing is foolish and not worthy of respect" without actually using those words, all Julie could hear was Michael's "And I suppose the girls should walk home from school, because their mother is too busy scribbling fairy stories at her desk to remember she even *has* children?"

Am I being unfair? Julie asked herself. Gavin hadn't said that; Michael had.

But it was the same attitude, wasn't it? *"Your work doesn't matter. It's stupid and foolish and female. Only big important men's work counts around here."*

"Nobody wants to read your scribblings."

Julie sighed, and pulled a kleenex out of the box to blow her nose. Then her phone rang. *Oh, too soon, Gavin,* she thought, but a glance at the screen told her it was Megan. She swiped the call open. "Hey, hon," she said, trying to sound normal.

"Hey Mom!" Megan said. "Is this a good time?"

"Yes, it is." Distractions were always good. "What's up?"

"I just wanted to check in about next week. I talked to Lori—she has a temp job that she can't leave till six on Friday, so we thought we'd just head up on Saturday. Is that all right? We can probably catch the mid-afternoon boat if we don't hit too much traffic."

Julie thought a moment. "You don't have ferry reservations?"

"No, do we need them?"

"Yes!" Julie said, then added, more gently, "Remember? I told you to make reservations two weeks before. The boats might all be full."

"In winter? I thought winter was the slow time."

"Yes, except right around the holidays." Julie forced herself to take a deep breath. "You'll probably be fine—but you might have to wait till the next boat if you don't make the afternoon one. And remember, Steph's party is that night."

"I know! We're both looking forward to it."

Julie didn't exactly believe that, but she appreciated both her daughters' willingness to humor their old mother and make nice to her friends.

"And we're both looking forward to having the run of your house while you hang around with this hot new squeeze of yours, who we still can't wait to meet," Megan went on.

"About that…"

"Mom! What? Did you dump him already?"

Julie blinked back another sudden tear. "I…I don't know. We had a little…disagreement this evening. You might just have me to kick around here after all."

"Oh no! I'm so sorry. Are you okay? You sound sad."

"I am a bit sad," Julie admitted. "And I don't know if we're through. It might have been a misunderstanding. It's too soon to know."

"Well, whatever he did, he better apologize if he knows what's good for him."

Julie smiled. "Thanks, hon."

"'Cause Lori and I will *mess him up* if he doesn't."

"There's no need for that," Julie said, though her heart warmed.

"Not if he apologizes," Megan said fiercely. "And not some sort of mealy-ass 'I'm sorry you feel that way' kind of apology either. A real one, and maybe some jewelry to go with it."

"I'll keep that in mind. Though I don't really need any more jewelry."

"Mom! Every woman needs more jewelry."

"If you say so."

Megan laughed. "Okay, fine, humor me, but I *will* be calling Karen to give her a heads-up." Then she grew more serious. "Truly, though, are you okay? Do you want to talk about it?"

"I am okay, I think; and no, I don't really want to talk about it right now. I was actually thinking about going to bed in a bit here."

"Well I won't keep you. But if you change your mind, I'm here, night or day."

"Thank you, Megan. I love you."

"I love you too, Mom." Julie was about to hang up when Megan added, "I'm serious, though. Lori and I will make him rue the day he made our mom sad."

Julie smiled as the line went dead.

STEPH

STEPH WAS CLEANING up her breakfast dishes Friday morning when her phone rang. She dried her hands and pulled out the phone; it was Ron.

"Hey," she said, putting the call on speaker and picking up a dish towel to start drying. "What's up?"

"Oh, I was just still thinking about Julie's great idea," he said.

"What idea was that?" Steph wiped her omelet plate and put it back in the cupboard. Something more to do with the parking meter issue? Which, of course, was a ridiculous thing and should be stopped, but to her mind, Julie had gotten a little extra caught up in the controversy.

Then again, Steph didn't run a business in town, so what did she know?

"No, the cookbook," Ron said, his strident tone conveying excitement—at least to someone who knew him well. "It's brilliant! I think we should move forward with it, the sooner the better."

"Oh-kay," Steph said slowly, to cover her confusion. *Now you think it's a great idea?* she thought. *Just a few days ago you were sure that no one would pay for such a thing.* "So…why are you calling me about this? It's Julie's brainchild, after all. And Alicia's working on the hand-lettering."

"Steph!" Ron cried. "Of course it's Julie's idea, and Alicia's handwriting is very nice, but *you're* our chef. *You're* the one who will have to test all the recipes, and who will know how they should best be written up, and all that. We have no book if you're not all in."

"Well, sure, I'm in," she started, but Ron cut her off.

"Are you busy right now? Can you meet me in town for coffee to talk about this? It's too hard to do it over the phone."

She started to shake her head, but the fact was, she wasn't all that busy today. She'd been thinking she'd spend some time working on the arrangements for the big Christmas party, but honestly, that was all pretty much already taken care of: the guest list had been created and the invitations were sent, with RSVPs already coming in; she was nearly settled on her menu; it was too early to begin shopping or prepping anything. This weekend she was going to drive up to Lum Farm and buy a Christmas tree, and maybe David would help her decorate it, but today…well, Steph didn't really know what she was going to be doing all day. "All right," she said, drying her coffee cup. "I'll head to town—where shall we meet?"

Ron paused. "Well, I was going to say the yarn store place, but that closed."

"It's the bread bakery now," Steph said. "They have tables, but no coffee. What about the bookstore? Or Brown Bear?"

"Those places are so noisy, we won't be able to hear ourselves think," he said. "Why don't you just come here? I'll make us coffee, and we can talk without being disturbed."

It would mean a longer drive, but again, it wasn't as though she had a full schedule or anything. And it would be nice to see Alicia as well, and see if she'd done any of the lettering yet. "Sure, that sounds fine," she said. "I'll head out in a few minutes; I should be there in under an hour."

"Great!" Ron said, and hung up without saying goodbye.

Steph smiled at the phone as she tucked it back in her pocket and turned to finish the dishes.

At Ron and Alicia's house, she pulled up to the front door and parked. Ron came out onto the porch as she got out of her car.

"Where's Alicia?" Steph asked, not seeing her car.

Ron shrugged casually. "Oh, she's off-island today; she had a hair appointment in Anacortes. Come on in—coffee's ready."

At their big dining table, Ron had piled a stack of cookbooks, presumably to use as reference; beside them was a yellow college-lined tablet and a Cross fountain pen. "What do you take?" he asked, standing in front of their big combo espresso machine/ filter coffee maker.

"Cream and sugar—lots of cream, just a little sugar."

He fussed around with the cups for longer than seemed strictly necessary, then brought them to the table. "Here you go."

Steph sipped. "Oh, that's good. Thank you."

Ron beamed at her. It still seemed strange to see him smile so openly—he was such a crabby-pants usually. "Yes. The trick is the exactly right grind on the beans—and of course the right beans themselves…"

Steph watched him more than listened to him as he explained his process. His hand shook almost imperceptibly. A tremor, or just nerves? Was he nervous about having her over—alone, without Alicia here? Surely they had put that brief flirtation from years ago behind them, never to revisit.

Surely they had.

Steph sipped again and set her mug on the table, then reached over for the stack of cookbooks. "Are you thinking something Orcas-specific?" She lifted a locally produced book off the pile and flipped through it. It was a gorgeous thing, with as many scenic photos of Lopez Island as luscious images of the recipes themselves. "Like this?"

"Maybe," he said, frowning. "I mean, we don't want to copy that exactly—and we're not farm-focused of course—but I like the local angle. I see them fly off the shelves at Darvill's."

So he really had given this some thought, after pooh-poohing the idea initially. Typical Ron. "I still like our soup angle, obviously," she said. "And the friends-sharing-recipes thing. I think we should lean into that, and then it will be even more clear that we're not copying the Lopez book." She set the book down and picked up an older cookbook, well-worn and clearly well-loved, on vegetarian cookery. "What's this? I'm not sure I've ever seen you guys make anything out of this one before."

Ron made a scoffing sound. "That's Alicia's, from before we were married. I only set it out there because, I don't know why, actually." His hand trembled again as he picked up his coffee. "I was just looking for themes. A cookbook has to have a theme."

"It does," Steph agreed, then leaned back in her chair and studied Ron. "So, let me just back up a moment and ask this: why the sudden interest? I thought you weren't into this idea at all, and now it seems like you're ready to take the reins and charge forward with it."

He gave her a hopeful smile. "I was hasty. That's all. It's a brilliant idea, and I've realized that I need more to do in my retirement. Editing a cookery book—"

Steph put her hand up. "Wait a second. Editing? Alicia's the only professional editor among us. Not to mention this whole thing was *Julie's* idea."

Ron sat a little taller. "Well, of course Alicia and Julie will have input—everyone will, it's a joint project, as we discussed—but I'm the only *university professor* among us. My name on the cover will certainly help sales."

"Ron, what were you a professor of?"

He gave her an *are you stupid* look. "Romantic literature, Steph—capital 'R' Romantic, of course. You know that."

"And what does Romantic literature have to do with cookbooks?"

"A book is a book is a book!" He flung his hand out in what was probably meant to be some grand gesture, but he nearly upset his coffee mug, only managing to restrain his hand at the last moment. "I mean, you're right—Alicia should probably be the assistant editor, and as I said on the phone, you have the most experience in the kitchen—but the underlying nature of *what is a book* remains the same, whether we're talking an analysis of the poems of Coleridge, or a middle grade reader, or a collection of recipes with narratives."

She picked up her coffee cup and cradled it in her hands, feeling the warmth of the beverage. Watching Ron, as she thought. After a minute, she said, "You know, I'm actually not comfortable with any of this—it feels too much like going behind everyone's back with something that should be, at best, a group project, if not Julie's thing entirely."

"We're just talking!" he spluttered, but she put her hand up again.

"And I'm also not comfortable specifically with you calling me over here to talk about editing something while Alicia, *the editor*, just happens to be away." There, that was as close as she could come to saying it without actually *saying* it. "I think it's great that you're excited about a cookbook—it's a fun idea, and it would be a neat thing for our soup group to do together, so I'd like to just table this discussion for now and reopen it when we're all together. As a group."

"But the next meeting is your big Christmas party!" he protested. "And we won't even be able to talk about it then, with all those other people there."

Steph sipped her coffee and smiled at him. "Is there some urgency with this project that I'm unaware of? We can talk about it at our first January Sunday soup gathering. Can't we?"

He exhaled sharply through his nose, not quite a snort but close to it. Then he seemed to regain control of himself, and returned her smile. "Of course we can. I merely became enthusiastic, and wanted to get going on what I felt was a splendid idea while it was still new and fresh." He cocked his head in a way that he must have thought looked winning. "You can't fault a man for his enthusiasms, can you?"

"Of course not," Steph assured him. "Like I said, I think it is a great idea too. And if I'm right about that, it'll be just as good an idea in January as it is today. Maybe even more so, when all the craziness of the holidays is behind us."

"Right. Of course." He took another sip of his coffee and set the cup back down on the table a little too solidly. He squared his shoulders. He looked her in the eye. Then he took a deep breath. "Steph—"

Before this, whatever it was, could go any further, Steph finished her coffee in one great gulp, set her own cup down, and stood up. "Well, thank you for the coffee—it was fantastic. I'm going to head home now. I'll see you at the party?"

Ron stumbled to his feet. His face showed both panic and relief. At least she hoped it was relief. "Uh, yes, of course! You'll let us know what we can bring?"

"I'm working on that now, I'll send an email by the end of the week. Bye!" She leaned forward and quickly kissed him on the cheek, moving away again before he could react.

On her way back toward town, she called Julie. "Are you busy right now?"

"I'm in the shop," Julie said. Her voice sounded strange—flat, and a little too quiet. Probably she had customers, Steph thought, until Julie went on: "It's deader than doornails here. I can talk."

She didn't *sound* like she wanted to talk… "Can I stop by? I'm heading into town right now."

"Sure. See you when you get here."

That was weird, Steph thought. *I wonder what's up?* Well, she'd find out soon enough—if it was anything.

JULIE

JULIE SIGHED AS she set the phone back on the glass counter. Did she want to talk to Steph about it? Was she ready to talk to someone? She hadn't been ready to tell Megan anything about it, last night. And what could she even say? *My boyfriend doesn't respect me?* How pathetic and juvenile was that!

Gavin had indeed called her last night, late—maybe he'd gone to the theater alone—but Julie, lying in bed reading, hadn't picked up. He'd left a voicemail; she hadn't listened to it.

He'd called again this morning, but hadn't left a message this time.

In the cold, sober light of morning, she asked herself if she was making a big deal out of nothing. There was no rule that said a couple had to admire every single thing about each other. Was she acting like a child? Was she being unfair to Gavin, overreacting because of how Michael had been?

But no, she didn't think so. This wasn't just some little random, unimportant aspect of her life, like whether she preferred flannel or percale sheets, or how she arranged her refrigerator shelves. This was her *art*, her *creative work*. The very expression of her soul, if she were being honest with herself.

Gavin had belittled her essence, her spirit. He'd called it dishonest, implied that she should feel ashamed of her work. Work that not only fed her soul, but it provided a pretty decent livelihood as well!

No, this wasn't pathetic and juvenile.

It was heartbreaking.

Well, thank goodness she'd found this out sooner rather than later. Imagine if she'd fallen much more deeply in love with him. Imagine if she'd introduced him to Megan and Lori! Bad enough that she'd brought him to a soup group to meet her friends, and that she was involved in the parking meter fracas with him.

Julie groaned as she thought about their political work together. Fortunately, that all seemed to be under control. Maybe the issue would just quietly fade away in the new year, and she'd never have to see Gavin again.

It would be too bad to never be able to use the library, but, oh well. She didn't go there all that often these days as it was.

By the time Steph arrived, Julie had talked herself down off the ledge yet again, and faced her friend with something like a smile. "Hey, come on in. What's up?"

"I'm not sure. I'd like to run something by you, if that's all right?"

"Of course. Pull up a stool."

Steph told her a slightly unsettling story about Ron—ostensibly trying to horn in on the cookbook idea that Julie had had and had already mostly forgotten about in her heartbreak, but underneath that, something more? Perhaps? "I don't know what to make of it, or if I'm even just imagining it," Steph concluded. "I know he was kind of sweet on me when we first met, and I know I flirted back probably a bit too much, but I thought we both decided—without actually talking about it—that neither of us were the least bit interested in having an affair, or of leaving our spouses, so we sort of quietly agreed to put the whole thing behind us."

"Maybe too quietly," Julie said. "But it sounds like he got the message this time?"

Steph shrugged. "I hope so, but again, we didn't talk about it directly. I just got this weird vibe off him. Maybe I'm overreacting, like I said—maybe I made the whole thing up, and he really was just talking about editing a cookbook."

"No, trust your gut. If it felt like he was coming on to you, he probably was."

"I was surprised that Alicia wasn't there—that she was off island entirely. I didn't think he ever let her that far out of his sight."

"Yeah," Julie agreed. "What if he needs a sandwich made or something?"

They both chuckled, though it wasn't all that funny. "So, thanks for the perspective," Steph said. "And what do you think I should do now—anything?"

"Like what? Mention it to Alicia?"

They grimaced at each other.

"Don't do anything for now," Julie went on, making a decision. "You can consider this his one warning. If he creeps on you again, then you should scream bloody murder, metaphorically speaking. Tell Alicia, tell the whole group. Yes, maybe that would blow up our soup parties, but do you really want to continue in a situation where you're always fending off unwanted attention? Where you're always on the lookout to avoid being caught in the hallway and kissed by Professor Pepe Le Pew?"

Steph burst out laughing. "You have such a way with words!"

"Thanks." Julie gave her a weak smile. "I'm glad to know I've still got something going for me."

"Okay, I knew something was wrong," Steph said. "Do you want to talk about it?"

Julie sighed, and made a decision. "I don't, but I also do." She looked at her friend, perched on the uncomfortable stool. "Let's go back to my house."

"But the shop!" Steph looked scandalized.

"What do you think 'back in ten minutes' signs are for?"

"I thought you didn't do that."

Julie shrugged. "Special circumstances. Besides, I haven't seen a customer all day. I think they're all scared off by the no-parking signs for the Solstice Parade. I wish the county would make it clearer that the parking ban is for *tomorrow*, not today."

She took Steph back to her house and they settled in the living room. Steph refused a cup of coffee or tea—"I'm too caffeinated already"—so Julie just launched into it.

"That sucks," Steph said, when she'd explained everything. "What an ass. And what's he got to brag about, anyway? No library degree despite that being all he ever wanted, just a bunch of money from doing work he hated because he couldn't explain to his college girlfriend that he didn't want to be a banker?"

Part of Julie wanted to defend Gavin against this assessment, but the rest of her had to admit that it wasn't unfair. "I just feel like such an idiot," she said instead.

"Good god, *why*? You're an amazing woman. He doesn't deserve you."

Julie smiled at her friend; even if Steph's own marriage was clearly not ideal, she had immediately grasped the problem here.

"He seemed so—promising, I guess. But what really steams me is that I wasn't even looking for him! I wasn't looking for a relationship at all. I was fine, I was happy, I was complete. And now I'm all, all…" She stopped, blushing, but made herself go on. Thank goodness she'd decided to talk to her girlfriend about it, and not her daughter. "I'm all heated up inside. I thought all of that had gone to sleep with menopause, but, sheesh."

Steph patted her arm affectionately. "That's not a bad thing, hon."

"It's a terrible thing! Now I'm all worked up with no place to go."

"Just because Gavin wasn't the right man to go the distance with you doesn't mean that there isn't someone else out there for you. Someone who respects the badass, clever, creative woman you are, *and* wants to toss you over his shoulder and haul you off to bed."

It was Julie's turn to burst out laughing. "Now who's the one who has a way with words?"

"I'm serious. I predict that, when it's time to tell your life story, the Gavin chapter will read like, 'He was a twit, but I will be forever grateful for him for waking my libido back up.'"

"I don't even want to think about it," Julie said. "It's too depressing. I just feel like I should have known better. I should have seen the signs, or something."

Steph shook her head. "No, the way to get to know someone is to actually get to know them. You can't shortcut that. Most guys don't walk around with 'I'm a twit who doesn't respect women's creativity' tattooed on their foreheads. You have to actually take a risk to get to see that part. And you did! And that's great."

"It doesn't feel great."

"I know it doesn't." Steph gave her a gentle smile. "I know it sucks, and I'm not trying to discount that, or blow off your feelings. I just don't want you thinking *you* did something wrong here, that's all."

"Thanks." She returned the smile. "Well, that's what's going on with me. I guess I should get back out to the shop in case a customer happens by."

"Yeah, that was a pretty generous ten minutes."

"That's the beauty of it," Julie said, getting up and handing Steph her coat. "If you don't put a time on the sign, then the ten minutes could have started anytime." Though it did still feel weird to have put the sign up at all, as much as she felt better for having run the whole issue by Steph—and having gotten her unqualified support.

Steph laughed as they headed out of the house. "I'll never understand the complexities of running a business."

Chapter 11

JULIE

Saturday morning arrived. The day of the parade. Julie woke early, but brought her coffee back to bed with her; the shop didn't open until eleven, an hour before the parade was to start. And she was all ready.

Boy howdy was she ready. Without a boyfriend taking up all her spare moments, she'd had plenty of time to get all the books carried up to the shop, arranged fetchingly in her windows and on the various display surfaces, and extra stock stored close at hand behind the counter.

Now all there was to do was wait till time to open.

Fergie had been extra cuddly since Gavin's departure. Julie appreciated the comfort. "And people think cats are cold and aloof creatures," she murmured, scratching Fergie's ears.

The cat purred.

Eventually, Julie finished her coffee and rolled out of bed. Those books weren't going to sell themselves.

When she turned off the shower, she paused, listening to a strange sound coming from outside somewhere. *If I didn't know better*, she thought, *I'd almost think that was...*

It better not be.

She hurriedly got dressed and ran out to the street.

"What are you *doing!?*" she screamed at the workmen who

were jackhammering up the entire sidewalk in front of her shop. Different workmen from two months ago; these were younger fellows, but they still wore county hard hats and vests.

The one wielding the machine stopped and stared at her. Blessed silence descended on Eastsound. "Emergency work order," he said, gesturing at the no-parking signs up and down the street.

"Those signs are for the parade!" Julie yelled. "Which starts in two hours! The whole town is turning out—you can't just—why are you even here? It's a Saturday!"

He shrugged and looked at his fellow-worker, who shrugged back, then said, "Sam said it was an emergency. Can't wait till Monday."

"Sam?" Julie said, incredulously. It couldn't be…

"Oh, here he is now," said the second worker, looking relieved.

Julie turned to see a silver-haired man striding up the undamaged part of the sidewalk toward them. He wore a pristine fleece jacket and blue jeans which had clearly been ironed. He flashed her a predatory smile and stuck his hand out as he approached. "Sam McLeod," he said.

Julie almost shook his hand out of sheer polite reflex, but yanked her hand back just in time. "Mr. McLeod, what is the meaning of this?" she asked, struggling to keep her voice from trembling with emotion.

His smile did not fade; his hand dropped easily to his side, as if she had not just rebuffed him. "And you are?"

"Julie Pessel. This is my shop, which no one can get into with this mess in front of it, and we have an injunction against this work!"

"Ah, yes, of course." He somehow managed to look even more pleased with himself as he shook his head in mock-sadness. "Unfortunately, I fear there's been a bit of a misunderstanding. We have a water main break underneath the street here, which needed to be seen to immediately. Judge Varela's injunction only covered the improvements to the town that our team has been working to get on the ballot."

Improvements? Julie narrowed her eyes at him. "How convenient—a water main break right where you want to put parking meters?"

"These things happen when you've got so much aging infrastructure." He shrugged, giving what he probably thought was an innocent expression. "Anyway, if you'll kindly step out of the way so Brian and Jose can get back to work…"

"Wait a minute," Julie said, stepping even closer to the jackhammer. Brian, or so she assumed, shrank away from her without letting go of the heavy tool. "A water main break?" she said to Sam.

He was working very hard to keep that affable smile on his face, she thought. "Yes, Ms. Pessel, that's what I said."

"So does that mean the water is turned off right now?" She gestured at the torn-up concrete under the jackhammer. "I mean, that's how you repair a water main, right? You turn off the water, dig up the pipes, find the leak, fix it, and then turn everything back on again?"

Now it was Sam McLeod's turn to narrow his eyes. "Well, yes, that's an oversimplification of course, but more or less how it goes. I'm real sorry for the inconvenience, but surely you understand—"

Julie smiled triumphantly. "Oh, I do understand perfectly, Mr. McLeod. The only thing I'm confused about is why you're lying to me right now."

His smile fell away entirely. "Now, wait just a minute here—"

"Because," she went on, "my house is right behind my shop, and I just finished taking a shower. When I turned off the water, the jackhammer was already going."

McLeod blinked and looked at Brian, then at Jose. Both workers shrugged, but only Jose, unencumbered by a heavy tool, was able to take another step backward, closer to their work truck.

"And furthermore!" Julie continued, catching sight of what was in the bed of the work truck. "Can anyone explain to me what all those parking meters are doing there?"

"You idiots!" McLeod suddenly screamed at the workmen, startling everyone. Brian now leapt back, letting go of the jackhammer, which clattered to the rubble below.

"Hey, man, we were just doing what you said—" he started, but McLeod cut him off.

"Not one word!" he yelled. "If you want to still have a job Monday morning, you'll shut your mouth *right now*."

The workers exchanged worried glances with each other, but neither of them spoke again.

McLeod seemed to visibly gather his poise before turning back to Julie. He even pasted on another smile, phonier than ever. "This isn't over," he said, and then his smile grew reptilian. "Despite the incompetence of *some people* on my team, I think you'll find that my research has been thorough and far-reaching. In fact—"

"What's going on here?" asked a familiar voice.

Julie wheeled around. There, standing at the edge of the path that led to her house, stood Gavin, his arms full of books.

Despite herself, despite everything, her heart gave a *thump* of delight at the sight of him. She forced herself not to smile. "*This* fellow," she said, pointing at McLeod, "who does not even work for the county last I checked, appears to have invented a fake water main crisis and brought in some fake county workers in order to march ahead with his entirely inappropriate parking-meter project. And on Solstice Parade Saturday, at that!"

"Is that true?" Gavin asked, stepping close enough for Julie to see the books he was holding. *What in the world…?* Fully half of them appeared to be by Libby Perrine, her favorite author. And they clearly weren't library books.

She shook her head—too many mysteries, and she didn't want to lose sight of the important problem. "Well?" she said, turning back to McLeod. "Tell him."

"I don't answer to the *assistant librarian*," McLeod said snottily, giving the books, and Gavin, a disdainful look. "I don't answer to any of you. And I have some very important business to attend to, so I'll be on my way." Then he leered at Julie. "Remember what I said, Ms. Pessel: this isn't over. In fact, you may have another surprise already waiting for you." He turned on the heels of his city shoes and strode back down the sidewalk.

Brian and Jose gave each other a confused glance, then withdrew and began talking in low tones, clearly unsure whether they should resume their work or not.

"Don't," Julie told them, raising her voice to be heard. "Just—just don't. You've made enough of a mess already." She looked at the rubble leading to her shop's porch and suddenly wanted to cry. She was supposed to open in an hour! Would that be enough time to find some more pallets or boards or something to make a makeshift bridge to her stairs? Would anyone be willing to brave such a bridge?

"Um," Gavin said. Julie turned to him. "I went to your house, but you weren't there…"

"We need to call Leslie," she said to him, making her tone all-business. "I don't know if she can get hold of Judge Varela on a weekend, but—"

"Leslie's already gone for the holidays," Gavin said with a frown. "She won't be back till after the new year."

"Well, do you know how to get hold of the judge? Someone has to stop that man!"

Jose and Brian were watching Julie with something like fear in their eyes. Then they exchanged another glance, and went to their truck, climbing up into the cabin and slamming the doors behind them. Brian pulled out a cell phone and called someone. Julie turned away; at least they'd stopped for now.

How did one disable a jackhammer? Was there some sort of battery or fuse or wire that they could pull out of it? This one wasn't plugged into anything; did it have a gas tank?

"I can try calling the judge," Gavin said doubtfully. "I might only have his work number, though."

"Well, where *is* Leslie? We can still call her on her cell—she didn't travel to the *moon*, did she?"

Gavin shifted the books to one arm, apparently trying to free up a hand to find his phone, but there were too many of them.

"And what's with the books?" Julie asked.

"Um, can we go to your place? I don't want to set them on the ground here, and they're getting heavy." He gave her a helpless, tentative smile. "I'll explain everything, but in private maybe?"

The county truck started up, and Brian backed it out into the street, then slowly drove off. "Huh," Julie said. "They left their jackhammer." She looked back at Gavin. "Okay. We can go to my house."

Inside, Gavin carefully set the books on her coffee table, in two large stacks. "Whew. Thank you."

She folded her arms across her chest and stayed standing. "All right, we're inside and the books are safe. So. Explain."

He nodded, but pulled out his cell phone. "I will—but you're right, we should try to get hold of Leslie first. She went to Disneyland with her kids and grandkids." He found her number and dialed, then left a brief message. After he hung up, he said, "Straight to voicemail."

"Hm."

"Anyway. The books." Gavin looked nervous, yet hopeful. Also…abashed? Julie thought she saw an expression on his face she hadn't seen much, not since they were first getting to know each other. Shy, awkward, uncertain of himself. "I was trying to make a grand romantic gesture."

Despite herself, Julie let out a small snort of laughter. The ice that covered her heart cracked a little. "A grand romantic gesture? Gavin, this isn't a rom-com movie."

"I know, and we're not teenagers, but—Julie, I screwed up. You're the best thing that's ever happened to me, and I never wanted to hurt you. I tried calling, and you didn't pick up, and I totally understand why, I'm not complaining about that. But I needed, I mean, I wanted a way to get you to listen to me, just so I can explain—then you can send me away forever, but at least hear me out first?"

"I'm listening," she said, keeping her voice even.

He nodded, gulped, and went on. "I...I know Libby Perrine is your favorite author, so you've probably read all those books, but I got ones I hadn't seen on your shelf, and then a couple other authors who are supposedly similar, and—Julie, I want to help you create a book group again, and start with your favorite Libby Perrine book!" He stumbled to a finish and grinned at her.

"Oh Gavin." Julie sank down onto the couch and shook her head.

"No?" he asked, his voice small.

"Sit down." She patted the cushion beside her; he took it, sitting carefully not-too-close. "I mean, that's very sweet and very thoughtful. The idea of a grand romantic gesture at all, and the fact that you not only know who my favorite author is, but you know how much I miss having a book group."

He looked even more hopeful.

"But," she went on. "As lovely as this is, it doesn't tell me what I really need to know."

"I know! So will you let me explain?"

"I'm listening," she said again.

"Okay. Thank you." He smiled at her and cleared his throat. "I'm sorry, Julie—let me just start there, again. I'm sorry I didn't understand what your books were really about—the books you create, I mean—and I'm sorry I didn't deal better with my own surprise about it. I—this is no excuse, but I really don't deal with surprises well, or change, or stuff like that. That's on me, and I've been working on it, and I obviously have a lot more work to do, but I'm still trying. I want to get better. If you...if we...if you can give me another chance, I promise that I will try even harder to be the kind of man you deserve as a partner. I want to deserve you."

"Thank you for that," she said, leaning back against the arm of the sofa and studying him, partly just to move away from the heady scent of him. Her whole body yearned to reach out, to pull him into her arms; but there was still something missing here. "But, can you tell me why it was such a terrible surprise to you that my books are fiction, not reference materials?"

He blinked and gazed back at her. "Um, just, I thought they were one thing but they're something else?"

"Yes, I get that, but why does that matter so much? Or at all? Do you have something against fiction? Against creative writing? Or against humorous writing? I'm trying to understand this here."

Gavin shifted in his seat, and looked at the double stacks of books on the coffee table. Had he somehow bought them all, in the last day and a half? Surely Darvill's didn't stock Libby Perrine's entire oeuvre, and there wouldn't have been enough time for Amazon to have delivered them. Had he gone off island? However he'd done it, she was impressed, in spite of herself. She felt more of her heart's ice slowly begin to thaw. "I...well," Gavin said, "I told you, I don't have a lot of experience with reading fiction. But I want to do more! That's why I thought the book group would be a great idea." He tried another smile.

Julie exhaled, almost a soft sigh. "Do you know what you actually said to me? The thing that upset me so much?"

He cocked his head. "I think? I...said I was surprised you'd made up the countess or whatever?"

"You called it fake. You called my creative work fake—which is basically calling me a fraud, a cheat. A liar."

"I don't think that!" he protested, his eyes widening.

"Are you sure?"

"Of course I'm sure!" He looked panicked. "Julie, you're the most honest person I know. You would be the last person in the world I would call a liar."

"But do you see how it sounded to me? Gavin, you disdained not only the thing I do for a living, but the work that comes from my soul. The work that gives me delight. Yes, it's light and kind of silly, but it gives me great joy to create it. And, from what I can tell, people enjoy reading it. In fact, I've been looking forward to selling a lot of them during the Solstice Parade—except now I'm not sure if anyone will even be able to get into my shop!"

"I can help with that!" he said, looking like he was barely restraining himself from leaping to his feet. "I can help you figure out a way to clear a path to your stairs."

"Thank you, and I will take you up on that." Now he looked like he might fall over in relief. "This isn't resolved," she added, but put a hand on his arm to soften her words. Oh, how she wanted it to be resolved…but not at the cost of him not getting it fully, all the way down. "We need to deal with the emergency of the moment, and get my shop open. After the parade and the tree lighting, we can talk more about this. I need to explain more fully why what you said hurt me so much, and I need to know that you get it. All the way."

"Thank you," he said, glancing down at his feet. "I will do everything in my power to get it—and never let it happen again."

"Okay." Julie got up. "Let's go see what we can do. We've got those pallets from the last time, though we'll need more than that; I might have some plywood in the shed in back."

He followed her out to her paper-making shed, where they found a few planks and a ratty sheet of plywood, which they dragged out to the front of the store. Gavin immediately began arranging the lumber and pallets, but it was clearly not enough. "I can drive out to Island Hardware and get a few more boards," he offered.

"We can check at Ace first," Julie said, glancing up the street to where the smaller, in-town hardware store was. "I can just walk up…" She trailed off as she stared again up the street. Something was wrong, something was different… "Wait a second," she said.

"What is it?" Gavin asked.

Julie was already marching up the street. "That bastard!" she yelled, when she was sure.

Gavin caught up to her. "What? What's wrong?"

"My car! My car is missing. I parked up there," she pointed across the intersection just past Mijitas, "because the street closure ended here, for the parade."

"There's signs all the way up now," Gavin said warily. "As far as I can see."

"The bastard had my car towed," Julie said. "That's what he meant when he said there was another surprise in store for me."

"Do cars ever even get towed on Orcas?" Gavin asked, puzzled. "Where would they even take them?"

"I have no idea!" Julie flung her arms in the air in frustration. Then she took a deep breath and turned to Gavin. "Okay, this is serious. This is war. We have to stop him. I don't care what we have to do or how much money or influence he has, but Sam McLeod does *not* get to just stomp all over everyone else to get what he wants."

Gavin stared back at her. "I don't know whether I'm scared of you right now or very, very impressed. Either way, I'm at your complete disposal. Just tell me what you need me to do, and I'm there."

Julie shook her head, even as a large icicle in her heart melted. "We'll use your truck if we need to go to Island Hardware. We'll get my shop open. We'll get my car back. And we'll *stop Sam McLeod.*"

THEY WERE PUTTING the finishing touches on the makeshift "patio" leading to Paper Magic's porch, complete with two large pots with succulents in them to go beside the stairs, when Gavin's phone rang. "It's Leslie," he said, sounding relieved.

They had a brief conversation, mostly Leslie talking and Gavin nodding. When he hung up, he told Julie, "She's going to do some phoning around, but one of us will probably have to go to Friday Harbor on Monday, to get another signed injunction—a more detailed one. She says we should make copies of it this time and put them up all over town, and that we should probably call another community meeting to tell everyone what happened. She also said we should take photos of everything."

Julie looked at the plywood patio. "Damn, I wish I'd thought of that before we covered up the worst of it. For that matter, I wish I'd gotten a photo of the parking meters in the back of that county truck!" If it *was* even a county truck...

"At least we can get one of the jackhammer." They had pulled the offending machine to the side, and leaned it against her shop's porch, near where the pile of rubble had been so recently removed. "It doesn't matter—it's still obvious enough what happened here. And we can tell the judge everything that those workers and Sam told you—lying about the broken water main, towing your car. Oh, and about that: she says to call the Orcas Towing guy."

"The guy who pulls everyone out of ditches every time it snows?"

Gavin smiled. "Yeah, him. Even if he didn't tow it himself, he'll know where your car is."

"Great." She smiled back at him, then glanced down at her watch. "It's almost eleven—I'd better get this shop open!"

"What can I do to help?"

Julie started to say "You've done enough for now, thanks" when her stomach growled loudly. "Huh," she said. "I guess I never had breakfast."

Gavin stood taller. "I'll head down to Brown Bear. Quiche? Or should we go straight to pastries?"

Julie laughed. "If there's a peach croissant..."

"Say no more." He paused for only a brief moment—two days ago, this would be where he would have leaned in for a kiss—

then turned and marched down the street.

Julie watched him go as another large shard of ice fell away from her heart. He even had an adorable *walk*, damn it. Oh, she missed him. He was clearly truly sorry—he was taking that much of it seriously, at least.

Would it be enough? Was he going to get it all the way? Or was this just another might-have-been?

Would Megan and Lori have to mess him *all the way up*?

She supposed time would tell.

THE DAY FLEW by. Julie barely got half her peach croissant eaten before the crowds started pouring into her shop, and she had to set her chocolate muffin aside for a slow moment, which never arrived. She didn't even get to see the parade right outside her shop, she was too busy ringing up sale after sale.

Gavin stuck around for the first half-hour, helping pile new stock onto the tables and shelves when they ran low, but then he got another call from Leslie. "She got hold of Judge Varela and he said he'll sign a new injunction today if I can get over there!" he told her, breathless, when he'd hung up.

"Can you get there and back today? Is the inter-island boat even running?"

"I don't know but I'll find out!" And then he was gone, leaving her to her flurry of customers.

Mid-afternoon, Alicia and Steph showed up, having come to town for the tree lighting. "I thought you might be bored and want some company," Steph said, grinning around at the crowded store. "But this is better!"

"This is better indeed," Julie agreed, "though I can hardly keep up. And I've been having to give people rainchecks on gift wrapping—I'm just too busy to do that."

"I can wrap gifts," Alicia said.

"Me too," Steph added. "I'm great at it. Where's your paper?"

Soon, her friends had set up a gift-wrapping station on the

shop's tiny front porch, which somehow seemed to attract even *more* customers, all of whom wanted to buy gifts for every literature lover or aspiring writer and artist on their lists. Julie was beginning to wonder if she was going to run out of stock after all, but then suddenly it was five and time for the festivities to begin.

"You guys," Julie said, pulling both friends into a three-way hug. "You saved my butt today."

"Our pleasure!" Alicia said, grinning at her.

"Yes," Steph echoed, but her gaze searched Julie's face. She clearly wanted to say more—had something else happened with the Ron situation?—but wasn't going to do so in front of Alicia. "Let's get over to the green," she said instead.

Julie quickly locked up, saving the tallying of the day's amazing sales for later. Then they hurried across the street and onto the village green. Julie had just stepped foot on the grass when Steph grabbed her arm, looking worried. "There's Gavin," she said quietly, into Julie's ear.

"That's okay," Julie said, and then to both her friends she added, "He helped me a ton this morning. And…he made a grand romantic gesture."

"He did?" Steph asked, disbelieving, as Alicia said, "He did?" with innocent delight.

"I'll tell you everything later—let's get dinner after the lighting, okay?"

"If we can get in anywhere!" Alicia said, looking around at the crowd packing the green.

"If we can't, I'll cook us something," Julie promised. "For now, let's go see what Gavin got accomplished in Friday Harbor."

"In Friday Harbor?" Steph asked, more confused than ever.

"I'll tell you later!" Julie repeated, walking up to Gavin.

He turned to face her when she was a few feet away, and his whole face lit up with joy.

The icicles in her heart melted the rest of the way, into a little puddle at the end of her left big toe, then dissipated entirely.

Chapter 12

JULIE

"I FEEL SO honored to be invited back to another soup club meeting," Gavin said a week later, as Julie drove them out toward Deer Harbor.

Julie laughed. "Don't be—I mean, yes, it is an honor, but this isn't really a soup meeting. Steph has a big Christmas party every year—"

"I know, I know, you explained that." He patted her leg to soften the abruptness of the interruption. "I guess what I really mean is, I feel so honored to be invited back into your life."

Julie smiled over at him, then returned her eyes to the road. "Well, who can resist a grand romantic gesture?"

"Are you talking about the books, or the new watertight injunction?"

They both laughed together. Julie felt the fizzy bubbles in her bloodstream again. Her body had certainly welcomed Gavin back into her life—and her bed—without hesitation. Her heart was not yet entirely convinced, but was more than willing to consider the question.

She and Gavin had had several good, honest conversations over the past week. He did seem open to putting in the effort to make this work, even if he still didn't fully get why what he had done had hurt her so much. To be fair, she wasn't quite sure herself—beyond the obvious. But they were both working earnestly to achieve a deeper understanding.

This evening she had packed up some things in preparation for spending at least a few nights at Gavin's cozy little house. Julie had arranged to leave her own cottage—and cat—under the care of her daughters, who had indeed made the afternoon boat and were going to meet them at Steph's party. The girls were also planning on staying on the island till nearly the new year. Julie was looking forward to spending quality time with them every day, of course; the whole point of her daughters' visit was to see their mother. But there would be long sweet winter nights spent with Gavin...something she was very much looking forward to.

And the new injunction did indeed seem watertight. In the week since Gavin had scrambled over to meet the judge at his home on San Juan Island, all the no-parking signs had come down, and no one had heard anything from Sam McLeod. Julie's car had even been retrieved, and at no cost: the fellow from Orcas Towing had grumbled about "certain people overstepping" and "making trouble for everyone" as he returned her Subaru wagon completely unharmed.

There was still the matter of the torn-up sidewalk in front of Paper Magic, and the abandoned jackhammer, and the parking meter issue coming up on some future ballot, but all those things could be dealt with in the new year. For now, Julie looked forward to her favorite party of the year—and not just because of Steph's prowess in the kitchen.

"Too bad your daughters didn't get here in time for us all to drive out together," Gavin said, as they made the turn in West Sound.

"Oh, actually, they're fine with it. Lori told me it's good they have their own car, in case we old folks want to leave early; they won't have to hold us back."

"Do you think that's true?"

"I'm guessing it's the opposite, actually," Julie said with a laugh. "*They* might want to leave early and find some party with an average age rather closer to theirs. I'm surprised they agreed to come at all, to hang out with us fogies."

"Well, I do look forward to meeting them, and getting to know them," Gavin said, only sounding a little bit nervous. "Assuming they hang around the party at least a little while."

"There'll be plenty of time while they're here," Julie said. "But they're good girls, they'll probably stay a while tonight. They do like Steph."

When they got to Steph's house, signs directed them to park next door, at Lynne's. Julie barely managed to squeeze her car into a spot behind Lynne's garage. "Are we that late?" she asked, stepping out of her car and reaching into the back seat for her rum balls. "Brr, it feels even colder here than it did in town."

"I think it is," Gavin said, shivering. "The wind's coming up." He pulled her into his arms and held her tight. "I'll warm you."

"Or, we could go to the party, which will be indoors and presumably heated. And maybe even be offered a warming beverage."

He laughed.

"Do you think it's going to snow?" she asked, as they walked out onto the road to Steph's driveway. "The ground feels almost crunchy."

"It's not supposed to," Gavin said, but he dug his phone out of his pocket. "Huh—now it gives it a twenty percent chance, by ten p.m. Maybe we *do* want to leave early then."

"My Subaru is all-wheel-drive," she said. "It'll be fine."

Steph greeted them at the door. "Come in, come in! Brr!"

"Yes, I know," Julie said, giving her friend a hug before holding up the rum balls. "Where do you want these?"

"I'll take them. I've got desserts in the dining room this year," Steph said, pointing, and then disappearing with the container into the really very impressive crowd.

"Wow," Gavin said, taking off his jacket and looking at the completely stuffed coat rack, and the bench that was also piled high with coats and wraps. "Is the whole island here?"

"Sounds like it! Come on, let's find something to drink."

They both dropped their coats on the towering pile and headed into the house. They hadn't gone more than a few steps before Julie ran into the owner of the dress shop two doors down from her store, and someone also hailed Gavin. After a few short conversations, Julie tried to steer further into the house in search of the drinks and appetizers—and her daughters, who had texted from the ferry landing long enough ago that they were surely here somewhere. "You really do want to do a Steph-meal in order," she shouted at Gavin, hoping he could hear her over the din.

He seemed to, but then he was again greeted by someone he knew. Julie thought she recognized the man—someone who worked at the library?—and then Ron and Alicia were at her elbow. "Finally!" Alicia yelled, pulling Julie into a hug. "How was the drive? We should have carpooled. Is it snowing out in Olga yet?"

"I don't know, we were in town. Gavin's app said there's a small chance of snow, later tonight..."

"You don't have any wine!" Ron hollered at her, and disappeared for a moment, returning with two full glasses of red. He handed one to Julie and then frowned at Gavin's back. "This is for him, when he wants it."

"Thanks," Julie said, taking the second glass as well, though it would leave her no hands for munchies.

"It's the most drinkable thing here at the moment," Ron said with a grimace, nodding at the drinks table where there had to be thirty open bottles of—everything. "Potlucks, ugh."

Julie laughed and sipped her wine. It was, indeed, very drinkable.

Gavin finished talking with his friend and turned back around. "Oh, thanks," he said, taking the glass she handed him.

"I'll finish that for you when you've had enough," she said, as softly as she could in the din and still have him hear. "Come on, let's find some nibbles."

The appetizer spread was in the main, formal living room, on a long table set in front of a bank of windows that would have looked out over a glorious garden if it weren't pitch-black outside. Oh, and also if it weren't the dead of winter and anything was growing. But nobody was interested in looking outside. In addition to an entire village's worth of insanely delicious munchies, the room was decorated to the nines. A tall Christmas tree, heavily laden with ornaments, stood by the fireplace, in which a cheerful blaze crackled. The mantel was garlanded and festooned with more decorations. Mistletoe hung in strategic locations, including right over Gavin's unsuspecting head.

"Gotcha," Julie said, leaning up for a kiss.

He complied, pleased but a little confused. "Oh," he said, when she pointed it out. Then grinned down at her and kissed her again.

They filled plates at the appetizer table and looked around for a place to sit, or even perch, while they ate them. "Maybe there's more room in the kitchen," Julie said, starting to lead him in there.

"Kitchens are always the most crowded rooms at parties," Gavin said, but he followed her.

"Steph's kitchen is pretty large," Julie assured him. "In fact, here's—oh." She stopped in her tracks, not quite sure what she was seeing.

Or what she thought about it.

MATT

THIS HAD BEEN Matt's Season of Not Wanting to Go to Social Events, and this Christmas party was no exception.

He'd been doing a lot better since October, of course, having been to a number of soup group gatherings, and of course community meetings; but a big holiday bash was another thing altogether.

Especially this one, with mistletoe hung all over the place. As if there would be anyone for him to kiss.

As if he'd ever have anyone to kiss ever again.

But his father had been excited to come, and even if he hadn't been, Matt didn't want to let his friends down. The whole group had continued to be so supportive of him in his misery. Steph had phoned him this afternoon to make sure he was coming—and bringing his famous cheese straws.

"I can't believe you really need me to make cheese straws," he told her.

"Oh, I *do*. I really, *really* do," she said, making him laugh.

"Don't worry, I'm coming," he assured her. "Dad would never forgive me if we missed it." Although Dad would forget the whole thing within a week or two…probably. Matt was never entirely sure which things would stick in Gordon's memory and which would fade away. The most surprising recollections would pop up from time to time.

Especially if they had to do with pretty ladies, as his dad put it.

So Matt had dutifully baked a triple batch of cheese straws, packed them up carefully, and driven out to Deer Harbor. Mindful of his dad's condition, he'd gotten them there on the early side, so that Gordon could get settled comfortably somewhere, and maybe even be able to hear what people were saying to him. Steph's parties could get a little loud, he knew.

There were only a few guests there when they arrived. Matt even thought he caught sight of Steph's husband, David, filling a plate at one of the buffet tables, but the man disappeared without speaking to anyone.

Matt found a place for Gordon in the large breakfast nook off the kitchen, where Steph had set up what she called "backup munchies"—more appetizers, and some veggie side dishes, and a huge vat of mashed potatoes, for some reason. There was an overstuffed chair in a bank of windows, facing into the room. Several smaller chairs were arranged around it, and a low table sat before the grouping. Perfect. "Here you go," Matt said, helping his dad into the big chair. "I'll get you a plate of food, okay?"

"I just want your cheese straws," Gordon said.

Matt smiled at him. "We could have stayed home and eaten those. The whole point of coming here is to eat all the other stuff." He grinned at Steph, stirring something on the stove—perhaps it was even soup of some kind? Though soup was an awkward thing to eat at a party, despite everyone's joking about a soup contest tonight.

"Get him some of those meatballs, he likes those," Steph said.

Ah, that must be what the mashed potatoes were for. "On it."

Matt loaded up a plate for his dad with probably more than the old man would be willing or able to eat, but there were so many options—at least this way he'd have a choice, and Matt could eat the rest. He brought the plate back and then went to fill one of his own, with different things. Then he grabbed a glass of wine for himself and a sparkling cider for Gordon and joined him in the breakfast nook.

"Getting crowded out there!" Gordon said, happily chomping on a meatball. "Did I see Dolores Fischer come in?"

"You might have, Dad," Matt said, keeping a cheerful smile on his face as he wondered, yet again, what it must be like to slowly lose all your friends, and then lose the memory of having lost them. "Lot of people here."

Then he saw Julie walk in—except, a moment later, he realized it wasn't Julie. This woman was at least twenty years younger than her, and even lovelier, if such a thing were possible.

"There's your pretty friend!" Gordon said, beaming and pointing across the kitchen. The young woman was laughing with Steph as she took her coat off; an even younger woman was with her, also dark-haired, though her hair was cut pixie-short, and she was a bit less luminous. Were they sisters? They were clearly sisters.

Oh, I know who those women are... Matt thought, his mouth falling open. He had never met Julie's daughters, but he knew they were visiting for the holidays; this had to be them. He could hardly take his eyes off the older one, even before she turned and smiled at him across the room. Why did she do that? Oh, Steph had pointed him out to her...

Matt slowly regained control of his senses and his limbs, and then, eventually, his power of speech. "Dad, that's not Julie," he managed. "Those are her girls."

And then Steph had brought them over to Matt and Gordon. "This is Lori," she said, and the younger woman put out a hand and smiled. Matt shook it, and Gordon reached up. "And this is Megan," Steph said.

When his hand touched hers, Matt lost his words all over again. "Um. Ahem," he croaked, and smiled back at her. Had he ever seen anyone so beautiful in all his life? And there was that weird sense of already knowing her, because he knew Julie, but this wasn't Julie, but she also wasn't *not* Julie...

Megan laughed warmly and shook his hand. "It's nice to meet you, Matt," she said, and then greeted Gordon with equal affection. "I've heard so much about both of you. I'm so glad to finally get to meet you in person."

Matt struggled to remember what Julie had told him about her daughters. They both lived in Portland; what did Megan do? God, this would be so much easier if his brain would function.

Steph, the consummate hostess, caught on to Matt's plight. "Let me get you guys some wine," she said to Megan and Lori, and then pointed to the chairs around the low table where Gordon was sitting. "Have a seat and I'll be right back. Do you want white or red?"

"I want to see what's there—I'll come help," said Lori, and then she and Steph were gone and Megan had taken the chair right next to Matt, with Gordon on her other side.

"This is nice!" she said, looking around the kitchen. "Mom told me it would be a not-to-be-missed party, but you know—one can never trust one's parents, right?" And she gave Gordon a broad wink.

Gordon laughed and patted Megan on the shoulder. "I like this one!" he cried. "I've always liked her."

"Dad," Matt interrupted, before Gordon could say something even more embarrassing—like point out how "this one" was certainly not too old for him. "Are you enjoying the meatballs? I know you love meatballs."

"I do! Say, is there any of that meatball soup? With the macaroni in it?"

"I don't know, Dad," Matt said. "I can go look, but why don't you eat what you've got for now?"

It felt awkward to talk across Megan, maybe even rude, but she didn't seem to mind. In fact, she gave Matt the most understanding, sympathetic look before turning back to Gordon and asking him what other kinds of soup he liked.

She's not weirded out by his dementia, Matt realized. Heather had never been entirely comfortable around Gordon, and it had only gotten worse as his condition progressed. Despite saying that she understood why he repeated his stories and asked the same questions over and over, she had quickly grown irritated with him, answering him shortly or not at all. "I just told you that," she had snapped, more than once.

But here was Megan, already responding to one of Gordon's conversational loops as if hearing it for the first time.

Soon Lori returned, without Steph but with two glasses of red wine, handing her sister one. She took the chair on the other side of Gordon, who was unspeakably delighted at this turn of events. "I'm surrounded by pretty ladies!" he cried.

Matt gave Lori an apologetic smile, but she just laughed. "Who doesn't like to be called a pretty lady?" she said, before leaning in and seamlessly joining the conversation about soup.

He should have known that Julie's daughters would be comfortable and friendly—that's how Julie was, after all. And he was particularly glad that they were both so chatty. It helped cover up his own stupefying attack of shyness…or whatever it was. He could hardly glance at Megan without his heart rate picking up.

If she noticed, she didn't let on. She just kept helping her sister—and Gordon—carry the conversation, easing Matt in from time to time, making him feel comfortable as well. Eventually, he relaxed enough to join in more naturally.

In fact, he was so relaxed (perhaps it was the second glass of wine that had somehow appeared in his hand?) that he was telling a funny story about some clients when he happened to glance across the crowded kitchen and see Julie staring back at him, a bemused expression on her face. Her boyfriend Gavin stood just behind her; Julie turned quickly back to him, then returned her gaze to Matt…and Megan, who was leaning in quite close, he suddenly noticed. Probably just so she could hear better. Yes, that was certainly it.

Matt cleared his throat, smiled at Julie, and continued his story.

STEPH

STEPH SWEPT THROUGH her party, clearing used plates, refilling serving dishes, checking on the beverage supply. And playing social hostess as well: introducing people who should really know each other, drawing out the shy ones, making sure everyone was happy and having fun.

Of course David was hiding in his study. She should have known. She'd spotted him earlier, getting food, but then he'd vanished again.

It was getting to the point where people didn't even ask about him anymore.

Steph would have sighed, but she had her hostess-face on,

and she really did enjoy having a house full of people. It was like conducting a symphony, she thought, or cooking a complex multi-course meal: all the work, all the planning, all the practicing, all leading up to the moment where everything had to come together—and it did! It gave her such a good feeling to see so many people having such a good time, and largely due to her own efforts.

She even had a fun conversation with Ron and Alicia, who were in high spirits (well, Alicia was; Ron was as cheerful as he ever managed to get). And she got none of that weird vibe off of Ron that she'd gotten a week ago, so maybe that had been an anomaly—or just her imagination.

Well, she didn't really think it had been her imagination. So maybe Ron had gotten the message, at least.

All too soon, folks were starting to leave. "So early!" Steph had cried, when the first guests said their farewells, but they pointed out that it was after nine o'clock, which she couldn't quite believe. Parties went so fast!

"Ooh, it's starting to snow," someone said out in the hallway. Steph hurried over to check: yes, a light dusting was falling, making her front yard sparkle.

Word got around, and more people began looking for their coats. Steph resigned herself to reality, thanking everyone for coming, telling them to drive safely, making sure they had all their things.

And then came that part of the party where the remaining folks were few enough that they were all sitting in the living room together, enjoying the fire, finishing a last glass of wine or slice of cranberry tart, sharing a last few stories. It was most of the soup group (minus Lynne, who didn't stay up late), plus Julie's lovely daughters. Steph was surprised that Matt and his father were still here this late, but Gordon was bright-eyed and bushy-tailed, so clearly social activity was good for him.

And good for Matt. He'd not left Megan's side all evening—

and Megan seemed at least as happy about this as Matt did. Steph couldn't wait to get Julie alone to talk to her about this interesting development.

"Well, we should probably think about getting back..." Ron said, setting his empty glass down on the table beside him. Alicia frowned over at him, but sipped her own wine and nodded.

There was a knock at the front door. "Huh," Steph said. Surely nobody was arriving at the party this late—the last time that sort of thing had happened to her, she'd been in college. She got up, hurried through the front hall, and opened the door.

Her friends Duncan and Kate, who had left about ten minutes ago, were standing there. "I'm so sorry," Kate said, "but there's a tree down on Deer Harbor Road."

"A big one," Duncan said. "And the snow is coming down pretty thick now too."

"I'm not sure anyone will be out to clear the tree before morning," Kate added. "So we thought we should come back and check if there's any news on the community group, see if anyone knows anything."

"And warn the rest of your guests not to head out!" Duncan said.

"Come in, gosh, it's freezing out there!" Steph said, standing back to let them in. They stepped inside amid a flurry of snow. "Come get warm!"

She brought them into the living room, where everyone exclaimed at the situation and agreed that they were lucky not to have had the tree fall on them—it had clearly just come down, or more of the guests would have gotten trapped.

Alicia was already on her phone, scrolling through the Orcas Island Inclement Weather and Roads newsgroup, looking for word. "Here it is," she said. "Someone's already reported it."

"I told you we should have left earlier," Ron said, sourly. Alicia gave him another look, then returned to her phone.

"Yeah, here we go," she said after a minute. "The county sent a crew out, but the snow is already too deep for them to get there tonight—the truck got stuck in Crow Valley, and the tow guy is on the scene, trying to pull them out of a ditch. They're advising everyone to stay put tonight, even with chains."

"How deep is the snow?" Matt asked, looking worried. He got up and looked out the back windows, but it was pitch-dark outside.

Steph flicked on the lights that lined her garden paths. They barely glowed under deep drifts of snow. "Oh, wow. That happened fast."

Now nearly everyone was at the windows, marveling at the deep snow. From his chair, a gleeful Gordon said, "We'll have to sleep here tonight!"

Matt turned to his father, as if to contradict him, but Steph said, "Yes, he's right. Nobody should be out driving in that, even if there weren't a tree blocking the only road off this side of the island. We've got guest bedrooms..." She bit her lip, counting people. There were too many. "I'll call Lynne," she said, pulling out her cell phone.

Fortunately, her neighbor hadn't gone to bed yet. "Of course," she said, "but I've only got Ethan's room, and it's, um, a little crowded. It's available, though; I'll come over and help whoever wants to use it find their way in the dark."

"Thank you! Bundle up!" Steph said, tucking her phone back into her pocket. She counted again; removing one couple would help, but there were still too many... "I'll be right back," she told her guests, and marched down the long hallway toward the back of the house.

She rapped on the door to David's study. There was a faint light showing under the door, so he was still up. It didn't matter, though: she would have awakened him if she'd had to.

His door opened and he peered out at her, looking confused. "What is it? I still hear voices."

"Yes, there are still people here, and they're going to be here all night. There's a tree down on the main road and everyone's stuck. We have to make up both guest rooms…and your bed in here."

He blinked at her, as though she was speaking a foreign language. "That's my bed," he said at last.

"Not tonight it isn't. You'll have to bunk in with me." She turned to open the linen closet in the hall, and handed him a set of sheets. "Here, remake your bed. Let me know when it's ready."

She was already walking back down the hall when he called after her plaintively. "I can't have people in my study!"

"Yes you can," she said over her shoulder. "I'm not sending my guests out into the snow to sleep in their cars, and probably freeze to death, when we have perfectly good beds in this house."

Back in the living room, Lynne had arrived. Duncan and Kate had been deputized to stay with her; she quickly bundled them off to get settled.

"So," Steph told her remaining guests. "We've got two guest rooms, and David's office." She tried not to notice how everyone's eyes widened slightly at the mention of her present-yet-absentee husband. "Matt, you and Gordon should take a room; then Ron and Alicia can have one, and Julie and Gavin the other." She smiled at Julie's daughters. "Sorry, girls, but the couches in here are pretty comfy."

"We can sleep on couches!" Megan assured her.

Lori nodded. "The rug in here is nice and soft as well—and the fire is pretty sweet. I think this room is the best of all."

"Yeah," Megan agreed. "You're all going to be jealous of us."

"Good thing we still have all our luggage, too," Lori said. "See? I knew there was a reason we came straight here."

Julie gave her daughters a grateful smile. "Come to think of it, I have stuff for a few days myself."

"It's in your car, though," Gavin said. "Do you want me to go get it?" He had already leapt to his feet.

Steph didn't know exactly what had happened between them last week, but Gavin was certainly being on his best behavior.

And Julie seemed quite happy about it.

Julie thanked him, then turned to Steph. "What can we do to help?"

"Let's all make some beds!"

She went back to the linen closet and pulled out all the bedding she could find, distributing it between the rooms. There was barely enough; Lori and Megan were going to have to use sleeping bags, but they professed themselves delighted to do so. Then it was a matter of showing everyone where all their respective bathrooms were, and making sure everyone had what they needed to bed down for the night.

David reappeared, holding a bag of toiletries and a pile of clothing, looking to Steph for something—reassurance, guidance? He seemed so lost. "Go get yourself settled in our bedroom," she said, stressing the *our* just a bit, as she ushered Julie and Gavin into his study. They were new lovers; they'd be delighted to squeeze onto a daybed.

David, of course, used to sleep in the master bedroom with Steph. There hadn't been a definitive moment when he'd moved out...like so much else between them, it had happened slowly, gradually, imperceptibly. Until it was a done thing, without either of them ever having talked about it.

Without hardly noticing it.

"I'll be in soon," she added, as he slipped into her—their—bedroom.

She made the final rounds of her guests, finding everyone situated. Then she went around the house turning off the lights, casting barely a glance at all the dirty dishes in the kitchen, at the food still left out. She'd put away the most perishable things; everything else could wait till morning. Exhaustion finally made its presence known to her. God, sleep would feel nice.

Would she be able to sleep with David in the bed with her? After so long?

She turned out the last light, in the hallway, and went into the bedroom, closing the door behind her. David sat on the bed, at the foot, looking like a lost child. Still holding his little bundle of personal items. She looked at him, feeling the familiar muddle of frustration and affection.

"I'm sorry I didn't attend the party," he said, giving her a sad look. "I got…caught up in something."

"I know you did," Steph said, sitting beside him. There was no anger in her, no reproach, just…weariness. "You always do."

He just nodded.

"You can help me in the morning," she added. "We'll still have a house full of people, and I have no idea when the roads will be open again. I just hope we'll have power—I'm kind of surprised it's still on now."

"Okay," he said softly. "I'll help with the people. And with the generator, if we need that."

"Good." She patted his knee, and got up. "I'm going to go brush my teeth, and then we should turn in. I'm completely wiped."

"Okay," he said again. Then, "Where do you want me to sleep? Do you want me to make up a bed on the floor?"

Steph stopped in the doorway to their bathroom and turned around to look at him, surprised. "Sleep in our bed," she said. "With me. You remember how to do that, don't you?"

"I…don't know." He looked at her pleadingly. "Steph, I just don't know…much of anything."

She looked at him for a long moment. But the weariness threatened to drag her down where she stood. "David," she said at last. "I mean it: I've got nothing left in me tonight. And we're dealing with some chaos, unexpectedly hosting a group of people for who knows how long. But when this is all resolved…we need to talk."

He looked back at her, blinking, and then nodded. "Yes."

She searched his eyes. Was he still in there, the man she loved? The man she'd married, and built a life with? Moved to Orcas

Island with?

Steph had no idea. But she was ready to find out.

LYNNE

LYNNE HADN'T MET Duncan and Kate before tonight, but she'd spent some time talking to Kate at the party after Steph had introduced them. She had liked her a lot, so she'd offered the couple her guest bedroom, such as it was. "Sorry it's such a mess," she told Kate, as she started taking at least a few of the excess embroidered pillows and tapestries off the bed. Duncan was out in the living room talking to their babysitter on the phone. Lynne could see the relief on Kate's face as it became clear that the babysitter was fine staying the night at their house, and that their children were enjoying the adventure of it all.

"It doesn't look messy to me," Kate said. "We're just so grateful to you for taking us in. When we suddenly saw that tree in the road right in front of us…" She blew out a breath. "I'm just glad Dunc was able stop in time."

"Me too. That must have been so frightening," Lynne said, beginning to fold one of the larger wall hangings.

Kate took a corner of the piece in her hand and peered closely at it. "Is this your work? It's astonishing."

"Yes," Lynne said, and almost automatically started to minimize her own efforts—to explain how she was relatively new at embroidery, it was just a hobby; to point out the goof-ups and mistakes in the piece.

Kate gave her a warning smile. "None of that, now. Remember what I told you earlier."

Lynne shook her head ruefully. "It's funny, because I'm not like this professionally; I never was. When you're one of the few women in your entire medical school, you learn pretty fast to stop apologizing for yourself."

"So channel that energy and self-confidence into your creative work and tell me about this piece."

Lynne took a deep breath. "It's called 'Deep Autumn.' It's not exactly representational, but I wanted to convey what the island looks like when the seasons turn and the light gets lower. When the big-leaf maples go brown, and the hay fields get mowed, and the evergreens are still green. When all the wildflowers are long gone, but the landscape is still full of color, if you know how to look for it, how to see its quieter beauty."

Kate was nodding with every word. She pointed to one side of the piece, moving her finger along in a slow line. "This back here: I see some low hills, and chunks of limestone. And maybe a small barn, or hay shelter?"

Lynne couldn't help the grin on her face. "Yes! Exactly. You see it!"

"I do. And quite a bit more—in this piece and the rest of the tapestries you're clearing off the bed like they were so much laundry." She looked at Lynne. "My gallery is booked through the end of April, but we have an opening in May. Would you be interested in a solo show?"

"Yes. Yes, I would love that," Lynne said, before her mind could get in her heart's way.

ALICIA

"Mmm, comfy." Alicia stretched out in the queen-sized bed, wiggling her feet in an attempt to warm up the cool sheets.

Ron came in from the bathroom and started undressing on his side of the bed. "Small, compared to what we're used to," he said sourly. "And I wish I'd known this was going to happen—I'd have brought my toothbrush."

Alicia turned her head on the soft pillow and gave him a look. "Do you ever have anything nice to say about *anything*? Ever?"

Startled, Ron stopped, his dress slacks in one hand. "What do you mean?"

She almost muttered *Never mind*, but maybe she'd had just enough wine to not let it drop this time. "Nobody knew a tree was going to fall—nobody knew it was going to snow like this. Yet Steph cheerfully opened her house to us when she was obviously exhausted after throwing a party entirely by herself, and made *eight extra people* comfortable. She's given you and me the best bedroom—the only one with its own private bathroom. You know that Julie and Gavin are sleeping on a daybed in David's office, right? Are they complaining?"

"Well—" Ron started, but Alicia was on a roll.

"Matt has his elderly dad with dementia to take care of, in an unfamiliar setting—twin beds, and a bathroom down the hall. But did he complain either? No. Julie's daughters, who are not children but are grown-ass women in their thirties with presumably real beds at home, are acting like it's a treat to be put in sleeping bags on the living room floor! But you are whining because you don't have your toothbrush, and you might have to sleep several inches closer to your wife than you're used to. Well, don't worry, I'll stay off your side of the bed. You won't even know I'm here." With a final huff, she turned on her side facing away from him and closed her eyes.

"Huh," he huffed in return, and then was silent for a long moment. Eventually she heard him finish getting undressed, laying his clothes over a chair. He carefully crawled into bed and shut out his light without another word.

MATT

"I'M THIRSTY."

Matt looked over at his dad on the matching twin bed. "You are? That's awesome." Gordon hated drinking liquids of any kind, particularly in the evenings, claiming that it just made him have to get up and use the bathroom in the night. "I'll go get you a glass of water."

"Can I have some more of that soda?"

Nope, no sugar for you at bedtime, old man, Matt thought, but he only said, "I'll see what I can find."

He got up and pulled his jeans back on, then tiptoed out into the darkened hallway. He didn't see any lights under any of the bedroom doors on his way to the bathroom.

Once there, though, he relented, feeling like kind of a jerk for withholding what his dad really wanted. What would be the harm in ginger ale or something else without caffeine? He wouldn't drink more than a few swallows anyway.

So Matt continued on toward the kitchen. As he passed the living room, he thought he heard Lori and Megan whispering to each other, but he wasn't entirely sure. He walked as softly as he could beside the wide opening into the room.

In the kitchen, he turned on the tiny light over the stove, then looked around for a small drinking glass. Of course every glass in the place was dirty; he washed one in the sink, dried it, and then opened the fridge. The fridge light shone startlingly brightly, flooding the room with its antiseptic glare. Matt quickly grabbed a bottle of some kind of fancy organic carbonated juice drink and poured a few inches into the glass, then shut the fridge door. He had to wait, blinking, for a minute to regain his night vision, and then again once he turned off the stove light.

On his way past the living room, he heard another whisper: "Who's there?"

"It's me, Matt," he said, standing in the doorway. "Sorry to bother you guys—my dad was thirsty."

"Do you need any help with anything?" A shape sat up, backlit by the ghostly snow-light coming through the big picture windows behind her. Megan: her long hair shone.

Matt felt his heart thump deliciously. "No, thank you. Are you guys comfortable here?"

"We totally are." As his eyes adjusted further, he could see her smiling at him. Her sister was a second shape, lying beside her.

"Yes, super comfy," Lori put in, from the floor. "This is way more room than we would have had at Mom's house; we're scheming about how we can stay here for our whole visit."

"Uh, I have a guest room," he blurted out, before he could stop himself.

Megan laughed softly. "Thanks, but I think Mom wants us close by."

"Except on the nights when she's at Gavin's!" Lori said.

"Yeah, she's giving us her bed those nights."

Matt stood there, holding the soda-juice, not wanting to leave. He was just staring at Megan, drinking in her loveliness even in the dim light, as he had done all evening. Embarrassed, he looked away, up at the ceiling above her.

She had set her sleeping bag directly under a garland of mistletoe.

Even more embarrassed now, Matt yanked his gaze away from the perilous trap, but Megan had seen his look, so she looked up as well.

Her smile grew. "Matt, it was so nice meeting you tonight, and I hope we get to see a lot more of you before we go back home." Then she lay back down and snuggled into her sleeping bag. "You'd better get your dad that drink before he wonders where you've gone."

"Um. Yes. Will do." He cleared his throat. "I do hope we see each other again soon too. Goodnight, both of you."

"Goodnight," both sisters whispered.

Matt tiptoed down the hall to his father.

JULIE

THEY'D MADE LOVE SO, so quietly, entangled in the cozy daybed. Now they lay spooned, murmuring sweet nothings and letting their breathing return to normal. Julie knew she should be feeling sleepy, but she was still abuzz with everything—being snowed in here at Steph's house; the enjoyable party; her wonderful daughters. Her life, expanding before her in so many unexpected ways. Gavin.

"Thank you for letting me meet Megan and Lori," Gavin whispered, after a few minutes.

She smiled in the dark. "You're welcome." She snuggled closer to him. "They liked you."

"I'm glad; I like them too. They are clearly remarkable women." He wrapped his arm more firmly around her waist; she nestled her arm over his, holding him close. "Meeting them…I think I understand something I didn't quite get before."

"Oh?" She wanted to turn around and see his face, but she also didn't want to budge from this uber-comfy position. "What is that?"

He took a breath. "Creativity. No—that's not quite it. Let me see if I can explain." He paused, thinking. "You created them. I mean, I know it's much more complicated than that."

She laughed. "I should say!"

He chuckled as well. "Bear with me. Pretend it's a metaphor. It's just—well, okay, first literally, you grew them in your body. Then you raised them—yes, with whatever help you got from their father, and teachers, and anyone else in their lives, but it's clear even from what little I know that it was mostly you. Then, they grew up, and became their own selves, but they're still a part of you. They still obviously love you *and* like you; they still want to be close to you."

She caressed the back of his hand as it cradled her belly. "I'm lucky. Not every mother has this."

"Lucky, maybe, sure; but what I'm saying is that it's not just luck. It's what you did, the good job you did—creating and raising them. And then, when you were done with that job, you took that enormous, amazing, boundless creativity of yours and moved on. You created your whole shop, as well as the books you make and sell in it."

"Well…" she temporized, but he squeezed her gently.

"What I'm really trying to get at is that—Julie, I've never created *anything*. I've never even taken the risk to really do what I want for a career, much less create children, or even get all the way to a marriage. I just…hover around the edges, judging other people's creations. And I never really got that about myself before, until I met you, and got to know you, and fell in love with you—and then thought I'd lost you."

Now she did turn around in his arms, holding him close and putting her nose against his before giving him a quick kiss. Dim light peeked around the curtains; she could just barely see the outlines of his face. "I believe I've seen evidence of a garden at your house. A garden is an act of creation."

He snorted softly. "Okay. I planted some things. It's a start, maybe." He leaned forward and kissed the tip of her nose. "But, despite what it sounds like, I'm not trying to make this about me. I'm trying to tell you that I think I'm at least farther along in understanding just what kind of an asshole I was when I got all judgy about your creations. I think…I think it was jealousy, and a feeling of, I don't know, not being good enough. Not being *for* anything. I've done this for so long, it's almost reflexive. I was judgmental of Jennifer for wanting to make lots of money, so what did I do? I went and showed her I was better at it than she was. And then I was judgmental of Elizabeth for wanting to be a romance writer. She probably wasn't wrong, not letting me read her work, and refusing to move in with me. I totally would have thought I was being supportive of her writing, but I know now that I didn't respect it, and I wouldn't have taken it seriously. Wouldn't have taken *her* seriously."

He pulled her close, now, stroking her hair as he tucked her head under his chin. "I don't want to do that to you, Julie. It wasn't just a grand romantic gesture, buying those books. I actually do want to help you start a book group. I want to know what excites your creative mind. And…maybe…I want to figure out what might awaken my creative side." He gave a soft sigh. "If it's not too late for me."

Julie held him tight, her heart melting. "Gavin Jones, it is absolutely not too late for you. I would love to accompany you on your creative journey."

He kissed the top of her head. "Thank you for giving me a second chance."

She squeezed him tightly. "Thank you for showing me you were worth it."

They fell asleep in each other's arms, as the snow blanketed the house and all the world around them.

~ o ~

READ ON FOR A SNEAK PEEK OF

Love and Lemongrass

Book 2 in The Island of Second Chances

COMING SOON!

STEPH

Twenty-nine years ago

There he was again. The cute blond fellow that Steph had seen at least a dozen times already, at the dim sum place where she regularly picked up a Combo Box Number Six to eat in the park on her all-too-brief lunch hour.

They'd noticed each other the first time, smiled tentatively at each other the second time, said "Hi" the third time, and then… that's where it had stalled out. Just another "Hi" each time.

Steph had had quite enough of this, she'd finally decided last week. She was going to break the impasse, take matters into her own hands. Frustratingly, since she'd made this resolution, he hadn't turned up.

But here he was! Walking in as she was leaving with her lunch, just as cute as ever, and smiling shyly at her like he did every single time…

"Hi!" she said brightly, clutching her Combo Box. "Great to see you again!"

"Uh, yeah, hi," he mumbled, still smiling but now glancing down at his feet. He moved to step around her on his way to the counter.

Steph moved just enough to block his route as another customer came in and walked around them both. The cute blond guy looked up at her, clearly confused. At a loss. "Uh," he said again.

"Sorry!" Steph said, grinning widely, conveying, she hoped, a complete lack of sorrow. "But I made myself a promise, and I'm not one to go back on promises. To anyone."

The man blinked at her. "You're not?"

"Nope, I'm not," she said quickly, not letting herself lose her stride even though when she'd planned this all out and rehearsed it in her imagination, he was supposed to say *What was the promise?* She forged ahead. "I promised myself that the next time I saw you, I'd introduce myself." She held out the hand not holding her lunch. "I'm Steph Hancock."

He stared at her hand for an uncomfortably long moment before producing his own. "David Palmer."

She took his hand and shook it warmly but firmly. While still holding onto it, she said, "Nice to meet you, David. I'm about to go eat my lunch in the park across the street. It's such a pretty day. Would you like to join me?"

Now he looked panicked, and she felt him trying to pull his hand away. She let it go but amped up her smile, and didn't move out of his way. "I. Um. Usually take it back to the office?" he finally squeaked out.

"Where do you work?"

"Smith Barney. The brokerage house?"

She nodded. "That's not far from my office. Do you actually have to go right back, or can you take a few minutes?"

"I…suppose I could take a few minutes." He looked less panicked now, but more confused. "Why?"

For crying out loud, do I have to spell it out? "Because we see each other here all the time, and we nod and say hi, and I'd like to get to know you better." She gave him another hopeful smile. "I'm not a serial killer, I promise."

His eyes widened. They were light blue, almost sky-colored: gorgeous. "I didn't think you were a serial killer! You're too—" And then he clamped his mouth shut as his cheeks colored.

"I'm too what?" Steph asked sweetly. *Pretty? He was going to say I'm pretty!*

Maybe?

"Uh, too...female," he stammered. "Serial killers are almost exclusively male."

Steph snorted with laughter. "Oh, so you did notice!"

His cheeks reddened further, and more customers kept filtering into the tiny takeout joint; now a line was forming at the counter.

"Get your lunch," Steph went on, finally moving out of his way. "I'll wait here, and we can walk over to the park together."

"Okay," he said, and gave her another fragile smile.

After a minute, Steph stepped outside to wait on the sidewalk. It was getting very crowded in there, and noisy as well. Besides, this was the only door. It wasn't as though David could slip out the back and flee from her.

Even though I'm totally not a serial killer, she told herself.

Once he'd emerged and they'd settled on her favorite park bench, Steph opened her box of dim sum and pulled out the pork bun. "Mmm," she said, around a fluffy mouthful. "Perfect as ever."

He had gotten a different combo; number fourteen, she thought. Heavy on the seafood. "Yes," he agreed. "They do a good job there."

She snapped her bamboo chopsticks apart and picked up a siu mai dumpling, popping it in her mouth. "The best. I have friends up in the city who say Yank Sing is the best, but frankly, I've never been as impressed with them as I am with this little hole-in-the-wall down here." She grinned over at him. "Or maybe it's just because I can walk here from my office, and familiarity breeds contentment."

He looked briefly confused, then laughed. "Oh! That's funny."

"Thank you." Okay, this was all still fairly awkward, but at least she'd made him laugh.

"Where do you work?" he asked.

She wanted to cheer: the man asked a question! He was showing interest! "A-1 Insurance, just over there." She pointed across the street with a chopstick. "The most boring job in the history of the world, and I'm happy to have it. Not many jobs out here for English majors, I'm afraid."

"You're an English major?" His confused look was back.

"Was. Graduated from Stanford last year, and couldn't find a single company that was looking for someone who could analyze a Victorian novel and delineate its themes, or even diagram a sentence. And before you ask, no, they don't make you diagram sentences in college—though I could do it in a heartbeat if anyone needed me to. Fifty cents a sentence, or three for a dollar." She gave him a hopeful smile, then added, "That was another joke. You could laugh again if you wanted to." *You're even cuter when you laugh.*

To her surprise, he did laugh. "You're a very interesting person, Steph."

"Thanks!" She ate another siu mai. It was the combination of the ground pork and ground shrimp that made it, she thought, already wondering if she could learn how to make them herself. "So what do you do at Smith Barney? Are you a broker?"

Those blue eyes widened. "Oh no. An analyst. I…uh…they don't let me talk to the customers."

"They don't?"

He smiled broadly. It was like the sun had come out after a cloudy morning. "That was a joke too. But it's also true. I'm a little, uh, shy."

"You know? I had actually noticed that," she said, gently.

She asked him more questions—easy ones, not too intrusive—and offered little tidbits of information about herself. When they'd both finished their boxes, he started to seem nervous again, glancing over at the tall building where his office was. So she made sure to exchange numbers, both home and cell.

Well, her cell number. He didn't have one. "I don't, um, talk on the phone much. Nobody needs to reach me—well, I'm usually either at work or at home, so it didn't seem important to get yet another line."

"Fair," she said. "So, what do you say: lunch next Tuesday? Same place, same time?"

"I'd like that," he said, with no stammer at all.

Fifteen years ago

"ARE YOU DISAPPOINTED?"

Steph reached across the table and took David's hand. He squeezed hers, and she squeezed back as a few tears leaked out of her eyes. "Yes. No. I don't know." She shook her head and said again, "I don't know. Are you?"

He exhaled a soft sigh. "I think I'm 'yes and no and I don't know' as well."

"It would have changed so much."

"It would have."

The waitress came to their table. Steph asked for a coffee, with plenty of cream; David asked for the same, and a plate of strawberry mini-muffins to share. She jotted their order down and stepped quickly away. Steph wondered if she saw lots of couples like this, in here. So close to the clinic as it was.

"But I think I was ready for such a change," Steph said. "I mean, I wasn't, when we thought the decision had been made for us. I totally freaked out."

David gave her a kind smile, a loving smile. "You did. To be fair, I did too."

"Not half as much as I did."

"Well, I've always been quieter than you," he teased.

She smiled back at him and wiped away a tear with the hand he wasn't holding.

The waitress came back with their coffees. "Your muffins will be along in a minute."

After she left again, Steph ventured, "Well. We could always adopt."

"We could. Do you want to?"

"Yes. No. I don't know." She stirred cream into her coffee and took a sip. At least she wouldn't ever have to give up caffeine, even temporarily. Or brie, or sushi. Or wine! See, there was always a bright side, if you just took the time to look for it. "We could look into it. But there's no rush."

"There is no rush," he agreed. "But we could, when you're ready—look into it, I mean. Or I would be happy to do the research, and let you know what I find out. When you're ready."

"Thank you." She took a deep breath, and another sip of coffee.

The waitress brought the mini-muffins. Steph took a long time tearing one apart, dabbing butter on its still-steaming interior, letting the butter melt, taking a bite. Her mind deconstructed the recipe almost automatically. It would have been so much fun to teach her child how to cook, how to bake. To share all her kitchen insights, her love of flavors, her appreciation for food made by others and her delight in making it herself.

But would her child have been interested? You never knew, did you? Steph's mother had not been able to interest her, or her brother or sister, in her own hobby of heirloom rose cultivation. Steph enjoyed gardening, of course, but pretty much exclusively of edible plants. Gardening was a means to an end, and the end was cooking.

Cooking had been Steph's passion for as long as she could remember. From the earliest days when her mom had let her sit on the kitchen counter beside the stove, stirring the Campbell's chicken noodle soup as it heated up; through when she had followed her first recipe to make something from scratch (grilled cheese sandwiches with tomato jam), when she could barely read; until her first invented meal, in junior high: a riff on her mom's meatloaf, making it spicier, and also into meatballs, which she served over pasta with a homemade sauce at the family's Sunday dinner. Only after everyone had remarked on how delicious it was had her mom told everyone that Steph had created the dish herself, with no help.

Cooking still gave Steph's life its richness, its delight. It was her creative outlet. David worked long hours, now at a smaller, more specialized brokerage firm, and still as an analyst. Steph still worked in insurance administration. It was tedious and repetitive, but it paid well, she was good at it, and when she left the office at five o'clock sharp every day, she never had to give her work a thought until the next morning.

When she'd missed a period, thirty-six-year-old Steph had looked at thirty-seven-year-old David and said, "We need to talk about something important."

When the period showed up two weeks late, they were already well on their way to wrapping their hearts and minds around the idea of having a child. Though they'd been married nearly twelve years, it had always seemed too soon…there was always time to think about it…later.

Suddenly, later was now. So, without fully committing one way or another, Steph went off birth control, and they agreed to see what happened.

What happened was more irregular periods, weight gain, and a year of doctor's visits and tests…and finally, almost an hour ago, a diagnosis of late-onset PCOS—polycystic ovary syndrome. Steph was not technically infertile—miracles did happen—but the doctor advised that it would be best if they assumed that she was. She'd offered Steph and David a referral to a fertility doctor.

They'd declined. "For now," Steph said. "I just need to absorb this for a while."

The doctor smiled at them both, her face filled with empathy and care. "I understand. I'm here if you need me—for anything."

"Thank you."

Now Steph looked at David across the table. "You're not eating any muffins," she said.

His smile, even his sad smile, was still like the sun coming out.

"I'm really not all that hungry."

"You know, I'll never understand that." She gave him a watery smile back, and tried not to think about what their child might have looked like.

Nine years ago

DAVID WAS ON the couch when she got home from work. Wrapped up in a blanket, staring at the television, which was tuned to a game show, with the sound off. He was shivering.

Steph set her purse on the entry table and sat on the other end of the sofa. David didn't look at her, but from this angle, she could see he wasn't really looking at the TV either.

He was just staring. At nothing. At the abyss. At his darkness, somewhere in the middle distance, where it seemed no one could reach.

And still shivering, though the room was overly warm.

Eventually, she got up, went into the kitchen, and returned with a mug of hot chocolate. She set it on the coffee table in front of him. His gaze flickered; he seemed to just now register her presence.

"Rough day?" she asked, softly.

He nodded.

"Did you talk to your boss again?"

He shook his head.

Steph forced back her frustration, schooled her emotions. Calm, peaceful, unchallenging. "It's bad for the whole team, if they let certain members get away with bullying. Because that's what it is: bullying."

He shrugged.

"You're by far the most valuable member—not just of the team, but of the whole damn brokerage house. I hope they know they're going to lose you if they can't get this under control."

Now he turned and blinked at her. "I can't quit this job," he whispered. "We need it."

"We actually don't," she said quietly. Calmly. "We enjoy the money, but we're doing fine. We would be fine if you didn't work for a year. We would be fine if you didn't work for ten years." She nodded at the mug before him. "Drink your cocoa."

He picked up the mug and took a sip. Then he set the mug back on the table.

Steph looked at the TV. The game show contestants were very excited about something, hopping up and down. Maybe the hopping was part of the game? She didn't understand what the contest was, but the colors—of the studio set, of the contestants' clothing, of the host's clothing—were certainly very bright.

Was it a Japanese game show?

She turned back to David, who had relaxed slightly, and had stopped shivering. After another long moment, he picked up the mug and took another sip. This time, he held onto the mug, and continued sipping.

Steph let out a breath. He was talking (well, whispering), drinking his hot chocolate: they'd gotten around the edge of this one. Probably.

When he finished the mug and set it back on the coffee table, she said, "I'm going to go start on dinner. Are you going to be okay in here for a while?"

He turned and gave her a ghost of a smile. "Yes. Thank you." And then, "I'm sorry."

She slowly reached out a gentle hand and touched his arm. "No need to be sorry. You're safe, and I love you."

"I love you too."

In the kitchen, she took a few more deep, centering breaths, and wondered whether to call his therapist tomorrow. He'd been doing so much better, for so long...but they kept coming back to this.

Workplaces were supposed to be accommodating, both by law and just because of simple human decency. Harassment, of course, was not supposed to be tolerated at all…well, that was the theory, anyway.

She wondered what motivated these dude-bro-asshole brokers to pick on the analyst upon whom they relied for the information they needed to actually, you know, serve their clients and be successful in their business. But who ever said bullies were rational creatures?

Steph poured herself a half-glass of wine and stared into the fridge, part of her mind figuring out what to make for dinner while the rest of her pondered how to fix this. Not how to fix David—only he could do that—but what she could do to make their situation better.

They already let him work remotely two days a week, but was there really any reason he had to go into the office at all? His work was nearly entirely independent, and even without the bullying, the office was a distraction; he'd told her many times that he got twice as much done on his two days at home than in the three office days. Not to mention the commute time. Maybe the firm would consider shifting him to entirely remote? Or, failing that, only going into the office occasionally—for all-hands meetings, face-to-faces with his boss, that sort of thing?

There was still city living to take into account, though. And this house, however comfortable, was cheek-by-jowl with neighbors on all sides, traffic, noise, chaos, interruptions. David was never so relaxed and, well, himself, as when they were in their vacation home on Orcas Island.

Steph shut the fridge, sipped her wine, and thought.

Eventually she went back into the living room. "David?"

"Yes?" He looked up at her. The cocoa had restored some of his color, but he still looked so fragile.

"Let's move to Orcas full-time."

Notes and Thanks

Books are funny creatures. For one thing, they sure don't like plans.

Last October, I had three other books I was supposed to be writing: A book that's under contract with a publisher (and really, really late). Another book that is eagerly awaited by an excited audience—I can't set foot in Darvill's Bookstore here on the island without being asked about it. And a third book that I started about a year ago, a deeply personal book which I am slowly, carefully assembling, working hard to make it as honest and sharp and ruthless as possible, and also, maybe, beautiful.

Imagine my surprise when Julie and Matt and Steph and the rest of the gang just waltzed into my head out of a clear blue sky and demanded to jump to the head of the line. "Tell our stories," the soup group said. "Now."

"No," I said, and, well, you can see how that went over.

This series is set on Orcas Island, but it's an Orcas that's not entirely contiguous with the one we know out here in the real world. There are real businesses in the books, and then there are made-up ones. I played with some geography for the sake of making the story work. And, of course, so far as I know, there are no plans in the works for parking meters.

Thank you to Kathia Zolfaghari (and to her BFF Ava!) for the gorgeous, striking, perfect cover—and for all the advice and encouragement. Thank you to Spencer Ellsworth for the brilliant editing: the book grew, no kidding, ten thousand words longer after his careful, insightful feedback. Thank you to Laura Anne Gilman for her deft help with the cover copy. Thank you to everyone at Darvill's Bookstore for being such good sports about getting this book instead of the one you were waiting for! I promise I'll get back to that series…real soon now…

Shannon Page
February, 2025
Orcas Island, Washington

ABOUT THE AUTHOR

SHANNON PAGE LIVES on Orcas Island, with her husband, author and illustrator Mark Ferrari. The island is an amazing place to live, and to write. She's a versatile writer (which sounds much better than saying she can't make up her mind!), publishing novels of fantasy, cozy mystery, romance, and science fiction, as well as personal essays; for her "day job," she's a freelance proofreader and copy editor. She also loves to edit anthologies. In her spare time (haha), she cooks, gardens, plays pickleball, and takes *lots* of pictures of frogs. Visit her at www.shannonpage.net.